When twin boys are born, a servant with a grudge switches their birth order . . .

1366 A.D. – Kenric Fairfax is raised as the second son of the Earl of Shadowfaire. The day of his Knighting Ceremony, a tragedy takes place—and Kenric flees the north of England, putting his past behind him as he swears he will never marry. He becomes a trusted knight in service to Lord Michael Devereux, who asks Kenric to lead an escort party from London in order to bring his wife's sister home to Sandbourne.

Avelyn Le Cler has spent a year as a lady-in-waiting to Queen Philippa and finds the treachery at the royal court not to her liking. She looks forward to a summer visit with her sister Elysande, who will soon give birth to her first child. While journeying from London, Avelyn discovers a secret about Sir Kenric Fairfax that could change his life—if he believes her.

But Avelyn is plagued with doubts since she has no proof to present Kenric. As the couple falls in love, Avelyn knows she must reveal to Kenric the truth she has learned about his birth—even if it costs her everything.

Join Kenric and Avelyn as the truth rips them apart—but their enduring love brings them together again.

JOURNEY TO HONOR

Knights Of Honor
Book Four

Alexa Aston

Copyright © 2017 by Alexa Aston
Print Edition

Published by Dragonblade Publishing, an imprint of Kathryn Le Veque Novels, Inc

All rights reserved. No part of this book may be used or reproduced in any manner whatsoever without written permission, except in the case of brief quotations embodied in critical articles or reviews.

Table of Contents

Prologue 1
Chapter 1 10
Chapter 2 19
Chapter 3 27
Chapter 4 36
Chapter 5 45
Chapter 6 54
Chapter 7 62
Chapter 8 72
Chapter 9 81
Chapter 10 90
Chapter 11 98
Chapter 12 108
Chapter 13 118
Chapter 14 127
Chapter 15 137
Chapter 16 144
Chapter 17 154
Chapter 18 160
Chapter 19 169
Chapter 20 177
Chapter 21 186
Chapter 22 193
Chapter 23 204
Chapter 24 215
Chapter 25 223
Chapter 26 231
Chapter 27 238
Epilogue 244
About the Author 246

PROLOGUE

Shadowfaire Castle—May, 1342

GUSSALEN LOOKED DOWN at the woman in the bed, her hair damp with sweat from the many hours of labor she had endured. At least, this time, a child would be the end result. Poor Juliana had lost three babes in the four years of her marriage to The Brute.

"Guss?" Juliana's voice was barely a whisper now, hoarse from the piercing screams that had gone on since early morn.

"I am here, my lady," the nurse said. "I will not leave you. I will never leave you."

She took the noblewoman's hand and squeezed it encouragingly. Juliana let out a long sigh and closed her eyes, resting them until the next birthing pain struck.

The young woman would deliver soon. Gussalen had grown up accompanying her own mother to hundreds of births until she herself had wed and become a midwife. Her new husband died in an accident less than a month before she gave birth to their child. One look at the weak, mewling babe told Gussalen that the infant would soon follow her husband to the grave. Two days later, the priest buried the child next to her father. Gussalen had wanted to crawl into the hole with them—until word came from the castle.

The baroness' water had broken.

Gussalen answered the summons and delivered a beautiful, healthy daughter, but she could not save the mother. The master kept her on as wet nurse—and Gussalen never left. She raised Juliana from birth and attended the girl every day. The old lord, who had refused to marry after the death of his beloved wife, had not even let his daughter leave to foster, reluctant to part from his only child. Gussalen had gone from that household to Shadowfaire Castle seventeen years later upon Juliana's marriage to the Earl of Shadowfaire.

And then the nightmare began.

Within the first week, an array of bruises covered her sweet girl's body. The earl—tall, broad, and loud—enjoyed dominating women. Juliana had always been a timid flower. Quiet. Thoughtful. Fragile. She endured whatever punishment her new husband doled out in silence.

But the tears came when Gussalen brought a small meal to her mistress' bedchamber each morning. She couldn't imagine the horrors the earl subjected his wife to and Juliana never described them. The two women pretended nothing was wrong. She tended to her lady's body as best she could—all the while cursing The Brute under her breath.

She had seen him pinch the bottom of a passing servant. Watched him push unwilling women into darkened corners while everyone in the great hall ignored what happened. Gussalen had come across the nobleman fondling the breasts of a frightened girl that was no more than half a score.

That was when she put her foot down—and paid the price.

The girl had escaped. The earl had not been pleased. He backhanded Gussalen with such force that she found herself lifted off her feet. Her cheek burned in agony, sliced open by the man's signet ring. She bore the scar and reminded herself of her hatred toward him every day when she briefly touched her fingers to her face and traced the memory.

Injuring her hadn't been enough to please The Brute. He had dragged her by her braid to the larder and slammed the door. Tossed her face down across a table and drew her skirts up past her waist. Forced himself upon her. She thought he might rend her in two, but she never whimpered, refusing to give him any satisfaction.

He'd ignored her after that. Gussalen made sure to give him a wide berth.

In her heart, though, she plotted revenge. For herself—and for Juliana. Gussalen thought of poisoning The Brute and smiled when she imagined his twitching body jerk, foam coming from his mouth as everyone in the great hall looked on in horror. Or she would slip into his bedchamber and stab him in the heart, twisting the baselard until the hilt reached his chest. She imagined sneaking down to the stables and loosening his saddle's straps. Just enough so that it would come apart as he galloped across the field as he led the hunt. In her mind, she pictured him falling from his steed and being trampled by all those behind him, his body broken beyond repair.

Yet she had acted upon none of these desires. The time would come when Walter Fairfax, Earl of Shadowfaire, would pay for all that he had done to her and his wife.

Tonight, the debt would be collected. She had yet to decide just how.

Juliana's eyelids fluttered open again. She gasped. Gussalen drew back the bedclothes to the foot of the bed and saw a head beginning to crown.

"'Tis time, my lady. You must push."

"I don't know if I can, Guss. I think I would rather die than give birth to . . . *his* child."

"No!" she said fiercely. "You will not die. You will live where your own mother did not and be a good mother to this child. It's as much yours as his. More so, because you have nurtured it all these months. Now push!"

Juliana began straining, tiny whimpers escaping her parched lips.

Gussalen looked over her shoulder. The bedchamber still remained empty. When Juliana reached her sixth month without miscarrying, Gussalen had gone to The Brute and told him the best chance for him to see a child from his wife would be for the countess to spend the rest of her time in bed. Alone. With no distractions. At two score and having already seen one wife and three other children put into early graves, the nobleman readily agreed, desperate for an heir.

That day, Gussalen moved Juliana to a new bedchamber and isolated her. The Brute had not visited once during the last three months. She had gone downstairs and brought up all of Juliana's meals. She bathed her mistress and cared for her. No one knew how large the countess had grown. Even now, The Brute drank himself silly in the great hall, awaiting news from Gussalen that his son had arrived. She had personally told him this morning that by nightfall, he would, once more, be a father.

So Gussalen helped the babe slip from her sweet lady's womb—and believed another would follow. Even Juliana did not suspect since she had never come close to bringing a babe to full term.

The infant arrived in a slick rush of water and blood. As Gussalen slapped his bottom to help give him life, he gave a lusty cry. She studied the infant, frowning.

He looked exactly like The Brute.

The boy proved much larger than the usual newborn, with a head full of dark hair. His coloring was that of The Brute. She already hated him upon first sight. Still, she cared for the infant as she had for so many others over the years. Cut the umbilical cord. Cleaned and swaddled him. Placed him atop a pillow on the floor since the bed was soaked in sweat and blood.

And waited for the next one.

Juliana shrieked in pain again as the second child came out. She raised her head weakly to try and see what had happened, but exhaustion caused her to fall back into the pillows.

The Brute had a second boy. This one had the fair coloring of his mother and a sparse bit of blond hair atop his head. Gussalen had to slap him several times before he let out a soft mewl. She readied this babe, as well, smiling. It would serve the earl right if this one became his heir.

In that moment, her decision became clear. She would do it. Why not? No one would know, not even her sweet lady. Juliana had passed out from the strain of the births. Gussalen said a quick prayer to the

Virgin Mary, hoping this one would survive as she wiped him clean and wrapped him tightly. What a huge joke on The Brute if this frail, little mite was destined to be the next Earl of Shadowfaire. She placed him beside his brother. He looked dwarfed alongside the other child.

She took a damp cloth and swept it across Juliana's face. Pushed back her hair. Placed both babes next to a bare breast. Naturally, the greedy firstborn started guzzling, conquering the challenge of sucking without any trouble as he latched on to his mother's breast. Gussalen knew this one would take everything in life—whether 'twas offered to him or not.

Even with her guidance, the fair twin had trouble finding his mother's nipple. Gussalen feared he might not last the night if he did not learn to suckle, but she determined to let the earl know this weakling was his heir. Finally, the babe understood what he needed to do and began nursing quietly as his brother noisily drank inches away. She cleaned Juliana up as best she could and covered her and the babes with a clean linen sheet.

Slowly, Juliana came around as Gussalen bathed her face again. The countess looked down at the two bundles cradled next to her. Hope radiated from her smile.

"There are two?" she asked, wonder evident in her voice.

"Yes, my lady. Both boys. One thrives. The other?" She shrugged. "Not so much."

"I want to see them."

Gussalen pulled the tiny brute away. Milk dribbled down his chin. She held him out for inspection as he howled angrily.

Immediately, Juliana cringed. "Oh, he's so like his father." She bit her lip. "Put him aside, Guss. Let me see the other boy."

She placed the dark one down and lifted the fair one, who remained quiet, his large, blue eyes studying his mother.

This time, the mother smiled. "Oh, he is so sweet." Juliana reached her arms out and claimed the babe, cradling it close to her.

"You hold the firstborn, my lady," Gussalen shared. "I hope he has a kind nature and will be a good lord to his people."

"I do, too, Guss." Juliana gazed with love at the child in her arms.

Gussalen made her next decision. "I fear you are one of those women who will not produce enough milk for the two of them. You will need a wet nurse. I had one waiting just in case. May I fetch her?"

The noblewoman nodded. She cooed softly to her babe as Gussalen crossed the room and stepped out into the corridor.

A heavy woman from the estate waited in the hallway. She had already borne two other children, the last coming almost two years ago. Gussalen had spoken with her about weaning her youngest so she could care for Lady Juliana's babe.

"I hope you are ready," she told the woman. "There are two of them. One will have no trouble nursing. It's the firstborn I am concerned with."

The woman nodded. "My youngest took some time to catch on. Do not worry, Gussalen. I will care for both babes as if they were my own."

"Focus on the older one," she cautioned. "He will be heir to Shadowfaire. Come in now."

She led the woman into the bedchamber and to the bed.

"This is the woman I told you about, my lady. She will be wet nurse to both boys."

"I thank you," Juliana said quietly as Gussalen took the child from her and gave him to the wet nurse. "The heir."

She gave the new wet nurse a few more instructions and indicated the second boy, making sure the three were settled in a chair in the corner of the room. After some coaxing, both babes suckled at the unfamiliar breasts. Gussalen nodded her approval to the woman and returned to the bedside.

"I need to tell your lord husband that he is father to two boys, my lady. First, I want to change your sheets and put you in fresh clothes. Comb your hair. You will want to look your best for him."

Juliana let her do as she wished. Gussalen wanted everything perfect before she ventured downstairs to see The Brute. She even stopped by her own chamber and tidied up before she descended the stairs.

The evening meal had just ended and servants cleared the dishes away. Men moved the trestle tables back against the walls. She spotted The Brute standing with a group of his soldiers and made her way toward him. As she suspected, he had a cup in his hand and, from his flushed face, she knew he'd been drinking all day.

He caught sight of her as she approached. "You'd better have good news for me."

"The countess did her duty, my lord," Gussalen assured him. "She has given birth to not one boy, but two."

The Brute gave a shout of approval. "Did you hear that? I have two sons!"

He lifted his cup and had those near him toast to the health of his children. He slapped a few backs and pinched a passing maid's bottom.

"Would you like to see the twins, my lord?" she asked. Her heart raced at the deception she would now put into motion.

The earl nodded and followed her from the great hall.

Gussalen led him up to the bedchamber. The babes had finished nursing and now lay sleeping, one on each side of Juliana. As expected, he ignored his wife and snatched up the larger one that favored him. The child did not appreciate being grabbed so roughly and loudly bellowed his displeasure.

The Brute smiled. "See? This one has a good set of lungs on him. He'll make a fine warrior. We shall name him Kenric. 'Tis a strong name for a strong heir."

"But my lord," Gussalen said, shaking her head sadly, "you do not hold the firstborn." She indicated the other sleeping infant. "This is the babe who is your heir to Shadowfaire. Surely you wish to hold this son, for he will be far more important than the second born."

The shock on the nobleman's face gave her more pleasure than she'd imagined. The Brute looked to the smaller, pale babe that resembled his wife and back at her in disbelief.

"Nay. It cannot be. *This* one has a strong, lusty cry. *He* should be earl."

Gussalen frowned at him. "Nay, my lord, Ask your wife."

The Brute glared at Juliana as he possessively held the darker babe to his chest. "Tell me now. I order you. Which one is heir to Shadowfaire?"

Without hesitation, Juliana pointed to the tiny babe who had awakened at the shouting and fussed. "*He* was first to claw his way from my womb. He shall make a fine knight, my lord husband, as the true heir to Shadowfaire."

The Brute looked as if someone had punched him in his gut. All the bluster fled from him. Disappointment darkened his face.

He glanced down at the babe in his arms. "At least I have a strong second born son in case the first weakling dies." He thrust the babe into Gussalen's arms and stormed from the bedchamber.

Juliana gasped in horror at his brash statement. She lifted the child and cradled him in her arms, kissing the babe's forehead and smoothing down what little hair he had.

Gussalen secretly smiled to herself. The sickly runt might not hold the title of firstborn for long, but she would do everything in her power to see that this scrawny babe lived to become earl, simply to spite the present one.

"Take both babes across the hall to the chamber I have prepared for them," she ordered the wet nurse who cowered in the corner. "I shall be with you shortly."

The woman scooped up the fair child from his mother and took the darker one from Gussalen and exited the bedchamber.

She went to the woman who was more her girl than the babe she'd given birth to so many years ago.

"Do not weep, my lady," she comforted, stroking the silky, blond hair. "He has two sons. He may very well leave you alone now."

She watched as Juliana understood her words. Relief washed over the noblewoman. "Do you really think so, Guss?"

"I do, indeed, my lady, and 'twould be a huge blessing. But we have something important to discuss. He did not name the other babe. What would you like to call him?"

Juliana thought a moment. "Roland. After my father. I only wish he'd lived to know this child."

Gussalen put an arm around her charge. "I am sure your father looks down from Heaven above and approves. So Roland the Fair is the elder and heir, and Kenric, the younger brother, will serve him." She stroked Juliana's hair. "You did a fine thing today, my lady, giving birth to two boys."

And the Earl of Shadowfaire had believed what he had been told.

CHAPTER I

Longshire Castle—June, 1363

KENRIC FAIRFAX STOOD at the foot of the stairs that led up to the keep, awaiting the arrival of his family. He had mixed feelings about seeing them again. The last time they had spent time together occurred five years earlier when they put his father into the ground.

He had not returned to Shadowfaire since.

Walter Fairfax had been a difficult man, swift to anger and hard to please—yet he had been a good teacher to his son. Kenric left his home to foster with Lord Forwin at Longshire well prepared. He sat a horse and rode better than any boy his age and understood various nuances of swordplay. Since he was large for his age, he had a strength that enabled him to be skilled at archery from a young age. Kenric had met with nothing but success under Lord Forwin these last ten and four years.

His twin had not fared nearly as well.

Roland Fairfax did not favor his brother in any way. Where Kenric stood tall and sturdy, Roland proved weak in body and was more than a head shorter. He was timid around horses and couldn't seem to understand the strategy to use in order to best an opponent with a sword. Roland sneezed constantly and fell ill often. He nearly died thrice—and that was before they left at age seven to foster together.

His brother had only spent a few years training as a page. He was so slow at completing tasks that Kenric stepped in many times and speedily polished the last pieces of armor so that his twin would not suffer the consequences. Yet Roland never once thanked him. The older Fairfax boy was arrogant and condescending—when he wasn't lying. More times than Kenric could count, Roland had done some mischief and blamed the outcome on his brother.

As Kenric matured, he realized Roland must be jealous of him for being smarter, stronger, faster, and better at anything the two attempted. Since his twin was now the earl, he hoped that would be enough to satisfy Roland.

Kenric had his own life to lead—and his own destiny to fulfill.

The sound of hooves beating against the earth drew his attention. The Fairfax colors danced in the breeze as the expected party arrived from Shadowfaire. For once, events focused on him. Kenric would participate in the Order of Knighthood Ceremony on the day he turned one and twenty. By this time tomorrow, he would have become a full-fledged knight of the realm.

Tossing his shoulders back and standing a little taller as the riders drew near, he noticed his uncle riding next to his mother. Kenric closely resembled Uncle Doran, who physically was cut from the same cloth his brother, Walter, came from. The three Fairfax men all possessed thick, dark hair and hazel eyes. The trio also hovered above six feet, though Kenric had turned out to be the tallest of them all.

Doran Fairfax had never married. He'd returned to his childhood home to guide the new earl as Roland assumed the title at the tender age of ten and six. Kenric had never trusted his uncle. He believed the man was a second son who longed for the mantle of power to be placed upon his shoulders—and Doran had gotten his wish with his older brother's death. Though Kenric had not visited Shadowfaire in several years, he believed Roland was a puppet and Uncle Doran the string master and true authority behind the title.

As his uncle moved to help his sister-in-law from her horse, her eyes locked with Kenric's. The wintry blue eyes had never warmed to him. While Roland cuddled in their mother's lap, Juliana Fairfax would push Kenric away if he tried to join them. She told Roland stories and gave him treats but never did so with her younger son. Kenric often wondered what he had done wrong to be kept at such a distance both physically and emotionally.

He stepped over to greet her and kissed her offered cheek.

"Thank you for coming, Mother. Uncle." He shook hands with Doran.

Then he turned and noticed Gussalen, the nurse who had tended to his mother's every whim since childhood. The old woman glared at him with hate before she spat on the ground.

"Brother," Kenric acknowledged.

Roland climbed from his horse, looking pale and frail in the summer sun. Kenric noticed his twin had not grown in height since their father's funeral mass. Roland barely came to his shoulder. His brother's frame had not filled out and his fair hair, so much like the blond of their mother's, had already begun to thin and recede.

"Who is that?" Roland asked.

He glanced over his shoulder as the baron and his daughter descended the steps to meet their guests. Lord Forwin had given Kenric time to greet his family privately but now came forward to welcome the new arrivals.

"Surely, you remember Lord Forwin," he said. "Lady Jannet, his daughter, accompanies him."

"She was merely a babe when I was here as a page," noted Roland. He smiled. "She has grown into quite a beauty."

Kenric shrugged. He had little contact with the girl, though she'd hung around the training yard in recent months, mooning over barechested soldiers as they partnered in various exercises. She'd proven a distraction to the men. They showed off for her, trying to impress her and win a smile. He wished the captain of the guard would ask her to leave, but even Kenric realized Jannet was an only child and notably spoiled.

"I extend a warm welcome to you all," Lord Forwin said. "We are delighted that Kenric's family could attend his Order of the Knighthood Ceremony."

"My lord, may I introduce to you my mother, Lady Juliana, and my uncle, Sir Doran Fairfax? And also my brother, Roland, Earl of

Shadowfaire." Kenric left unspoken how Forwin knew exactly who Roland was and that he had abandoned his training at Longshire many years ago to run home to his mother's skirts.

"'Tis a pleasure to meet you," the nobleman said. "Of course, I met the previous earl on several occasions when he brought the twins to Longshire." He paused and turned, drawing Jannet closer. "And here is my lovely flower. My daughter, Lady Jannet."

She made her curtsey and Kenric watched Roland's eyes gaze at her in approval. It occurred to him that Roland also turned one and twenty tomorrow. As the earl, he would need to find a wife in order to have children and pass along his title and the estate. He bit back the smile that threatened to escape.

So, Roland found Jannet interesting.

Little did his twin know that the young noblewoman had a vile temper and was used to ruling the roost since her mother had passed along a good half a score ago. Kenric observed his mother pick up on Roland's interest. He waited for her to make a move for her favorite son.

"We are so pleased to have you visit Longshire Castle," Jannet told them. "Please, come inside. We have bedchambers prepared and refreshments awaiting you."

His mother linked arms with Jannet. "And we are delighted to be here, my dear." She turned. "Come, Roland. Help Lady Jannet and me up these stairs."

Roland sprang into action, attaching himself to Jannet's other side, and they ascended the stone stairs. Lord Forwin and his uncle fell in behind them, with Kenric bringing up the rear.

When they arrived inside the keep, Forwin asked Kenric, "Do you know where your assigned chamber is? We cannot have your ritual of cleansing take place in the noisy barracks."

"I have been instructed as to which bedchamber I should use. Thank you, my lord." He looked to his uncle. "I will see you tomorrow, Uncle Doran."

Kenric moved toward his mother and brother. "Thank you again for journeying to Longshire. I am sure you are in good hands with Lady Jannet. I must excuse myself now to prepare for the ceremony."

He mounted the stairs and counted the number of doors along the corridor until he arrived at the appointed room. Once inside, he stopped and stared at the clothing awaiting him on the bed.

A white vesture, symbolizing purity, was spread next to a red robe, which stood for nobility. Both the hose and shoes, black in color, represented death. Once he had completed his ritual bathing, he would don this set of new clothes. His shining sword and shield rested beside the clothing. Kenric had polished the pair himself, not trusting the task to a page.

A knock at the door drew his attention. He opened it and admitted a row of servants, each carrying two buckets of steaming water which they dumped into the wooden tub at the far end of the room. Lady Jannet brought up the rear. In her hands, she carried a large bath sheet, scrubbing brush, and a cake of soap. She dismissed the servants and closed the door.

Facing him, she said, "I am here to help you in your bath."

Kenric did not like the gleam in her eye.

"I thank you for the offer, my lady, but I believe I can manage."

Her eyes narrowed. "But as lady of the house, I am expected to help visitors bathe."

He laughed. "I am no visitor, Lady Jannet. I have resided at Longshire since I was seven. In fact, I remember you as a babe. You began to walk about the time I arrived."

"I am a grown woman now, Kenric Fairfax, or have you not noticed?" She thrust her bottom lip out, a seductive look in her eye.

Kenric remembered his friend, Hudd, warning him about Jannet. *"She's trouble, that one,"* Hudd had said only days ago.

He decided to focus on the religious aspect of the experience and hoped that would discourage her.

"I do appreciate your thoughtful offer, my lady. But I need to concentrate on the ritual of bathing. I must thoroughly cleanse my body as a symbol of purification, as well as prepare my mind for the long prayer vigil which follows. I can't have distractions from my task while I ready myself for God."

"Is that what I am—a distraction?" She licked her lips slowly.

"A pretty girl is always a distraction," he teased, hoping to lighten the tension filling the room.

Jannet closed the gap between them. Before he realized what the girl meant to do, she locked her hands behind his neck and pulled him down to her. His lips briefly brushed against hers before he jerked away.

"No, my lady. This isn't proper. We are not betrothed. You mustn't—"

"I love you, Kenric," she declared. "My love is deep and rich. You are the man for me. No other will do."

Her declaration came from nowhere and startled him to his core.

"Father has not given me to another. He has waited for the most advantageous match." Her eyes danced as she studied him. "But you are soon to be a knight and come from a respected noble family. You are the best of all his soldiers and I know he thinks highly of you."

Kenric knew he must discourage her and be gentle about it. Jannet was not only physically frail but he thought, mayhap, mentally fragile, as well.

"I am flattered, my lady," he began, pausing when words failed him.

"I do not wish for flattery," she snapped, then took a deep breath and looked at him imploringly. "Why do you think I have come to the training yard so frequently, Kenric? It was because I wanted to watch you fight. See how quickly you dispatched your training partners."

Jannet reached a hand out and ran it seductively along his arm. "Do you know what it does to me when I look at you? See your sleek muscles ripple as you engaged in combat?" she purred. "View the sweat glistening on your torso? Ah, Kenric, my love began for you many years ago. And now that I am a woman, 'tis time we came together as one."

Her fingers glided up his arm slowly, causing him to stiffen. "I want to feel you inside of me. Call out your name. Do whatever it takes to possess you. To make you mine."

The gleam in her eyes frightened him even more than her words.

Kenric thought quickly. "But I could provide no home for you, Lady Jannet. You are a most beautiful woman who deserves the best of what life has to offer. Wealth. Jewels. A titled, handsome husband." He let his words sink in before he continued. "My brother, Roland, is a man who could give you these things. As my elder brother, he holds the title in our family, as well as a fortune and vast estate. Roland confided in me how smitten he was with you. You might wish to consider his suit, my lady. I know him well and I saw how taken he was with you upon his arrival. Roland would treat you better than the king treats Queen Philippa. You would do well to be open to the possibility of a union with Roland."

Kenric only hoped his words might have an impact on Jannet. Marriage to her—or any woman—was the last thing on his mind as he stood on the cusp of realizing his dream of becoming a knight. To be tied down to one woman, especially one as delicate and demanding as Jannet, would be a living nightmare.

She began to pout, reminding him of a small child who had been denied her way. He wished her to be gone from his sight before she turned even more reckless in her behavior.

"At least promise me that we may dance together at the celebration after the ceremony."

He could see little harm in promising the girl a dance. But he hoped she would consider attaching herself to Roland. Kenric would make sure he told his brother that Jannet might be interested in him.

"I would be honored to partner in a dance with you, my lady."

She bit her lip. "You now know what I think of you, Kenric Fairfax. I wish to know you better."

"Know that I will serve and protect you and your household. I will make my pledge to do so tomorrow. For now, though, I must prepare myself for the upcoming ceremony."

Jannet took the hint and bid him good evening. He saw her to the door and relief washed over him when she passed through it. Kenric closed and bolted the door and leaned against it.

Mayhap, Roland would draw her interest. Kenric had done his best to plant that seed in her mind. His brother was handsome in a soft way. Roland favored their mother while he resembled their father.

The thought brought him to a halt. Kenric remembered the coldness between his parents. He'd never witnessed a single sign of affection between them before he left for Longshire or on his brief visits home. His father had flagrantly bedded other women in the castle and on the estate. Kenric wondered if that was why his mother had never shown him any fondness or warmth. Did he remind her so much of her unfaithful husband?

Kenric also blamed Gussalen, the old woman who always lurked in the shadows. She had lied about him to his mother on many occasions and blamed him for things Roland did. He had always taken the punishment in silence, knowing he was the stronger of the two boys.

It caused him to believe he'd stumbled upon the reason for his mother's dislike. She had transferred her feelings toward her husband upon the child who was his mirror image.

He stripped off his clothes and climbed into the hot bath, pushing the past aside. It was more important to reflect on what the new day would bring and not be caught up in things he could never change.

As he scrubbed his limbs, Kenric focused on his future. More than anything, he had dreamed of becoming a great knight and adhering to the code of chivalry. He longed to prove his prowess on the battlefield. He decided, in that moment, to commit fully to knighthood and never let love or marriage become distractions. He, Sir Kenric Fairfax, would serve king and country till his dying breath.

He rinsed the last of the soap from his skin, raw and red from the vigorous scrubbing. Reaching for the bath sheet, he stood and dried himself before dressing in the clothes on the bed.

Now it was time to head to the chapel for the Night Vigil.

Placing his sword in one hand and his shield in the other, Kenric made his way down the stairs and outside of the keep. Within minutes, he reached the empty chapel. Silence hung heavily in the air, while lit candles rested upon the steps leading up to the altar.

He made his way to the altar and placed his sword and shield upon it. Lord Forwin had told Kenric he had a choice of kneeling in submission or standing for the ten hours of prayer that now came.

Kenric decided to stand tall and proud.

He offered many prayers to the Virgin Mother. He asked that he stay humble but, over time, hoped he might become the best knight in all the realm.

More importantly, he begged for the coldness that surrounded his heart to thaw where his mother and twin brother were concerned. Kenric wanted to be free of sin—and that meant being free of anger and resentment toward his blood kin. They had made the effort to attend his knighthood ceremony, so it was up to him to forgive them for all past transgressions against him. He asked the Blessed Christ to lift away his burden of sin.

Kenric slowed his breathing as he meditated. A calm surrounded him as if the dove of peace descended upon him and he put aside all petty feelings lingering from his childhood. What mattered was that he would be his own man, a knight sworn in service to both his king and Lord Forwin, his liege lord.

Tomorrow would be the first day his life truly began.

CHAPTER 2

K ENRIC SENSED SOMEONE'S PRESENCE and slowly opened his eyes to find the Longshire priest had arrived in the chapel. It surprised him that the time spent in prayer consecrating himself to his knight's life mission had passed so quickly.

"Good morning," Father Peter said. "I hope your vigil went as you wished. You have an air of tranquility about you, my son."

He smiled. "It did, Father. Despite having been on my feet for many hours and receiving no sleep, I have a strong sense of purpose and have reconciled my past with what my future will bring."

"'Tis exactly what your vigil should have accomplished. I believe you will make a fine knight, Kenric Fairfax."

"Thank you, Father."

The priest excused himself and went about readying the chapel for the morning mass and ceremony. Kenric squatted and rose several times and then shook his feet. He walked a few laps about the chapel to get his blood circulating again.

Workers from the castle and the surrounding estate began to arrive, followed by the soldiers from the garrison and then the nobility from both the castle and Kenric's relatives from Shadowfaire. Father Peter signaled for the doors to be closed so that the mass could commence. Kenric followed the ceremony since he read and spoke Latin, but he knew most of those present did not. He doubted even Roland knew what was being said. His twin had not enjoyed their lessons in reading and writing and hadn't mastered even the simplest of Latin verbs to conjugate.

Father Peter began to speak again, this time, addressing those in attendance in English so that all might understand his words.

"My homily usually revolves around the scriptures that have been read. But today is a special day in the life of Kenric Fairfax, squire to Lord Forwin at Longshire Castle."

Kenric sensed the eyes of those gathered falling upon him.

"I speak to you today of what it means to be a knight, for not every man can walk this path. A knight is a man of honor who possesses great combat skills and conducts himself with courage—whether he feels brave or not. Most of all, he values loyalty in himself and in others. A knight is guaranteed a place in heaven due to the loyalty he shows, both to our king and the Church."

The priest continued. "A knight adheres to the code of chivalry. He always defends a lady and is charitable to the poor and helpless. He never avoids a dangerous path out of fear and is prompt for any engagement of arms, be it in battle or a tournament.

"He defends the Church and remains devoted to Her throughout his life. He loves his country and is generous to all he meets. He champions the right and the good against injustice and evil." Father Peter paused and directed his gaze to Kenric. "And if he breaks his oath in any way? Then he has committed a crime against God and will be eternally damned for doing so."

Kenric took in the man of the cloth's words and knew he would always hold them dear. He would strive to be a man of honor and never stray from his knightly oath.

Prayers and communion followed the homily. A sense of urgency filled him once the last person accepted the Host.

"'Tis time to begin the accolade," Father Peter announced. "Lord Forwin?"

Forwin rose, along with the captain of the guard and Kenric's uncle. It surprised him that Doran would participate in the adoubement ceremony, but it pleased him that a member of the Fairfax family would be involved.

The three men made their way to the front of the chapel. The priest blessed the sword and shield before Doran took possession of them. He motioned for Kenric to join them.

His uncle conducted the ceremony as those present watched in rapt silence.

"Kenric Fairfax of Shadowfaire, have you undertaken to accept the accolade of knighthood offered to you?"

"I have," he responded.

"You have been deemed fit for this by your peers and have indicated your willingness to accept this honor. Do you now swear by all that you hold sacred, true, and holy that you will honor and defend the Crown?"

"I will."

"That you will honor, defend, and protect all ladies, and those weaker than yourself?"

"I will."

"That you will only draw your sword for just cause and enshrine in your heart the noble ideals of Chivalry?"

"I will."

"That you will honor and protect our king and the Church?"

"I will."

"And do you swear the oath of allegiance to your liege lord, Forwin of Longshire?"

"I do."

Doran held the sword out to him. Kenric kissed the hilt and dropped to his knees.

"Then having sworn these solemn oaths," his uncle said as he struck Kenric with the side of the sword on his shoulder, "once for Honor... twice for Duty... thrice for Chivalry... I dub thee Sir Kenric Fairfax. Arise!"

He stood while his sword was girded on and new spurs attached to his heels.

"Accept these spurs, which symbolize your devotion to the high ideals of Chivalry and Justice. Wear them honorably and proudly, and may they never be hacked off in shame or degradation."

Pride washed over Kenric as he turned to face his liege lord.

"I welcome you into my service, Sir Kenric," Lord Forwin told him. He held out his hand and both men shook.

Applause erupted throughout the chapel.

Forwin put a hand on Kenric's shoulder and turned to face the crowd. "The Order of the Knighthood Ceremony is not complete without a celebration. I bid you all to adjourn to the great hall to break your fast and then accomplish your tasks by the end of the morning. For once the noon hour approaches, we shall feast all day long and into the night. There shall be music and dancing—with plenty of wine and strong ale," he added.

"And whether or not Sir Kenric and his fellow knights have a clear head on the morrow, a tournament has been arranged to allow him and the others a chance to demonstrate their knightly skills. So make haste and return to the keep."

"My lord?" Father Peter interrupted. "A closing prayer?"

Forwin nodded. The priest gave a final blessing and mass ended.

"Go in peace," he told those assembled.

Many, especially Kenric's fellow soldiers, came forward to congratulate him. He accepted their well wishes with a huge smile. All the years of hard work as both page and squire had brought him to this moment. He would forevermore be a knight.

Finally, only his family remained behind in the chapel. His mother brushed dry lips against his cheek, showing little emotion. His uncle shook his hand. Kenric decided the person he most wanted to make amends with was his brother.

"Would you care to ride with me after we break our fast?" he asked his twin.

Roland thought a moment and then agreed.

They returned to the great hall for a simple meal. Kenric excused himself after they had eaten in order to change his clothes. He arranged to meet Roland in the stables in a quarter hour.

He arrived first and had both of their horses saddled and led outside the structure. Roland greeted him and they mounted the horses.

Kenric led his brother from the bailey and out the gates of Longshire. They rode to the end of the property as he pointed out various things of interest. Roland, however, seemed bored by their conversation.

"We should water our horses since the day grows warm," Kenric suggested. He led them into the woods and found the nearby stream often used for this purpose. Both horses lapped greedily at the water.

Roland collapsed upon a fallen log. He threw out his legs in front of him and braced himself with his hands.

"So, how is Shadowfaire these days?" Kenric asked. "Do you enjoy being the earl?"

His brother's sneer showed his disdain. "Every day is the same, which means that I am usually bored. What I long to do is go to court."

"Why?" If he had been born a minute earlier, he would be earl. Kenric thought owning land and a castle would be immensely satisfying, not parading around the royal palace with other fawning courtiers.

"Who cares about how much wheat is brought in or how many sheep are shorn? Numbers mean nothing to me. Running an estate is not something I wish to occupy my time, much less the rest of my life."

Kenric could see how his brother's disinterest would come into play. His short attention span would not suit the job at hand.

Roland waved a hand in the air. "Doran likes those details, so I don't have to fuss with them." He grinned. "And that means I have plenty of free time."

"What do you do with this time? Do you ride? Hunt? Work with the steward to improve the estate?"

Roland laughed. "I spend some hours in the village each week. A recent and very pretty widow has caught my eye."

His gut clenched. He did not like to hear that Doran had control of the estate and that Roland neglected his duties simply to dip his wick into a new widow. His twin had always fancied himself something of a ladies' man. Fresh anger at how Roland wasted his life brewed within him.

Kenric took possession of his reins and mounted Firefall, riding off without a word. He supposed Roland would never change. The Earl of Shadowfaire was a man who lived in the moment and shirked responsibility whenever possible. Kenric dug in his newly-won spurs and Firefall raced across the meadow, clearing the wall flawlessly. He had wanted to put things right between him and Roland before his brother's departure. Instead, bitterness brewed inside him.

If only he could have been firstborn . . .

He pushed the thought aside, knowing it wasn't right to dwell on jealousy. He needed to focus on his new status as a knight and put aside wishful thinking.

"Kenric! Wait!" Roland called out, riding after him.

Slowing his horse, Kenric brought it around as his brother drew near. Immediately, he saw Roland did not have control of the animal. It worried Kenric that they approached so fast.

Before he could spur Firefall on to meet them and slow the renegade horse, he watched as Roland's mount cleared the stone wall. Roland, already half out of the saddle, fell to the ground as his horse galloped away. Kenric let the beast fly by as he galloped to where his brother had landed.

Roland lay crumpled on the ground. His arm stuck out at an odd angle and Kenric knew it must be broken. He braced himself for the blame that would be hurled his way.

Leaping from Firefall and bending low, he helped Roland to his feet. His brother cradled the injured arm as he unleashed a torrent of curses. Kenric let his twin expel his anger before he brought an arm about Roland's shoulders to steady him.

His brother shrugged it off and let fly a few more choice words. Looking at him with hatred, Roland said, "It's your fault, this pain I suffer from. You rode off and left me. What if I had been unable to find my way back to the keep?"

Kenric lost his temper. "You know where you are, for you spent a few years here at Longshire—that is, before you ran home to Mother's protection. So what if I left? We are not far from the castle." He pointed to it over his shoulder. "You can see it from here. Are you truly so helpless that you cannot return on your own?"

Roland's eyes widened. "I knew you hated me, Brother. That you have since we fought our way from the womb. I realize you are filled with misery and jealousy simply because I am firstborn and privileged to be called Earl of Shadowfaire. You did everything to undermine me when we were children, but I will have no more of that. I *am* the earl! You are but a lowly knight and will never amount to anyone of value." He walked away, holding his arm close against his body to keep from jarring it.

Kenric paused, giving thought to his brother's words. He had protected Roland from the time he understood that he was the stronger of the two. Yet at every turn, his brother thwarted him. From the time they could walk, Roland was constantly bragging how he would one day become the earl.

Mayhap jealousy still lay in Kenric's heart, though he knew he was free of hatred. More than anything, he felt sorry for Roland, a man who would never be happy, no matter what he did or how much wealth he accumulated. At least Kenric had a purpose in life.

"Roland. Wait."

Kenric took Firefall's reins and hurried toward Roland. Reaching his twin, he saw hatred burning in Roland's blue eyes. Ignoring it, Kenric said, "Let me help you onto my horse."

"Nay. I want nothing from you. I wish to be gone from here, a place that only holds miserable memories for me. I never fit in here. The other boys laughed and made fun of me. And *you* led them in their taunts."

"I never did such a thing, Roland. I always tried to look out for you, as a brother should." Kenric kept his voice calm. His anger had died, replaced by pity for the weak man before him.

"I didn't wish to attend your ceremony," Roland continued, his voice dripping with venom. "I thought it a waste of time. As did Mother," he tossed out. "But Uncle insisted we come. Now look where that has gotten me."

Kenric had no answer. He fell into step with Roland, leading Firefall behind him. They walked in silence until they reached the keep. When they entered, Kenric steered Roland into the great hall. He spied his mother and uncle in conversation with Lady Jannet.

"Call for the healer," he told them. "My brother has taken a bad spill from his horse."

His mother rushed to Roland's side, fussing over him. Lady Jannet motioned for a servant and requested that the healer come at once to Lord Roland's bedchamber. The two women, one on each side, led the young earl from the room.

Doran gave a weary shrug. "Typical."

"He blames me, Uncle."

The older man snorted. "Of course he does, Kenric. He desires to be you. And I wish you had been Walter's heir. Roland is weak in body, spirit, and mind. He has no interest in becoming a good lord to the people of Shadowfaire. He would rather rut and gamble with others like him at the royal court. I have half a mind to send him there to do just that."

"I have heard that court can be a wild place. 'Twould not do to allow him to go there alone, Uncle. He could land in much trouble."

His uncle's brows shot up. "And if I did? Mayhap, he would drink himself to death. Or lapse into another of his many ailments. Mayhap, he might catch a fever—or be challenged and fight a duel where he would lose his life. That boy should never have been named firstborn. Walter should have looked at the both of you and insisted *you* had arrived first and would be the future earl. He treated you as if you would be. He was hard on you, but he taught you all you needed to know."

Doran clasped Kenric's shoulder. "My brother knew that one day you *would* become the earl." His fingers dug into Kenric. "Be ready. That day may arrive before you know it."

CHAPTER 3

"YOU SHOULD NOT be miserable at your own feast," Doran told him before he stabbed a bite of veal with his dagger and popped it into his mouth.

Kenric looked about from where he sat at the great table on the dais. He had never partaken of a meal while seated here since it was reserved for the noble family in residence and guests of distinction. He could see all of the great hall from this perch, people dining upon the wild game, fish, vegetables, and fruits from the six courses which had come from the kitchen.

"Mother refuses to speak to me," he told his uncle.

Doran glanced over at his sister-in-law and turned back to Kenric.

"Juliana often acts like a petulant child. She is as bad as Roland at times—or worse." His uncle picked up some of the hare and chewed thoughtfully. "And you cannot tell me you miss having Roland present at this banquet. 'Tis your time to shine, my boy. Your father would have been most proud of you today."

He looked to the far side of the dais, where his mother sat next to Lady Jannet. The healer had found it necessary to re-break Roland's arm in order to set it properly. Kenric had listened to his twin's screams of agony, guilt flooding him as he waited in the corridor. His mother exited the room long enough to scold him as if he were a child before returning to her favorite son's bedside.

The healer had appeared after that and told Kenric that Roland would be fine. She had given him something to make him sleep and the Earl of Shadowfaire would not awaken until tomorrow morning.

But Kenric knew his brother's wrath would not have cooled by then.

He took a drumstick of roasted chicken and ate it, not tasting the bird.

"You realize nothing you can do or say will ever change Roland's feelings toward you," Doran pointed out.

"I know." Kenric sighed. "I fear I will never see Shadowfaire again, for he would never welcome me within its gates. Besides, I am in service now to Lord Forwin. My home is here at Longshire, along with the rest of his knights and soldiers."

At that moment, Lord Forwin rose and held out his cup to the assembled crowd. The hall grew quiet.

"I ask you to raise a cup in honor of Longshire's newest knight." The nobleman faced Kenric. "To Sir Kenric. May he have good health, a long life, and much happiness."

"Sir Kenric!" the people echoed, toasting him.

He bowed his head, humbled by their support.

"'Tis time for music and dancing," announced Forwin. "Musicians, you may begin," he commanded.

Music filled the air as servants began clearing the dishes and men moved the trestle tables back against the walls to make room for the merriment. Kenric watched his mother draw Lord Forwin aside and excuse herself. She left the room without glancing in her son's direction.

"Come, Sir Kenric. It's the round dance."

A serving wench took his hand, pulling him down to the floor. Though dancing was condemned by the Church, it remained a favorite pastime in England. Even nuns participated in it from time to time.

Kenric stepped to the circle forming and joined hands with those gathering. Soon, he was caught up in the lively music as the group executed the complicated footwork as one. He'd always been skilled at swordplay and found dancing to be much the same. His body moved in time with the music as he tapped and spun. The more he danced, the more he enjoyed himself and put his troubles behind him.

He begged off after finishing four dances in a row in order to grab a tankard of ale. Hudd, his closest friend at Longshire, joined him.

"So how does it feel to be Sir Kenric?" Hudd teased as he tapped his cup against his friend's.

Kenric took a long swig before answering. "The same—other than my seat at the feast. And that place of honor is only for today. Tomorrow, I will join Lord Forwin's other knights and eat among the soldiers. Still, I appreciate the expense the baron has gone to in order to provide this feast of celebration."

"It's a fine way to celebrate your birthday, my lord," Hudd said.

His friend's words, though meant to be kind, deflated Kenric's high spirits. He might be making merry with food, drink, and dance—but his injured brother, who shared this day with him, was tucked away in pain above stairs.

"I wish to dance, Sir Kenric," Lady Jannet said.

Hudd rolled his eyes since his back was turned to her and mouthed, "Be careful." He excused himself and hurried off, taking Kenric's tankard with him.

Kenric reached out and took the girl's hand, placing it atop his forearm. "Let us go enjoy the music, my lady."

He led her to the center of the great hall. The song had changed to a rotundellus and couples now paired off from the large circles.

As they danced, Kenric became increasingly uncomfortable as Jannet gazed up at him in rapt adoration. He looked out across the floor, not wanting to meet her eye.

"My lord, look at me," she demanded.

He lowered his eyes to hers. "Aye, my lady?" he said, keeping his voice neutral. He didn't want to encourage attention from her in any way that might be misconstrued.

"I love you," she stated bluntly. "Now that you are a knight, we must marry."

Kenric surprised himself by keeping his feet moving. He said, "I shared my views with you earlier, my lady. I have no intention of marrying now or at any other time. My brother holds the family lands and title. I have committed to being a knight. I will not pursue a home with a wife and a family. Instead, I want to remain in service to your father."

A blush crept up her neck and stained her cheeks. "Am I not pretty enough?" she asked. "Is my bosom not large enough? Do I—"

"Nay, my lady. You are perfect as you are," he reassured her. "I am merely stating facts to you. I have not even been a knight a single day. I want to dedicate myself to service. I am not interested in women."

Her eyes narrowed. "But you go with the other soldiers to the village. I know 'tis there you find women to pleasure you."

He shrugged. "I do not deny it. That's the way of men, but it doesn't mean I plan to marry any of them."

"Kiss me," she commanded.

"Nay, I cannot." He halted his steps. "You will make some man a good wife one day, my lady. But 'twill not be me."

She glared daggers at him and flounced off. Kenric could feel the eyes of others upon him as he moved from the center of the room. He spied Jannet marching toward her father. They conversed less than a minute before she nodded and left the great hall. Lord Forwin scanned the room and motioned Kenric over. He quickly responded, his step confident, but his heart hammered in his chest. What if the baron dismissed him? Or worse—what if the nobleman demanded that Kenric enter into marriage with his daughter?

When he reached his liege lord, the man said, "We should adjourn to a quieter place, Sir Kenric."

"Of course, my lord."

The two men left the great hall. Forwin led him toward the steps that went up to the bedchambers on the floor above and to where Kenric believed they would speak—the solar.

As the noise and music began to fade behind them, the nobleman said, "My daughter tells me that she has feelings for you. Are they returned?"

Kenric tread lightly as he replied, "Lady Jannet is a fine girl and you have much to be proud of, my lord. Although I am flattered by her attention, I have no plans of settling down and offering marriage to any woman. I am committed in mind, body, and spirit to my knightly oath and your service."

Forwin's fingers laced behind his back as they reached the upper corridor and started down it. "I thought as much. You are a soldier at heart, Kenric, with a good head on your shoulders." He gave Kenric a wry smile. "But you are a second son. I must confess that I want a title for my girl. As a matter of fact, I have been in negotiations recently for that very event to occur. Just today, I received a missive that an agreement of terms has been struck with an earl of my acquaintance who is connected to the royal family. I believe he and Jannet will suit admirably."

Relief poured through Kenric as the tension left his body. "Then congratulations are in order. I think that would be for the best, my lord. Lady Jannet will have an esteemed place in the kingdom as a countess."

"In a different household where you will not be," Forwin pointed out. "I know that she's headstrong. I have let her have her way far too often, but what was I to do? She was a motherless child and I did what I could to make it up to her."

"You have been a wonderful father to your daughter. I know she will appreciate the match you've made for her."

They arrived at the solar. Forwin invited him inside, ushering him through the door.

Kenric saw that Jannet awaited them, seated in a chair by the fire, her finger lazily circling the rim of a wine goblet. She stood eagerly, a smile on her face, believing she had gotten her way again and that her father had brought Kenric to the family's private quarters to discuss their upcoming vows.

"Sit," her father instructed.

She did so warily, glancing from Kenric to Lord Forwin, concern registered on her brow.

"My dearest, I have spoken with Sir Kenric and I—"

Jannet leapt to her feet. "Do not listen to him, Father. He believes that I am a child who doesn't know my own mind. He thinks because he has no property that he could never be a husband to me. But I know a knight can purchase his own land if he has none of his own."

She gave them her most beguiling smile. "Surely you would not mind awarding Sir Kenric and me a parcel of land as our wedding gift? Or mayhap, we could simply live here inside the keep in a suite of rooms. You have no sons, Father. You could petition the king to name my husband as your heir."

Her lashes fluttered prettily. Kenric could see how Jannet had twisted her father around her finger over the years.

"This cannot be, child."

Jannet's jaw dropped. Kenric realized the girl had gotten her every wish before this moment. He said a swift prayer, thanking the Christ that a marriage had already been arranged for her.

"But I love him!" she cried, her voice rising with hysteria. "We are meant to be together. Forever."

"Nay," her father said. "Though Kenric is a good man and will be a great knight, I have bigger plans for you."

"Plans?" she said, uncertainty creeping into her voice. "What... plans?"

Forwin smiled. "I've arranged for you to wed an earl with vast wealth and royal connections next month. I have worked many months on the details and we have now settled the matter. You will be a countess, Jannet."

She crossed her arms. Her bottom lip shot out. "But I do not want to be a countess. I want to be *his* wife," she proclaimed. "Kenric is the most handsome man in all of England." She stomped her foot. "And I want him, Father. No other. Do you understand? Break off whatever you have arranged with this earl."

Forwin sighed. "I know your wishes, but you must bow to my better judgment in this matter, my little love. Your soon-to-be husband is wealthy beyond imagination. You are guaranteed to have a wonderful life with dozens of properties and hundreds of servants. 'Tis what I want for you, what I have always wanted for you—the very best. And now I can give it to you."

"I cannot change your mind?"

"Nay, child."

"Then I will refuse to marry this nobleman!" Jannet burst into tears and fled the room.

"She is not happy with you," Kenric said.

Forwin shrugged. "I didn't think she would be. I knew she would be upset, no matter when I told her the news. And I had no idea that she held such strong feelings for you."

"Neither did I, my lord."

"Women," the baron said, snorting. He moved to the sideboard and poured each of them a glass of wine.

Kenric took the offered cup and downed the contents in a single swallow.

"We should return to your feast, Sir Kenric," Forwin told him. "I hope the dark shadows of Jannet's storm will not upset your happiness."

"Nay, my lord. I am thankful at all you have done for me this day. I look forward to many years in your service."

They returned to the great hall. Kenric noticed the doors to the keep were now thrown open and he heard music drifting in from the outside.

"I believe the party has moved outdoors," Forwin said.

"Tonight is June's honey moon, my lord," he replied. "Dancing in the strong moonlight sounds very appealing."

"Put aside Jannet's silly notions and enjoy yourself," the nobleman declared.

Kenric did as instructed. He left the keep and found the inner bailey filled with people, some milling about in conversation while others danced. He joined in the fun, linking arms with two pretty girls and dancing for the next few hours.

Suddenly, a scream sounded. The music stopped. He saw a woman pointing to the parapet above. Kenric looked up and sucked in a breath. Lady Jannet stood balancing on the edge of the parapet, her eyes locked on him. The crowd murmured. Kenric felt their eyes burning into him and then looking back to Jannet.

He must talk her down, whatever the cost, promise her anything.

Even marriage.

"My lady," he called out. "Come down from there." He stepped away from the crowd and came to stand directly below her.

Jannet leaned slightly forward and her foot slipped. The crowd gasped. She clutched the stone behind her.

Kenric thought her face would show terror. Instead, the moonlight playing upon it revealed madness.

"I shall come up, my lady," he hollered. "We can talk with one another."

"Talk? Of what?" She laughed harshly. "I am done with talk, Kenric Fairfax. I told you how much I love you. How I worship the very ground you trod upon. You know I live for your smiles. I want to wed you and bear your babes."

Behind him, the group that was gathered murmured uneasily. Kenric hated that Jannet played to this audience. He needed to get her alone and try to reason with her.

"My lady, we should speak of these personal matters in private."

"Why?" she asked. "Why should I hide from the world how I feel about you?" Her voice rose in hysteria. "You are the man for me, Kenric. There could never be another but you."

"You barely know me."

"I know everything I need to know, my darling. You are perfect for me in every way."

"I am far from perfect, my lady, and I told you that you deserve a man better than I am. I wish to wed no one, least of all you, for I am dedicated to being a knight—not a husband. Your father has chosen your future mate already. Be a good, obedient daughter and wed the man he wishes you to. Come down from there now."

Kenric only hoped by mentioning her beloved father, Jannet would reconsider her words and actions. He believed that she would calm herself enough to step down from the parapet and away from danger.

She gazed at him longingly, a wistful smile on her face. "I love you,

Kenric Fairfax." Her voice rang out loud and clear. "If I cannot be with you, I want no other man."

Without hesitation, Jannet flung herself away from the structure. She sailed through the air gracefully, as a soaring bird, her clothing billowing out behind her.

Then she hit the ground with a thud, landing at his feet.

A shocked silence quickly erupted into screams from every direction. As chaos swirled around him, Kenric knelt and lifted the broken body to him, cradling the dead madwoman in his arms.

"Jannet!" a voice cried out.

He recognized the agony in Lord Forwin's single word. Suddenly, the baron stood beside Kenric. Falling to his knees, the nobleman wrenched his daughter from Kenric, rocking with her in his arms, tears spilling down his cheeks.

Then Forwin's eyes met his. "What have you done?" he accused, his eyes raging.

Kenric had no words of comfort for his liege lord. Only shame filled him.

"Get out!" Forwin cried. "Get off my lands! I wish never to lay eyes upon you again."

With a heavy heart, Kenric rose and stepped away from the grieving man as he held his only child close. Sorrow swallowed Kenric whole as he saw the shocked faces glaring at him, blaming him for Jannet's death.

Unsheathing his sword, he held up his booted foot and hacked off the new spurs he had received only hours ago, although it seemed as if a lifetime had passed since this morning's ceremony. He did the same with the other foot as the hostile crowd watched. Picking up the damaged spurs from where they lay on the ground, Kenric decided he would keep them as a reminder of his lost honor.

He only hoped that one day he would be able to reclaim it again.

CHAPTER 4

London—May, 1366

AVELYN LE CLER sipped the last of her onion soup and returned the bowl to the table. She tore away a piece of bread the soup had been poured over and absently chewed it.

"And then he said to me that he wanted a kiss!"

"Hmm?" she said, turning to her table companion.

Sela Runford huffed in disappointment. "I don't think you've heard a thing I have told you, Avelyn. You will be gone this time tomorrow. Who will I share conversations with?"

"You are friendly with many ladies at the palace, Sela. You know everyone, from the lowest page to men of state. You're the one who introduced me to so many people when I first arrived at the royal court. If not for you, I would still be friendless, secluded in my bedchamber with no one but myself for company."

Her closest friend at court burst out laughing. "Avelyn, you really don't see it. 'Tis what I adore about you." Sela brought an arm about her friend and touched her cheek against Avelyn's. "You are one of the most beautiful women in London. Everyone is suddenly nice to me because they know *we* are friends. I fear it's the only reason any of the men pay attention to me. They simply want to grow close to you."

The words took her aback. "You're exaggerating, Sela. You are lovely to look at and you have such a sweet disposition."

"But I have been here for years. You are the new treasure, only coming into the queen's service last September. You are like a shiny, new bauble. People wish to know you. They have known me since I was a young girl because Father has been on the regency council since my birth."

Avelyn thought back on the last eight months. She had yearned to come to the court in London when she'd been buried in the countryside at Hopeston Castle. Her uncle, Geoffrey, had made that possible, gaining her a place in the queen's service since he and his wife, Merryn, were favored by the royal couple.

At first, she had enjoyed her time away from home, though she missed her mother and sister beyond measure. The queen had wished for Avelyn to stay at court during the Christmas season, so it had been a long time since she'd seen her loved ones. At least she had been granted permission to leave for Sandbourne tomorrow. Avelyn longed for the extended time with her family and was relieved she would not have to be a part of the royal court's summer progress.

"So what news do you have from your sister at Sandbourne?" Sela asked.

"Elysande feels quite large and awkward. She claims her belly is as round as one of her mares before they give birth." Avelyn shuddered. "I have seen those mares. If Elysande tells me the truth, then she may give birth to a full-grown man or woman come mid-June!"

Sela giggled. "You said your sister loves horses?"

Avelyn nodded. "She does. Elysande would rather be riding or in the stables than weaving tapestries or painting."

"That will change when her babe arrives," her friend said knowingly.

She thought on that a moment. "I know she will cherish her child, but I do not see Elysande ever giving up her horses. And Michael will indulge her in whatever she desires. He is madly in love with her."

Sela sighed. "I wish a man would see to my every whim. One who is handsome beyond words and as rich as Midas." She grew thoughtful. "I believe Father is ready to arrange a marriage for me. He hinted about it in our conversation yesterday. What if we never see each other again, Avelyn? I would be so sad to lose you when I have only just found you."

"Mayhap, you should come to Sandbourne and visit while I am there. You would be most welcomed."

Her friend frowned. "I'm supposed to go on summer progress with the royal court. You are most fortunate in that the queen is allowing you to visit your sister and her husband instead of traipsing about England during the hottest months."

"Well, Elysande is due to give birth soon." Avelyn paused. "I fear that I, too, will have a marriage arranged for me and these carefree days will be behind me."

"Will your uncle find you a husband and negotiate the marriage contract since your father has passed?"

She shook her head. "Uncle Geoffrey has placed me in the hands of the queen. He trusts she will know which suitor I should wed."

A servant brought them the next course. They shared a trencher of pork in wine sauce, both growing quiet with their thoughts. Avelyn had noticed the queen studying her during the past few weeks and believed her time as an unattached young woman was drawing to a close.

Agnes, Queen Philippa's chief lady-in-waiting, stopped at their table.

"The queen wishes to take a turn about the gardens. Be present to accompany her in a quarter of an hour." She paused. "And her favorite silk handkerchief has turned up missing. Have either of you seen it? It's yellow like the bright sunshine."

"I know the one you mean," Avelyn said, "but I have not seen her with it in days."

"Of course you haven't seen her with it," Agnes snapped. "It wouldn't be missing if you had." The noblewoman sighed. "Keep your eyes out for it." She looked to Sela. "And do not be late to the gardens."

Avelyn watched Sela boldly meet Agnes' gaze. The lady-in-waiting waited for Sela to drop her eyes in deference to her position. When Sela did not, Agnes huffed and stormed off.

"I was late only once," Sela muttered. "That old hag has never forgiven me—or forgotten it. And who cares if the queen lost a handkerchief?"

"Hush!" Avelyn warned, shocked by her friend's callous attitude.

Sela lowered her voice. "I'm simply saying that the queen has well over a hundred silk handkerchiefs. I don't understand the fuss made over one misplaced handkerchief."

She tended to agree with Sela, but Avelyn would never have voiced such an opinion. It seemed, since she had been at court, that the queen was always losing an item. Sometimes it was found and other times merely forgotten.

"Besides," Sela lifted her pewter cup and motioned for Avelyn to do the same, "here's to a glorious afternoon spent outdoors."

Avelyn tapped her cup against her friend's. "To a fine afternoon," she said.

"And for your trip to Sandbourne being a happy one," Sela added.

They finished their meal and then went to await the queen. Avelyn studied the growing group of women arriving in clusters. She had not found many of them likeable. Every female at court seemed to focus solely on gaining the attention of men. Avelyn had only formed a close attachment with Sela, who was near her in age as opposed to most of the other ladies-in-waiting. She thought it a good time to be granted a break from the routine of her days in London and enjoy time in the country with Elysande and their mother, who should arrive at Sandbourne by the time Avelyn did.

"Who will escort you to your brother-in-law's estate?" asked Sela as they waited for the queen's arrival.

"Elysande wrote to me that Michael has sent an escort party. It will be led by a knight named Sir Kenric Fairfax," Avelyn revealed.

"Is he handsome?"

"Is that all you think about?" she teased. "Actually, I know very few of Michael's men. Some were with us when Elysande and Michael married at Kinwick Castle, my uncle's home. I have yet to visit Sandbourne myself since I left the wedding and came straightaway to London with Uncle Geoffrey and Cousin Alys. That's one of the reasons why I am excited to see Sandbourne."

"So this Sir Kenric could be toothless," Sela said. "Or as old as the king."

Avelyn shrugged. "I have no idea. Elysande merely wrote that Sir Kenric would be the knight in charge of my escort party and that it was a guard of ten total to see me safely to Sandbourne. She said though Sir Kenric hadn't been at Sandbourne long, Michael trusts him implicitly and finds he's the most skilled knight Michael has ever known."

"You must send word and tell me of your adventures with this toothless knight. And of your new nephew or niece once they make their appearance."

Avelyn slipped an arm about her friend's waist. "I will, though I wish you would consider coming along with me."

At that moment, the queen came into sight. Avelyn found herself standing a little taller and holding her chin higher anytime she was in the presence of royalty.

Philippa scanned the assembled retinue until her eyes landed on Avelyn. "Lady Avelyn, I would have you take a turn about the gardens with me."

She quickly stepped away from the gathered ladies-in-waiting and went to the queen, making her curtsey.

"Yes, your highness." Her heart raced at spending time alone with the woman. They had been together in small groups before but never only the two of them with no others present.

The queen took Avelyn's hand and slipped it through the crook of her arm. "Let me guide the way, but I shall be grateful for your support as we walk."

"Of course, your grace."

They stepped onto the path that led toward the gardens. Avelyn glanced over her shoulder and saw the other women followed at a discreet distance. Sela gave her an encouraging nod.

"You do not seem nervous in my company," the queen said.

Avelyn was pleased that she'd hidden her nerves well. "I am happy to be in your presence, your grace. I suppose I should be slightly on edge, for we have never spent any time together. But you are always even tempered and kind to all you meet. I look forward to our conversation."

The queen nodded sagely. Avelyn hoped she had pleased the royal with her answer.

"So what do you think of court, Lady Avelyn?" asked Philippa.

She gave a careful reply. "I am privileged to be here, your highness. I'm grateful to Uncle Geoffrey for arranging for me to come to London, as well as thankful that you made room for me among your ladies-in-waiting. I had always dreamed of coming to London."

"But what do you think of the court itself?" the queen asked again. "Do you like it? Is the conversation stimulating? Or do you find it tiresome?"

"Oh, I could never be bored," Avelyn answered truthfully. "I enjoy music very much and have heard many fine musicians play during my time here. I've also learned to paint a bit and my embroidery has improved. Mother will be so pleased."

She paused. "But as to the company? I find most of the women only tolerate other females. They save all their smiles and attention for the courtiers present. Other than Sela Runford, my friend, and Alys de Montfort, my cousin, I miss close female companionship."

"You are honest and direct, my lady," the queen noted. "I like that—in a man or a woman."

They walked in companionable silence for a few minutes before the queen asked, "What of children? Do you like them?"

Avelyn could not hide her smile. "I do, indeed, your grace. I'm looking forward to leaving for Sandbourne on the morrow to be present at my sister Elysande's side when she gives birth to her first child."

Philippa nodded. "That's right. I remember that I granted you permission to do so. You are not going on summer progress." She thought a moment. "Then let me ask this. Do you want babes of your own, Lady Avelyn?"

"Aye, most certainly," she said with enthusiasm. "I've enjoyed spending time with my young cousin, Hal, one of Uncle Geoffrey's children. He's a whirlwind that never seems to stop, but he is precious beyond words. I hope I have children as happy as Hal, as well as sweet-natured."

The queen pursed her lips. "To have babes, you must have a husband. With that being said, is there anyone special you've met at court that you believe would make you a good husband?"

Avelyn felt a hot blush rise on her cheeks. "Nay, your grace. I have met many men. Some interesting, some kind." She bit her lip and decided to remain honest since the queen seemed to appreciate that quality. "Some arrogant and loud. But none that I feel I could love."

"Love?" asked the queen. "You do realize, my lady, that a love match is rare."

"I understand that, your majesty." She grew thoughtful. "But I have seen how Elysande and Lord Michael look at one another. I want that for myself with my own husband. Do you know that the earl wanted to marry my sister before he even knew her name? He thought he better learn it so that he could ask her father for her hand in marriage. 'Twas love at first sight for them both."

"Hmm. I had not known Sandbourne was such a romantic." She studied Avelyn. "Nevertheless, I myself was promised to the king before we even met. We came into the marriage total strangers. Yet from our vows, friendship soon grew. Trust followed—and then came love. Fourteen children later, we still are devoted to one another."

"And there is my lovely wife."

Avelyn turned and saw the king and his retinue striding their way. She realized, in that moment, as this was the closest she had ever been to the pair, that Queen Philippa was correct. The king loved his wife very much. The expression on his face spoke for itself.

She curtseyed as he approached and then stepped back a few feet. The king took his wife's hand and brushed a kiss upon her fingers.

"I see you are enjoying this fine May day, my love."

"We are, sire." Philippa held out a hand. "Do you remember Lady

Avelyn Le Cler? She is Geoffrey de Montfort's niece."

Edward eyed her a moment, squinting as he considered her. "I do. I remember meeting you, your sister, and mother. And I have watched you dance. You possess a grace and rhythm that many do not, Lady Avelyn."

"Thank you, your majesty." Avelyn locked her knees together to still their trembling. While the queen seemed motherly, King Edward was another matter. She did not enjoy his scrutiny in the least.

"The girl journeys to Sandbourne tomorrow to visit with her sister and help bring her sister's first child into the world."

"Ah, the world is a better place for each child that comes into it." He glanced over their shoulders. "I see Lady Alys in that gaggle of women, speaking of the de Montforts. Tell her that I am in need of more of the tonic she makes for my headaches. If you will excuse me, ladies." He winked at the queen. "I shall see you when we sup tonight, my dear."

Edward swept by them, his courtiers trailing after him. Avelyn turned and saw the fluttering eyelashes of the many women as the group of men approached.

"Come, let us continue," the queen instructed.

Avelyn could smell the scent of basil, lemon balm, and wisteria as they wound their way through the herbs. They then came upon bold, red geraniums and the fragrant scent of roses.

"You are quite liked by many courtiers," Philippa confided, a knowing look in her eye.

"I am?"

The thought surprised Avelyn. A few men had spoken to her upon occasion. Two had pulled her into an alcove and stolen a kiss, but she had pushed them away. She had been more embarrassed than anything—though she had wished she felt something more.

"Some have hinted to me. Others have asked outright for me to consider them as your future husband."

"I know not what to say, your grace," she said, wondering if Queen Philippa had already chosen a mate for her.

"Go to your mother and sister at Sandbourne then," the queen proclaimed. "Think long and hard what you might desire in a husband. I shall keep watch as we travel on our summer progress and consider what man would be the best match for you. When you return to me in autumn, then we shall compare thoughts. I hope by this time next year that you will be wedded and bedded and have your husband's seed growing in your belly."

Avelyn wasn't quite sure how she felt about that.

CHAPTER 5

AVELYN GLANCED AROUND the bedchamber that she shared with her cousin, Alys. She had very little to pack for her trip. Michael had thoughtfully provided for her trunk to be sent ahead to Sandbourne a week ago and it would arrive before she did. She gathered her comb and small hand mirror and placed them in the bundle with her change of clothing. Sela had let her wear some of her kirtles and *cotehardies* this past week. Avelyn had returned them to her friend after breaking her fast a few minutes ago.

"Are you sure you do not mind stopping at Kinwick?"

She hugged Alys. "Of course not," she told her cousin. Alys might be young in years, but she possessed a wisdom and self-confidence well beyond her age. She looked upon the girl as a sister. They had grown close in the months Avelyn had lived at court.

The only disagreement between them had involved her friendship with Sela Runford. Alys, who had already spent a year in the queen's service before Avelyn's arrival, did not care for Sela. She couldn't give Avelyn a good reason for her to avoid Sela's company, only stubbornly warning Avelyn not to become too close with Sela.

Avelyn added, "I will enjoy seeing Uncle Geoffrey and Aunt Merryn again. And the baby. How old is he?"

"Edward is over two months old now. I can't wait to meet him myself, though I wish Mother would have had another girl. With little Edward added to Ancel and Hal, I'm quite outnumbered," Alys complained good-naturedly.

Avelyn laughed. "You and Aunt Merryn are a formidable team. I don't see the two of you ever losing ground to the de Montfort men."

"Mother is quite unstoppable. Grandmother told me of how Mother's labor pains began on Judgment Day. Though her pains increased steadily, she continued to render her decisions till she'd seen every laborer with a complaint. Only then did she take to her bed and let Tilda fuss over her while she gave birth to Ancel and me."

She shuddered. "Merryn is definitely a woman to admire." Though Avelyn knew she wanted children, she hoped she wouldn't give birth to twins. Having two small babes at the same time seemed overwhelming to her.

Alys continued. "She even supervised the harvest after giving birth. Grandmother said Mother was out in the fields a week later, ordering people about, while Ancel and I lay in a basket nearby. She would watch carefully at how the workers performed and how much yield was accrued even as she took time to nurse us."

"We all can learn from Aunt Merryn's example. Are you ready for our journey?"

Her cousin nodded. "I'm even more ready to get home and back to learning more about herbs. I know Mother still has much to teach me."

Avelyn laughed. "You already are the person at court that others seek out when they have an ailment. Even our king! You have a remedy for everything—queasy stomachs and headaches. Bruises. Sprains."

Alys frowned. "Not baldness. I wish I could find a way to cure that. 'Twould make me the most popular girl in the land." She twirled in a circle, her eyes dancing in merriment.

A knock on the door interrupted their conversation. A short page with a cowlick stuck his head in when she called out, "Come."

"Be ye Lady Avelyn? If so, your escort party has arrived and they seek your company. I can carry down what you need for your journey."

"Thank you." Avelyn handed him her bundle.

Alys did likewise but held on to a small case. Avelyn knew her cousin stored precious herbs within it and never let it far from her sight.

Sela appeared in the doorway, out of breath, crossing paths with the page as he left.

"Oh, I'm glad I found you before you left." She embraced Avelyn, juggling a folded bundle in her arms. "Is your offer still good?" she asked.

"My offer?"

"To visit at Sandbourne!" Sela cried.

"I know Elysande and Michael would be delighted for you—"

"May I come with you now?" Her friend's face glowed with excitement. "I discussed it with Father and he had no objections. He spoke to the queen within the last hour and she said she would excuse me from the court's travels. We can be together all summer long."

Avelyn hugged her friend. "Of course, you may come. Alys is also traveling with us. We'll be stopping to call upon my uncle at Kinwick for a night before venturing to Sandbourne."

"Father assured me that he would take care of forwarding my things. I packed what I would need until then."

"You can also borrow anything from my wardrobe till your trunk arrives," she assured her. "Oh, we're going to have such fun together, Sela."

Alys said curtly, "We'd best be on our way or the page might think we're lost." She left the chamber and Avelyn fell into step behind her. She hoped Alys would make an effort to be friendlier to Sela.

Avelyn turned to speak to her friend, but Sela wasn't behind her. Puzzled, she retraced her steps and bumped into Sela as she quickly rounded the corner.

"Where were you?" she asked. "I thought we'd lost you."

Sela giggled. "I passed Sir Bede and had to tell him farewell."

"I should've guessed a man was involved. Come, we need to catch up with Alys."

Alys stood waiting for them, tapping her foot, a look of disapproval on her face. Avelyn and Sela rejoined her, and the three wove their way through the maze of corridors. They caught up with the page, who lingered impatiently. The moment he saw them, he took off again, shaking his head.

Finally, they arrived in a courtyard and Avelyn saw a group of men sitting on horseback. Her eyes skimmed the guard and she spotted two soldiers she recognized.

And then she saw him.

He sat atop the largest horse but he would have to, for he was a large man himself. Even on horseback, she could see how tall and powerfully built he was. Then he laughed at something one of the men said. His smile was as dazzling as the diamonds the queen wore about her neck. Avelyn's heart fluttered erratically as never before. Her reaction to seeing this stranger with thick, dark hair and olive skin was like nothing she had experienced.

Alys broke away from them and reached the soldiers first. "I am Lady Alys de Montfort. Might I ask who leads this escort party to Sandbourne?"

Avelyn could have told her who did before he swung from his horse.

The knight towered over the young girl. "I am Kenric Fairfax, my lady, the leader of these men. If you are the daughter of Lord Geoffrey de Montfort, then I can tell you that I have met your father when he visited my liege lord at Sandbourne. He's a most impressive man." He smiled. "And he brought young Hal with him."

"You survived your encounter with my brother?" Alys asked, her eyes bright. "You must be made of strong stuff, my lord."

"Hal occupied his time being the earl's shadow," the knight confided. "He probably called out, 'Michael, Michael,' close to a thousand times as he followed the earl about. He is an entertaining lad."

"Hal can be a terror, but he is a sweet, loving boy," Alys replied. She pulled a parchment from her pocket and handed it to him. "This is from my father. He asks that you allow me to accompany your party and, while on your way, have you call at Kinwick. You may stay a night there and get a good meal in your belly before you travel on to

Cousin Elysande and Michael at Sandbourne."

The knight broke the seal and scanned the contents, a slight frown upon his face. Avelyn's breath came in short spurts as she watched him.

"You are most welcomed to ride with us, Lady Alys," Kenric Fairfax assured Alys, though Avelyn believed he was unhappy that her young cousin would accompany them for some reason.

Avelyn stepped forward to introduce herself and had to tilt her head far back as she looked up into his tanned face. Hazel eyes more green than brown stood out, drawing her in. Of all the men she had met at court, this knight was the most handsome man she had ever seen. Her mouth went dry and she found swallowing almost impossible. Avelyn struggled to find her voice.

And then she caught the impatience in his eyes. It broke the spell he had seemingly cast over her and she found she could speak once more.

"My lord, I am Lady Avelyn Le Cler, sister to the Countess of Sandbourne. Lady Alys is my cousin. And this," she indicated her friend, "is Lady Sela Runford. She, too, will be a part of our traveling party, as she has just gained the queen's permission to visit Sandbourne and act as my companion for the summer. I trust this will not be an imposition."

Fairfax stared down at her disapprovingly. "Do you have parchment to confirm that I am to take Lady Sela with us?"

"Nay, I do not," Avelyn said, her temper rising at a stranger questioning her so. "She has her father's permission. He sits on the king's council. And instructions from the queen that she is to remain with me at Sandbourne during the court's summer progress." She paused. "If you care to wait in line with the hundreds of courtiers that wish to see the queen in order to confirm this, I'm sure the rest of us can find something to occupy our time while you tarry the day away."

He continued to study her a moment. She wasn't happy with this knight's behavior and would make sure Elysande and Michael knew of it.

"Under your leadership, Sir Kenric, I believe that ten men can protect three females for a few days," she said, not disguising her displeasure.

Fairfax bowed his head. "As you wish, my lady. Have no worries. We shall deliver Lady Alys safely to her home and make certain you and Lady Sela arrive at Sandbourne unharmed."

Avelyn turned to her companions. "Then let us be off."

KENRIC FUMED AT the turn of events. He had been sent to escort Lady Elysande's sister from court, not a gaggle of women. Though he'd admired Lord Geoffrey upon meeting him, he didn't like the addition of a mere child to their escort party because children did not travel well. The road was no place for them, much less a female child. Though Lady Alys seemed well spoken and mature for her years, she wasn't even half a score. And then this sister to the countess had the audacity to blithely invite another featherhead from court at the last minute?

He never liked when things didn't go according to his wishes. As a knight, Kenric favored planning, paying careful attention to details. This would change the course of the journey he had already set, as he had not intended to pass by Kinwick.

And though his code of chivalry demanded that he protect women, he certainly had no use for them.

Especially after that night at Longshire.

Kenric glanced at his boots and the place his spurs should have rested. Guilt still ate at him daily.

No, from the detached feelings of his mother to the wiles of Gussalen to the insanity that Jannet's death had brought into his life, he had no desire to spend any more time than necessary in the company of women.

Ever.

He knew it was an honor that Lord Michael had chosen him to escort his sister-in-law from London to Sandbourne. Kenric had only been with the earl for a short time, so it showed great trust and favoritism for him to be tasked with this mission. Yet Kenric resented it all the same. He would rather spend his time training with the other soldiers at Sandbourne than escorting an empty-headed court beauty and her equally silly friend on the road for several days, much less a girl child who would probably whine while the two noblewomen complained about everything from the meals they ate to the ground they would sleep upon.

Kenric knew he'd better make the best of a poor situation—else this troublesome sister might spread falsehoods about him with the earl and countess upon their return to Sandbourne. He masked his rising anger and placed a pleasant look upon his face.

Turning to Lady Avelyn, he said, "The countess said you wouldn't wish to ride your own horse. I hope you and the others do not mind riding with another soldier. Especially since they were unexpected additions," he added.

"Nay," she replied, glaring at him as if he'd done something wrong.

"I know Sir Ralf," Lady Alys said. "I can ride with him." She walked to where Ralf's horse stood.

The knight reached down and lifted Alys into the saddle with him, helping her to arrange the box she carried.

"I can manage Lady Sela," another man volunteered. He grinned shamelessly at Sela and said, "I am Sir Martin, my lady." He dismounted and then escorted the woman to his horse.

Kenric glanced back at Lady Avelyn. She asked, a little too sharply for his taste, "And whom shall I ride with, my lord?"

"'Twould be my honor to have you ride with me, my lady," he said grudgingly. He had planned for her to ride with him all along since he would be her chief protector in their travels.

"Very well." She gave him a sweet smile, which only showed how fickle the woman was, because her voice had been laced with sarcasm moments ago.

He offered his arm and took her back to his horse. She stopped as they reached Firefall. Kenric saw fear in her eyes as she gazed up at the beast. He'd learned from the countess that her sister was not much of a rider, which surprised him. Lady Elysande was, mayhap, the only woman he had any liking and admiration for. She knew more about horses than any man he'd encountered. He believed himself quite knowledgeable about them, but through several conversations, she had taught him many things.

"I haven't been on horses very often," Lady Avelyn said. "The few times I have, it's proved uncomfortable and frightening for me," she revealed. She glanced back at Firefall. "This horse is the largest I have ever seen."

"His name is Firefall, my lady. I know he looks fearsome, but he's the most gentle of beasts. You will be safe atop him. I guarantee it."

Lady Avelyn nodded, as if she considered his words, but he saw she trembled. Then a calm descended over her. She stood taller, her shoulders thrown back, as if she had come to some decision known only to her. Leaning over, she stroked the horse tentatively at first and then more firmly.

"I'm Avelyn, Firefall," she told the animal, her voice low. "I have no treat to give you, but I'll appreciate you doing your best to get me to Sandbourne."

Kenric couldn't help himself. He laughed softly. "You're cut from the same cloth as your sister, my lady. She speaks to every horse on the Sandbourne estate as if they are human and can understand everything she tells them."

"She probably likes them more than most of the people who populate the place. Elysande has always favored horses over people."

"Shall we?" he asked, impatient to be on the road. They'd already wasted enough time dallying in the courtyard.

She nodded. Kenric placed his hands about her waist, easily spanning its slender width. He lifted her onto Firefall's back and then mounted behind her. He caught her looking to the ground, which most likely seemed a long way down for a woman who did not ride much.

Something stirred in him at that moment. He had an overwhelming desire to protect her and assure her that she would be all right.

Kenric wrapped an arm about the noblewoman's waist, drawing her to him, inhaling a hint of vanilla that clung to her hair and skin.

"Lean back into my chest, my lady. It will make for less bouncing and more comfort."

She did as he asked. Something within Kenric exploded, awakening him, a foreign feeling like nothing he'd ever known before. Suddenly, he wanted her.

Badly.

She looked over her shoulder at him, her teeth tugging in worry on her full, bottom lip. Kenric wanted to do the same. Nip it. Lick it. He wondered what she would taste like. He longed to bend and cover her mouth with his. Possess and plunder the sweetness within.

Lady Avelyn smiled at him with white, even teeth. His pulse skipped a beat as he became lost in eyes of sky blue.

Kenric blinked. He glanced over his shoulder to break the unnatural hold she had over him and called out, "We ride."

Firefall moved forward of his own accord, as if the horse knew what he wanted. The world raced by as they left the courtyard and wound their way around till they reached the open road.

CHAPTER 6

THE SCOUT KENRIC had sent out returned, assuring him that the spot they had stopped at on their way to London would be the best place to make camp for the night. Motioning for the men to follow him, he led them off the road and into the clearing. He swung down from Firefall and reached up for Lady Avelyn's waist. She tilted forward as he captured it and brought her to the ground. With reluctance, he released her—and wondered why.

They had not spoken while they rode. The clopping of the horses' hooves prevented it. He had allowed a brief respite in the early afternoon so the ladies could stretch their legs and tend to their needs, but they'd pursued no conversation in that brief interlude.

Yet Kenric had done nothing but think about the woman he held in his arms as they traveled away from the noise of London.

Avelyn Le Cler smelled divine. The scent of vanilla had invaded his nostrils, enveloping Kenric as they rode, tantalizing him. But that was only a small part of it. Her curves also called out to him. She had a petite frame, but her full breasts, tiny waist, and rounded bottom tempted him beyond measure. Having her pressed against him for most of the day had led to some very interesting fantasies that he'd had to pull himself from. He fought to concentrate on the road ahead, where danger could spring forth within seconds. As head of this escort party, he owed it to his men and the women they were charged with bringing back.

Before he could speak, Lady Avelyn began assigning tasks to the men. That did not sit well with him. He found it arrogant—a quality he despised in a man—much less a women.

"My lady?" he interrupted, knowing he must watch his words carefully. "Though you seem a natural leader, I'd have you allow me to instruct the men what they should do. We will hunt for dinner and cook the game caught."

"Your men may hunt, but we three will cook the food and clean the dishes, my lord."

Lady Sela, overhearing the remark, sputtered, a shocked look upon her face. Without thinking, Kenric burst out laughing at the noblewoman's reaction.

Avelyn glared at him. "You find it amusing that I would cook and clean?" she asked, her arms crossing defensively in front of her.

He quelled his laughter and tried to remove any sign of amusement from his face. "Nay, my lady. Simply unusual. I know of no noblewoman who cooks or washes dishes. Now, weaving tapestries or embroidering? That would be more believable."

"I like to cook," she stated. "My mother and I gardened together from the time I was a child. My interest grew from there. Mother says I have quite the green thumb when it comes to vegetables and herbs. That led to my wishing to cook."

"But men always provide meals during a journey," he protested.

"This is not my first time out on the road, Sir Kenric. I came from the north, the place of my birth. My sister and I accompanied our mother south when she came to marry her second husband. We traveled on the road close to three weeks." Avelyn shook her head. "You may see me as some spoiled court brat, my lord, but I know how to fend for myself. I believe this journey will be all the more pleasant if we act as a team."

"This journey is what I say it will be. One where I keep you safe. And the additional women."

He saw understanding dawn on her face. "So that's what is bothering you. Having my cousin and friend accompany us." She sniffed haughtily. "'Tis not your place to judge, my lord. The earl tasked you—"

"The earl did set the task, my lady," he interrupted. "And I take orders solely from him. Not you."

Avelyn laughed. "You act as if you are the best soldier in England and must follow your orders without any change in them at all."

Kenric told her, "I am the best soldier in England."

Her eyes widened. "You're serious. And here I thought you merely arrogant."

"Nay, my lady. I simply state a fact. I am the most capable of Sandbourne's men. It's why the earl tasked me to retrieve you and bring you safely back. Now, I ask that you allow me to conduct your passage to Sandbourne in the manner I see fit—and that includes what must be done when we make camp for the night."

Kenric stopped, suddenly aware that the entire traveling party had surrounded them, drinking in everything they said. He glanced around, seeing amusement in the eyes of his fellow soldiers, which caused his anger at the dainty beauty before him to grow.

Immediately, he began barking orders. He sent three men to hunt for their supper and another two to chop and bring back wood and start a fire. Another two would tend to the horses while the last pair was sent to gather water to boil the meat.

And he bristled when he heard Lady Avelyn trying to stifle her giggles.

When the last of the men departed camp, he turned back to her. "I won't have you question me and my authority in front of the men again."

She wiped the smile from her face. "Nay, Sir Kenric, I won't. If Michael charged you to fetch and protect me along the way, then you are the best of his soldiers. He loves my sister beyond words. You know that if you have witnessed them together. So to please her, I realize he sent his very best men—and you to lead them."

Kenric had definitely seen the looks pass between the earl and his countess, looks that conveyed a deep, abiding love. Small, special glances that only the two of them traded. He actually found himself almost envious and had brushed aside his feelings.

"So I'm not here to question you or your authority," Avelyn continued. "I'm here merely to aid you on this journey. For example, I can skin an animal, but it would be nice if one of your men did so. But I must insist that we three women cook the meal and clean up afterward. It's the least we can do to contribute in our own small way. Please."

He saw the stubborn set to her mouth and knew it made no sense to argue with her. "As you wish, my lady."

AVELYN WATCHED KENRIC head toward the horses. She did not like arrogance in a man, no matter how capable he was.

"Good riddance," she said under her breath.

Sela's eyes were round with surprise. "I've never cooked before, Avelyn. I haven't a clue where to begin."

Avelyn put an arm around her friend's shoulder. "Alys and I know what to do, so just do as we say. You'll see. It will be fun."

Sela's lips pursed as if she'd eaten something sour. "We have very different ideas of fun, Avelyn."

Alys looked worried. "I'm sorry I asked to come, Avelyn. Father thought it would be convenient for me to do so. Mother so wanted to see you before you went to Sandbourne. And they both thought a night of rest inside the walls of Kinwick would break up the journey."

Avelyn assured her cousin. "You are no bother, Alys. That knight is simply full of himself."

"Well, he is an imposing man," Sela pointed out. "And impossibly handsome."

"But why does he not wear spurs, as a true knight should?" Alys asked.

Avelyn hadn't noticed such a small detail. She looked over at him helping the two men he appointed to care for the horses. Sir Kenric had a natural air of confidence about him and was intelligent and well spoken.

But where were his spurs?

She knew both a sword and riding spurs were presented when a man became a knight. A disgraced knight, though, had his spurs hacked off.

Had that happened to Sir Kenric?

Surely, Michael would never have taken on a man of such dubious character. Avelyn figured there was more to his story—and she wanted to find out exactly what had occurred.

The small groups of men soon returned. They started the fire burning and put the water pot on to boil. The hunters returned with three rabbits and some wild onions they'd found. They skinned the rabbits and turned them over to the women without question, though she caught a bit of merriment in Sir Martin's eyes. Avelyn sliced the onions while Alys added some herbs from her box into the pot. Avelyn wanted Sela to chop the meat into small pieces, but her friend turned pale from the thought of touching the raw animal. Avelyn hurried with the onions and then saw to the rabbits, tossing everything into the pot. Within minutes, a fragrant smell encircled the camp.

One of the soldiers brought her their remaining bread. She looked at the amount and knew it wouldn't last even to Kinwick, which was another two days away.

"Sir Kenric?" she called out.

He came over. Avelyn noticed everyone watching them surreptitiously and determined she wouldn't get in to another spat with him with others present. She understood she had placed him in a bad light with his men and would do what she could to make amends.

"We are low on bread," she informed him. "The last of it will be gone after we break our fast on the morrow. We should try to buy some when we pass the next village or nunnery."

"Thank you for letting me know, my lady."

As everyone had completed the work given to them, they naturally began to seat themselves around the fire, awaiting the stew to finish cooking. Avelyn decided to put the others at ease.

"Since we don't know one another, we should introduce ourselves. I am Lady Avelyn Le Cler. I've been at King Edward's court since last

September, but I am a country girl at heart." She looked at Sir Kenric. "I enjoy embroidery and am quite good at it, but I'm a dreadful singer. I refuse to hurt your ears, so I will keep any songs to myself."

She turned to Alys. "Go ahead, Cousin."

Alys smiled. "I am Lady Alys de Montfort, daughter of Lord Geoffrey and Lady Merryn, whom some of you have met. Mother has taught me much about herbs and I am a healer."

"A healer?" asked Sir Kenric, doubt evident in his voice. "I find it hard to believe that one so young could call herself that. Are you even half a score, Lady Alys?"

"I am not, my lord," Alys said. "But Mother says I have a gift and I try to use it for good."

Avelyn added in support, "Lady Alys is well known about Kinwick and at the royal court in London. Even the king and queen ask for her personally. She creates tonics and other remedies for whatever ails them."

Alys beamed with the praise Avelyn offered. "The king does say my headache remedy rivals Mother's." The young girl looked at the remaining woman in their party. "And what about you, my lady?"

Sela blushed as the attention fell upon her. "I do sing a bit. And dance. I've spent most of my life at court since my father is one of King Edward's closest advisers. Because I live in London, I'm eager to see both Kinwick and Sandbourne and find out what country life is like." She paused. "I also hope to make some new friends while I am there."

"Let's hear from the men now," Avelyn said.

"I'll begin. I am Sir Ralf, cousin to Sir Martin and older than him by a year." He indicated the knight on his left. "My mother is a healer, so I have an appreciation for what Lady Alys does." Ralf elbowed his cousin. "Go ahead."

The man sat up. "I am Sir Martin, ladies, and have been with the earl for three years now." He glanced at Ralf. "As for my cousin, I believe I received all the good looks and manners in our family."

Everyone chuckled good-naturedly as Ralf punched Martin in the arm.

They went round the rest of the circle, each soldier sharing his name and a bit about himself. Avelyn committed the names to memory since she would be seeing them most days during her stay at Sandbourne.

Finally, they reached the remaining member of their group.

"I am Kenric Fairfax of Shadowfaire. My father passed nigh on seven years now and my brother, Roland, became the earl. I've been in service to Lord Michael for these last eight months." He fell silent.

Avelyn wanted to ask where he'd been before and where Shadowfaire lay. She wondered if he was close to his brother. But the air about him told her that Sir Kenric Fairfax was not opening the door for questions about his life.

Instead, she stood and stirred the pot. "I think our supper is ready," she declared.

Avelyn dished out the meal to each man while Sela and Alys gave them their bread. They ate in companionable silence until the last of the stew had been devoured. She began gathering the dishes to take and rinse in the nearby stream.

"These are too heavy for a woman," Sir Kenric proclaimed. "I will accompany you." He scooped up the majority of the dishes in his large hands.

As the men began bedding down for the night, Avelyn accompanied Sir Kenric to the nearby brook. He knelt with her and rubbed sand onto the cups to help clean them before they rinsed them in the cold water. As they gathered up the last of the dishes, she paused.

"What was that?" she asked, tilting her head. "I thought I heard a soft cry."

He grew still as they listened.

Avelyn heard the faint noise again. "It comes from over there," she said and stood to move that way.

"Wait, my lady," Kenric commanded. "Let me lead the way."

They walked closer and the sound drew only slightly stronger. Avelyn recognized it was a soft mewl she heard. Then she saw a sight that tore at her heart.

A small kitten had been left for bait near a trap. The ginger-colored animal cried pathetically. It was bound so that it could not even twist.

"You must do something!" Avelyn cried. She ran toward the kitten and set aside the cups she carried. She knelt and rubbed the top of its soft head. "You're to be rescued, my little one. The brave Sir Kenric Fairfax will see you set free. 'Tis what knights do—they help others in distress."

He placed the dishes he carried onto the ground before he pulled his baselard and bent, carefully cutting through the twine that bound the animal.

Immediately, Avelyn scooped up the freed kitten and brought it close, stroking it lovingly. The kitten began purring loudly and licked her hand in gratitude.

"We must take it with us," she said. "We can't leave it alone in the forest." She turned the furry beast and lifted its tail. "It's a boy," she said. Avelyn thought a moment. "I will call you Sir Kitten."

"What happens when the kitten becomes a cat?" asked her escort.

She frowned. "I hadn't thought of that. Hmm." Avelyn snuggled with the kitten and kissed the top of his head. It came to her. "I know. He can be Cattus."

Sir Kenric stared at her. "That's Latin for cat. You know Latin?" he asked, surprise evident in his voice.

Avelyn laughed. "Father insisted that Elysande and I both learn Latin." She nuzzled the kitten again and then looked triumphantly back at the man. "I'm afraid we're adding someone else to our traveling party, my lord, though at least you aren't being saddled with another female."

CHAPTER 7

"I SEE IT! I see Kinwick!" Alys cried.

"Not long now, my lady," Sir Ralf told her.

Kenric glanced over at the joy flooding the young girl's face as she caught sight of her home and pushed aside his guilt.

He hadn't wanted Alys de Montfort as a member of their traveling party when they'd departed from London, but the girl had proven to be helpful and friendly. She hadn't whined or been in a foul mood as he would have expected from a female her age. Alys had even tended to a deep cut Martin received when he skinned part of their dinner last night. The soldier's dagger had slipped, slicing a wound that concerned Kenric. Any time a man was injured, no matter how small it might seem, was cause for concern. Infection could set in quickly and prove deadly.

Young Alys had pulled a few herbs from that case she guarded and made a poultice. The girl had cleaned the damaged skin and stitched it up neatly before applying the poultice atop it. Her calm manner alleviated any fears Kenric experienced and Martin declared himself fit when they rode out this morning.

Kenric looked at the castle they would soon reach. Part of him regretted arriving at the estate so soon. The reason for that regret lay wrapped within his arms.

Lady Avelyn Le Cler had proven to be an interesting companion. She had managed the men in camp like a seasoned traveler. The food she prepared tasted better than any he had ever eaten out on the road. She had no courtly airs about her, treating everyone equally and with courtesy. Despite his initial impression, Kenric found his dislike of her melting like the snow on a sunny day.

They had talked quite a bit both yesterday and today as they continued their journey away from London. She proved to be a lively conversationalist with a quick sense of humor. It had helped the time pass much too quickly. Once they arrived at the de Montfort estate, he would need to release his hold on her.

Having the petite beauty in his arms for three days had only increased his desire for her. It almost seemed as if she'd been made to fit against him. The heady scent of vanilla wafted from her smooth, ivory skin, teasing him each time he inhaled a breath. His arm remained about her waist, drawing her snuggly to him. Kenric had never experienced such a strong longing for a woman. Any woman. It baffled him.

They arrived at the gates of Kinwick, which swung open before they could identify themselves. Obviously, they were expected. Alys called out a friendly greeting to the gatekeeper, as did Avelyn. Both women waved to several workers as they rode through the outer and inner baileys. Kenric supposed that Lady Avelyn had spent some time at her uncle's estate since she seemed to know so many of the people.

When they reached the keep, he spied Geoffrey de Montfort at the foot of the stairs. With him stood an exquisite woman, her hair afire in the late afternoon sunlight. The nobleman had a possessive arm wrapped about the beauty's waist, so Kenric assumed this was Lord Geoffrey's wife. Both Lord Michael and Lady Elysande seemed to think highly of Merryn de Montfort, so Kenric was curious to make her acquaintance.

Ralf assisted Alys from his horse and the girl flew into her mother's outstretched arms.

"I have so much to tell the both of you," she shared with her parents. Alys looked around. "Where are the boys?"

"Both are napping," her father said. "You'll see them soon and this lovely quiet will end. So take advantage of it, Alys, and tell us what you can."

Kenric climbed from Firefall and assisted Lady Avelyn to the ground. She handed Cattus to him and made straight for her aunt and uncle. They greeted her warmly, with open affection both loving and natural. A shadow of sorrow crossed inside him. He'd never been welcomed by his mother or brother in such a fond manner. Even while his father was alive, the earl had never once made a fuss over him.

He shook aside those thoughts as Martin brought Lady Sela down from their shared saddle. The noblewoman looked ill after three long days of travel. Martin escorted her to their hosts.

Avelyn wrapped an arm about the young woman. "This is Lady Sela Runford, my good friend from court. She is accompanying me to Sandbourne and, with the queen's permission, will remain for the summer. Sela, this is Uncle Geoffrey and Aunt Merryn."

Merryn placed a palm against the tired young woman's cheek. "You look exhausted, my dear."

"I am rather worn out," Sela admitted. "I've never spent that much time on a horse. In fact, I've never even left London. This journey has taken the strength from me. I can barely hold my eyes open and I'm sore in places that I didn't know existed."

"Tilda," called out Lady Merryn.

An older servant who hovered nearby stepped forward. "I'll take Lady Sela upstairs to the chamber we prepared for Lady Avelyn and care for her there."

"Please, let us share it, Tilda," Avelyn interjected. "No sense in making up another one. It will be less work for you, and Sela and I will enjoy being together."

"Be sure she eats something first, Tilda," Merryn insisted. "Then she's to retire. Poor girl. This trip has been quite draining for her."

The servant escorted her charge up the stairs and inside the keep. Kenric decided to step forward. He tucked Cattus to his chest.

"I bring greetings from Lord Michael," he said.

Lord Geoffrey's eyes lit up in recognition. "Ah, 'tis the indomitable Sir Kenric Fairfax." Geoffrey shook his hand and squeezed Kenric's shoulder in friendship.

"So, this is the dark knight that Michael has crowed about," said Lady Merryn. She turned and offered her hand to him.

Kenric took it and kissed her fingers. "A pleasure to meet you, my lady."

"Oh, the pleasure is all mine," she said, her eyes lighting in a smile. "My husband tells me that you're the most talented knight of his acquaintance and that you swing a sword better than any man he knows."

"Lord Geoffrey is too kind," Kenric murmured, though he enjoyed the compliment given to him.

"I think you would be proud of being acknowledged in such a public manner," Lady Avelyn pointed out as she reached over and claimed Cattus. "You do seem to have a rather high opinion of yourself. This only confirms it."

"Avelyn?" Merryn asked, frowning at her niece. "Have you forgotten your good manners during your time at court?"

"Nay, Merryn. I mean it not in an arrogant way. Sir Kenric himself told me matter-of-factly that he is the best soldier in England. It seems Uncle Geoffrey merely agrees with him." She stroked the purring kitten.

"Let us adjourn to the solar," Geoffrey said. "Sir Kenric, you must join us."

"I should see to my men, my lord."

Geoffrey waved over a soldier. "Gilbert is my captain of the guard. He can show your men where they may sleep tonight." He turned to the knight. "Gilbert, see that the Sandbourne men's horses are tended to and then show them where they may wash up for the evening meal. We'll dine in the solar instead."

"At once, my lord." The captain looked to Kenric. "I'll make sure your horse and your men are cared for, my lord."

Kenric saw that any protest would be swatted down. "Thank you. It's Firefall you deal with. He may be large, but his disposition is good."

He watched Gilbert begin to address his men and then turned his attention back to Lord Geoffrey as the earl said, "Shall we make our way inside the keep?"

The women linked arms and went ahead of them. As they arrived inside and throughout the long walk to the solar upstairs, many people greeted Alys and Avelyn. The servants looked busy yet happy in their work. He couldn't help but feel the atmosphere at Kinwick was unlike anywhere he'd ever lived.

They reached the solar, a warm and inviting place, and Kenric took a seat with the others. Alys immediately launched into tales of the royal court, sharing news about what had occurred since she'd last seen her family at Christmas time.

"While the queen kindly allows me time to choose and grind herbs, all her ladies-in-waiting keep me busy asking for remedies," she shared.

Avelyn laughed as she petted the ginger kitten in her lap. "It's not only those women who ask." She turned to her aunt. "Half the court beats a path to Alys' door, begging for her help. Even the king," she confided.

Kenric watched Alys' face light up. "Oh, Mother, the king really likes my headache tonic. He's sent for me several times and seemed most pleased with the results. And he's always asking about you. He is thrilled that you named your last babe after him."

Geoffrey groaned. "Just watch. He will somehow make his way toward Kinwick again this summer. If I have to entertain another summer progress, it might ruin me."

"No, Uncle. I can assure you that the court is steering far to the north and west this summer. The queen shared the route with her ladies-in-waiting not a week ago. By the time they swing back toward London, they won't have time to go out of their way to Kinwick."

"So what are your impressions of the royal court, Niece?" Geoffrey asked, a look of relief crossing his face. "Is it all you thought it would be? Or have unexpected matters changed your mind?"

Avelyn chuckled, a low, throaty noise that made Kenric's heart skip a beat.

"I have learned that I love country life far more than that of the city."

Her words surprised Kenric. He sat up, leaning his forearms on his thighs, eager to hear what she might say.

"Tell us what life there is like for you as a part of the queen's group," Merryn urged.

"The women are shallow," Avelyn explained. "I know that sounds judgmental, but all they think about is fashion. They spend hours discussing the various leathers used in shoes or what color ribbons they should buy. I have sat through endless talk about varying shades of blue and which makes a woman appear more elegant and comely. But more than anything, they love to discuss jewelry. First, you *must* wear jewelry, but it must be the *right* jewelry."

She laughed. "And, alas, I have none! Nor would I wish for any beyond the wedding band I will wear someday."

Alys chimed in, "Avelyn speaks the truth. Many of the women at court look down their noses upon others. Their talk is empty and pointless."

"If it weren't for Alys and Sela, I would have been lonely," Avelyn admitted.

Kenric ached for her in that moment. He understood loneliness and what it could do to one's soul.

"I am sorry it hasn't been what you expected," Merryn said.

"Oh, some things have been good. I adore the music. You know I don't sing a note that isn't off-key, but I enjoy listening to others sing and play. I've heard many outstanding musicians in my months at court. And I did find some who enjoy reading and talking about things that aren't so frivolous." Avelyn sighed. "But they are few and far between."

"Despite what Cousin Avelyn says, the men present pay her attention," Alys revealed. "She's always being asked to dance, and she moves with such grace and ease. The women at court are most jealous of her."

"They are?" Avelyn looked puzzled at her cousin's words.

"Of course," Alys confirmed. "Every handsome courtier, both young and old, wishes to speak to you and spend time with you. They are forever bringing you wine to drink and offering you sweet treats. They hang about you as bees buzzing about flowers."

Avelyn blushed. "I only thought them to be kind since I was new at court."

"They are kind because they want to get to know you," Geoffrey said. "And, mayhap, a few might wish to wed you."

"But I don't fancy any of them," Avelyn admitted. "I thought I was bored with country life and sought change—but at least I had a life there. I tended my vegetable garden. I sewed clothes and cooked. Everyone in the country has an express purpose. They have no interest in politics or power because those things don't put food on the table."

She stroked the kitten, now asleep in her lap. "I am happy that I've had this time at court and so grateful for you arranging for me to serve in the queen's household, Uncle. But, mayhap, 'tis time I came home." She shrugged. "Yet where is home? I don't know how long the king will allow Mother to run Hopeston alone. And since Elysande is gone from there, it wouldn't seem like home to me anymore."

Merryn put a hand atop Avelyn's. "Michael would certainly welcome you to come live at Sandbourne."

Kenric knew that would be true. His liege lord did everything in his power to make his countess happy. If that meant having his sister-in-law live with them, Lord Michael would welcome Avelyn Le Cler with open arms.

He thought how, in these private quarters, Lady Avelyn had revealed even another side to herself. She wasn't a spoiled court brat as he'd first thought, but more a woman of substance.

Which he found very appealing.

"I'm worried the queen won't approve of that," Avelyn said. "Before I left London, we spoke alone and she asked me about the various men at court and marriage. She told me we would speak again in the autumn once I returned. I fear that she'll choose for me some courtier who either has not a lick of sense and only cares about what he wears or worse—he'll be one of those who seeks power and speaks from both sides of his mouth."

Lady Avelyn looked totally miserable in that moment.

Kenric fought from interrupting. For if he did, he would speak up to claim her as his own.

What had Avelyn Le Cler changed about him?

He had no plans to shackle himself to some female—yet he wanted this one. Not only because he desired her physically more than he had any other creature, but because she had proven to be intelligent, compassionate, and full of life.

Geoffrey spoke up. "Let me see if—"

His words were lost as the door flew open. Two-year-old Hal de Montfort blew into the room like a strong gale. The servant, Tilda, followed him with a babe in her arms.

Hal shrieked in glee as he spied Alys and ran toward her. His sister caught him up in her arms and twirled about as he laughed. He gave her a sloppy kiss, and then he saw Avelyn. The boy wriggled so that Alys set him on the ground and he bounded over to his cousin.

Kenric saw the love on the boy's face as he cried, "Av-wyn, Av-wyn!" She set the kitten on the ground and scooped him up, a glow about her that told Kenric this one was meant for babes with her nurturing soul. He watched her introduce Cattus to Hal and teach him how to pet the kitten gently. Hal giggled as he did so.

Then the boy cocked his head and asked her, "Eh-wuh-sun here? Michael?"

"No," she told him. "They're at Sandbourne. Elysande is soon to have a babe, as your mother had little Edward not so long ago."

Hal looked to his mother, who cradled his new brother in her arms. He blew the babe a kiss. Then, as he glanced around the room, his eyes came to rest upon Kenric. Hal lost interest in the kitten and toddled over to him.

Kenric had never spent much time around children. He hoped he didn't frighten the boy with his large size.

"You know Michael," Hal told him.

"I do know Lord Michael," he assured the small boy. "He is my liege lord and Lady Elysande is my countess. So you remember me from your visit to Sandbourne?"

Hal squealed with delight and then started swinging his arm. It took Kenric a moment, but he realized that Hal played with an imaginary sword. The boy had watched Kenric and his father sparring in the training yard when they visited Sandbourne a few months back.

Geoffrey grabbed his son and placed him atop his shoulders, which pleased Hal to no end as he looked down from on high with a huge smile on his face.

Geoffrey grinned at his wife. "It seems it's time for Raynor to fashion Hal a sword." He turned back to Kenric and explained, "My cousin carved wooden swords for Ancel and Alys. He'll be pleased that Hal is ready for one. Though whether the world is ready for Hal to have a sword in his hand, although only a play one, only time will tell."

Kenric blurted out, "*Lady Alys* has a sword?" He couldn't imagine putting a sword into a female's hand, especially a young girl.

"Of course," Merryn said, as if a girl with a sword was the most natural thing in the world. She adjusted the squirming babe in her arms. "A girl needs to be able to defend herself as much as a man."

"Especially at court," Alys proclaimed, rolling her eyes.

Merryn pursed her lips. "I know that Raynor taught you a few defensive moves. I hope you haven't abused that knowledge, Alys."

"I wish Cousin Raynor had taught me some of the same," Avelyn chimed in.

"Why?" Geoffrey frowned. Kenric could see the earl wasn't pleased by his niece's words.

Avelyn gave a lofty wave of her hand. "You never know when it might come in handy, Uncle," she said vaguely.

"Has someone tried to take advantage of you, Avelyn?" Anger sparked in the earl's eyes. "I will flay the flesh from his back if anyone has touched you in an unseemly manner."

"Calm down, my love," Merryn said in a soothing tone. "Avelyn is just a woman who wishes to be prepared." She looked at Kenric. "Mayhap you could teach Avelyn how to defend herself, Sir Kenric."

CHAPTER 8

"Wake up, Sela. You must dress now."

Avelyn watched her friend start to stir as she gently shook her shoulder. Sela's dark hair spilled about her, a tumbled mess. She would have to braid it for her. Sela always had trouble awakening. Nights at the royal court spilled over into the wee hours of the next morning, many times till dawn. Avelyn was certain Sela had never been alert at this time of day.

Her friend rubbed her eyes sleepily and yawned. She glanced up and frowned. "Why do you insist I rise? It's earlier than a cock would crow." She rolled over and snuggled back into the pillow.

Avelyn lifted the bedclothes away, tossing them to the foot of the bed. Sela mumbled something and then didn't stir.

"Come. You need to dress for mass, then we will break our fast in the great hall. You are not at the Palace of Westminster. Country ways are much different than life in London."

Sela turned over, stretching lazily, and yawned again. "Actually, I do feel well rested." She sat up and swung her legs to the floor. Her stomach growled noisily.

"You will have one more day to rest up, for we are staying all of this day at Kinwick and will not leave till tomorrow," Avelyn shared. "Uncle Geoffrey sent word to Michael that we had arrived at Kinwick and will remain another day. He is eager for the Sandbourne men to spar with his own soldiers."

Without voicing it, Avelyn thought that her uncle was especially glad that Kenric Fairfax had shown up as one of the members of the escort party. As they dined in the solar together the previous evening, her uncle had again complimented the young knight and his skills so much that she was sure the man's head would swell and then burst.

But she was curious to see Sir Kenric in action. Her uncle was an experienced soldier, having fought in the wars in France on two different occasions. If he held Fairfax's fighting skills in esteem, then the knight surely was a talented soldier.

She helped Sela dress and then seated her so she could braid her long locks. Avelyn had to take time to plow through the tangled curls with a comb.

"I'm sorry my hair is such a mess," Sela apologized. "Tilda took it down and brushed it out for me. I was so tired from riding that I must have fallen asleep while she did so. 'Twould have been difficult for her to rebraid it for bed with me sprawled."

"Don't worry. I rather enjoy doing tasks such as this," Avelyn reassured her.

"I know your sister is eager for your company. I hope she doesn't mind our delay."

"Nay, she won't. It's only a single day. Besides, Michael would do anything for my uncle. Granting a favor of allowing us to stay an extra day so the men can train together is nothing."

"Why? Is Lord Michael in your uncle's debt?"

Avelyn began separating Sela's locks of hair as she explained. "Michael came to foster as a page into the household where Uncle Geoffrey and my cousin, Raynor, served as squires. The two took Michael under their wings and tutored him, something he never forgot. Then Michael came to Kinwick once he became a knight, wanting to serve under Uncle Geoffrey's leadership. No one but Uncle knew that Michael was destined to become the Earl of Sandbourne upon the death of his father."

"That's an interesting secret to keep," her friend mused. "If I was to be an earl, I would shout it to the heavens."

"That's not my brother-in-law's way. He is a very humble man. Then a short while after his arrival at Kinwick, Michael accompanied the de Montfort family to my sister's wedding."

Sela whipped around. "Wait . . . I don't understand. Your sister was marrying someone that was not Lord Michael?"

Avelyn laughed and turned Sela's head back into place. "Elysande was betrothed to another man and she was set to wed him. But she met Michael and they fell in love at that very first meeting. Then Elysande's betrothed died."

"Convenient," noted Sela.

"Oh, it became much more complicated," she assured her friend. "But in the end, Uncle Geoffrey petitioned the king on Michael's behalf, telling him what a wonderful knight Michael is and how he would be honored if his niece married such a man."

Sela smiled dreamily. "So they are a love match. That's so rare. I envy them."

"Uncle Geoffrey and Aunt Merryn have been in love forever. Since they were children. And Cousin Raynor fell in love with a woman he rescued from highwaymen in a forest. Beatrice is beautiful and smart, and Raynor tumbled hopelessly into love with her the minute he set eyes upon her. At least 'tis what I believe. They both say it took longer."

She paused. "I wish the same for myself, Sela—to find a man whom I love and want to spend the rest of my life with." Avelyn finished the last braid and tied a ribbon at the end.

"I don't know about all this talk of love," Sela said. "I only know I want to wed a handsome man so that we will have enchanting children. He must wealthy enough to keep me in beautiful clothes, but I would prefer that he's kindhearted, as well."

"Do you wish to remain at court?" she asked.

Sela shrugged. "It's all I know, having grown up in its midst. But who knows? Mayhap, I shall learn of country ways on this trip and find my own knight without Father's help." She thought a moment. "Why, it could even be someone such as Sir Kenric Fairfax."

Avelyn's gut twisted in a peculiar way. "What? Surely, you jest."

"Why not? He is, by far, the best-looking man I have laid eyes upon, and I have seen many a handsome man at court." Her eyes went soft and dreamy. "That dark, curling hair and strong jaw and chiseled cheekbones? Not to mention his great height and broad shoulders. I'm sure Sir Kenric is a man who would know how to please a woman."

"But don't you find him overconfident?"

"I like confidence in a man. And, after all, men will be men."

"Yet he is in service to the Earl of Sandbourne," Avelyn pointed out. "It doesn't seem Sir Kenric has the wealth or position you seek. I fear you must find a different suitor in order to please your father and yourself."

Sela gave her a mysterious, womanly smile. "Who knows? Mayhap, Sir Kenric does possess lands and a title—and keeps it in secret—as your brother-in-law did."

Avelyn stood, suddenly tired of their conversation. "Enough nonsense from you. Come. We'll be late for mass if we don't hurry."

She rushed them along to the chapel, where they entered just as the mass began.

Yet throughout the entire service, Avelyn wondered why it bothered her that her closest friend seemed interested in Sir Kenric Fairfax.

AVELYN WALKED TO the soldiers' training yard with Merryn, Alys, and Sela. Hal rode on Geoffrey's shoulders ahead of them, pointing out things and babbling about them, though no one paid him a bit of attention. Merryn had nursed Edward and left the babe behind with Tilda.

Alys carried a small basket for Merryn. "This contains things Mother and I might need in case any of the men are injured," she told Avelyn.

"They get hurt when they train?"

"Not often," Merryn assured her. "It's usually bumps and bruises to tend, but I like to be prepared."

They reached the yard. Avelyn saw it was filled with men milling about, talking with one another. She recognized the men from her escort party as they mingled with the soldiers of Kinwick. Her eyes swept the area till she located Kenric Fairfax. He stood with Gilbert, the captain of Kinwick's guard, his body relaxed even as he held a longbow almost as tall as he was.

"Come up here," Geoffrey called to them over his shoulder.

She saw a raised platform at the front of the training yard. Geoffrey lifted Hal from his shoulders and placed him on it before he swung up on it himself. As the women approached, he leaned down and grasped each one under both her elbows and whisked them to stand atop the platform.

"Oftentimes, I stand up here with Gilbert to observe the training exercises," he explained to Avelyn and Sela. "The height allows me to see over the entire area. I'm able to watch many pairs at one time and see where correction is warranted."

"Geoffrey says he's often up here, but I believe he's down among the men most of the time," Merryn revealed.

He laughed. "At times, I do like to show the men a thing or two."

Merryn sniffed. "Admit it. You spend most of your time down there sparring with the rest of them." She gave him a stern look, her eyebrows raised.

Geoffrey gave his wife a sheepish grin. He lifted her hand and placed a tender kiss into her palm. "You know me well, my love."

"Just promise me you won't train today."

He cocked his head. "Are you worried that Sir Kenric might best me?" he teased.

Merryn shrugged. "I merely think you should watch and see if there is anything new that these Sandbourne men might teach you and our own men of Kinwick."

He drew her close for a lingering kiss. Avelyn bit her lip, hiding her smile as she looked away. Her aunt and uncle made no secret of their great affection for one another.

Geoffrey broke their kiss. "I'm off to learn. I bid you a good day, ladies, and hope you'll enjoy what you see." He leapt to the ground and gave Hal's head a pat before he headed to where Gilbert and

Kenric spoke.

"My... goodness." Sela watched Geoffrey stride away and then looked over to Merryn. Then she glanced at Avelyn, her eyes round. "You did say they were a love match."

"They are forever kissing," Alys declared, shaking her head.

Merryn squeezed her daughter's shoulder. "You, too, will enjoy kissing your husband someday, my dearest."

The young girl crinkled her nose. "I doubt it."

The men began with target practice, using longbows made of yew that were over six feet in length. Merryn told them that this weapon had played a huge role in the victories the English had won at both Crecy and Poitiers, battles Geoffrey had taken part in. The archers alternated shots between Kinwick and Sandbourne soldiers, moving the target back each time to a greater distance. After several rounds, Kenric remained the lone representative from Sandbourne.

Avelyn watched carefully, noting how most of the men strained each time as they shot, their arms quivering—except for Kenric Fairfax. He seemed to press the entire weight of his body into the horns of the bow, using his bulk and height to his advantage. It didn't surprise her when he claimed victory in the contest.

He proved generous, though. She saw how he demonstrated several times to others how he maneuvered the longbow and explained how he sought the target. He, Geoffrey, and Gilbert then supervised groups of men in the exercise. She could see how his method of firing the weapon brought success to those he instructed.

Next, the men competed in throwing javelins. Only Sir Martin from Sandbourne came close, but Kenric still claimed the role of the man who tossed the weapon the greatest distance down the field. He and the other knights spent several minutes speaking with the Kinwick soldiers, who practiced, in turn, what they'd heard. Avelyn saw that, immediately, many of them tossed their javelins a much greater distance than before, thanks to the advice of Kenric and Martin.

Finally, the men began breaking into pairs. Hal came to his feet and began jumping up and down in excitement.

"Hal adores swordplay," his mother explained. "It's his favorite activity."

"I know nothing of it," admitted Sela. "I've never watched men train in any manner."

Merryn began pointing out different soldiers and the weapons they held, from lances to poleaxes, before she turned her attention to those holding swords.

"That is an arming sword. It's used for cutting and thrusting. And over there is an estoc sword, designed for stabbing." Merryn glanced around. "Do you see Alaric? He has a patula, which is a short sword."

"I didn't think the men would train today with real swords," Avelyn said.

"Many times they'll use a wiffle—a practice sword. Today, though, Geoffrey wanted them testing true weapons so he could pass along to our men any small bit that would aid them in becoming better at swordplay."

"At least they are putting on protective gear," Sela said.

Avelyn saw many of the men donned mail coifs and hauberks, some even fastening on protective shoulder plates. She hoped Alys would not have to bring out her medicine kit. Already, the air seemed charged with excitement as the men started up. The sound of clanging steel filled the air. She had to keep from flinching every time she heard the noise.

Her eyes searched again and found Kenric. Her heart pumped wildly as she watched him pull his clothing over his head. He tossed it aside and she stopped breathing.

Stripped to his waist, his bare chest exposed broad shoulders and sculpted muscles. A fine dusting a dark hair covered his chest, trailing down to a flat stomach. Avelyn couldn't help but stare.

Sela leaned over and whispered in her ear. "Even if he has no money or title, I would take him as is. I would pay him to have me. I have never seen a finer specimen of manhood. The women at court would fall at his feet with one glance."

Avelyn found her mouth dry and could not reply. She forced herself to breathe as Gilbert handed Kenric the largest sword she'd ever seen. He held it in both hands, swinging it to get a feel for it as he approached Alaric, a tall knight from Kinwick.

Alaric grinned at his opponent and, soon, the two men were caught in a dance of motion, thrusting and parrying. She couldn't tear her eyes away as the muscles in Kenric's back rippled and flowed. Her entire body stilled as only her eyes followed their duel.

Then Geoffrey interrupted them, asking a few questions. Kenric demonstrated some moves, slicing the sword through the air. Avelyn began watching his feet, treading as lightly as if he danced in the great hall as his sword cut through the air.

Kenric stopped and handed the bastard sword to Geoffrey. Gilbert then gave him two weapons and did the same with Alaric.

"Merryn, what do those men have?"

Her aunt turned her attention to where Avelyn pointed. "Ah, they each have an arming sword in their right hand and a main gauche in their left. That's a small dagger, but it can be deadly."

"Is it difficult to fight with two weapons and two hands?"

Merryn smiled. "Not by the looks of those two."

Avelyn focused on the pair of knights, locked in a duel of will as much as physical movement. Slowly, the entire training yard came to a halt to watch the two men battle one another. Cheers erupted each time one of them came close. She could see both sported a few cuts from close calls and it made her grow anxious. She didn't want Kenric to hurt Alaric, a jovial man with a quick wit and quicker smile, but she didn't want Alaric to injure Kenric either.

She didn't enjoy seeing these two warriors, no matter how skilled, pitted against one another. Fighting was beyond her understanding. Avelyn knew that men seemed to be a mystery in general, but she couldn't comprehend why they had to fight.

Yet despite her reluctance in watching the two men fight one another, she remained spellbound all the same. There was a beauty in their movements—the arc of a sword cutting through the air and the wave of muscles undulating across Kenric's shoulders and back. She continued to stare, her pulse pounding, her nerves frayed.

And then Kenric's arm shot out, so fast it was a blur. He jabbed Alaric's shoulder with the main gauche. Blood spurted from the wound.

Avelyn's insides turned as nausea flooded her.

Kenric jumped back and dropped his weapons as Alaric fell to his knees. Gilbert called a halt to the fighting. Merryn and Alys squatted on the edge of the platform before they jumped to the ground to rush to Alaric's aid. His hand had gone to the gaping wound in his shoulder. Blood poured between the knight's fingers. Merryn shouted orders as Geoffrey motioned for the crowd to step back.

Avelyn glanced to Kenric and saw the stricken look on his face. He turned without a word and strode from the training yard.

Without a conscious thought, Avelyn followed him.

CHAPTER 9

KENRIC HURRIED AWAY from the training yard. Anger at himself seeped deeply into his pores. He had not meant to injure Alaric. He had enjoyed sparring with the soldier, who tested him more than any man had since he'd met Geoffrey de Montfort during his visit to Sandbourne. The earl had extraordinary skills and patience, and he'd nearly gotten the best of his opponent. If not for young Hal calling out and distracting his father at a key moment, Kenric believed de Montfort might well have proven victorious in their match.

"Sir Kenric!" someone called from a distance behind him. "Wait."

He refused to turn around, for the reason he'd become so reckless lay in that lilting voice.

He'd been aware of Avelyn Le Cler from the moment she arrived at the training yard. It was almost as if he could smell her subtle scent of vanilla carried by the slight breeze of the May morning which came and enveloped him. With every contest, he preened a bit more as he bested both Sandbourne and Kinwick men alike.

Kenric couldn't understand why he felt the urge to impress this woman, only that it filled him till he could think of nothing else.

That need to stand out and gain her admiration caused him to be reckless. Careless.

"I said—*oh!*"

He heard the surprise in her voice and glanced over his shoulder without breaking stride, only to see her take a nasty tumble. Without hesitation, Kenric raced toward her.

She sat sprawled on the ground, her skirts hiked up to reveal trim ankles and very shapely calves. A hot frisson of desire ran through him.

Avelyn rubbed her ankle. "Stupid hole," she muttered.

Kenric saw she had stepped into a groove in the ground. "I suspect you've twisted your ankle, my lady."

She glared up at him. "Of course, I did. A woman knows when she's turned an ankle. She doesn't need a man to *tell* her she has done so." Her eyes narrowed. "Especially when she was chasing after said man and he deliberately refused to slow down to see what she wished to speak to him about."

He bowed his head. "I am contrite, my lady. I fear I didn't hear you because I was upset at myself." He knelt beside her. "May I?"

She shrugged. "If you wish."

Kenric grasped her calf in his left hand to steady her leg and fought down the thrill that rushed through him as his fingers wrapped around it. He gingerly touched her ankle with his right, feeling to see if it might be broken. Finding it intact, he slowly rotated her foot.

Her intake of breath caused him to halt. He met those blue eyes, fair as a summer's sky.

"I've twisted it," she informed him. "I'll put myself in Merryn and Alys' capable hands." She frowned and looked over her shoulder. "But first I need to get back to them."

Avelyn's hand reached out and covered his own, the one that still held the calf he couldn't seem to part with. "Why did you leave the training yard so suddenly?" she asked, her voice soft as silk.

He found he couldn't look away and answered her honestly. "I lost control. I was showing off. I should never have carried through with the movement. I could have touched Alaric with the dagger and withdrawn just as quickly without penetrating him."

Kenric swallowed. "But I thought to catch your attention and win your favor. In doing so, I lost focus."

Her rosebud lips parted. Confusion filled her face. "You wished . . . for *my* favor?"

"Aye."

Then the corners of her mouth turned up in a smile. "Do you

believe it worked?"

He held her glance. "I hope so."

Before he could think of the consequences, Kenric lowered his mouth to hers. Avelyn squeezed his hand as he slowly brushed his lips against hers. She started to speak and he took it as an invitation. His tongue eased into her mouth, running along her teeth. Then her own tongue met his and playfully dueled with him, causing his pulse to jump.

He brought a hand to the back of her neck and grasped the soft skin as he drank in her sweet taste. The heat of the sun burning into his back seemed to light a fire within him.

Avelyn's hand gripped his more tightly as her free one flattened against his bare chest. Her fingers seared into him as if branding him as hers for all time. His hands moved to cradle her face as his tongue now warred with hers, fighting for possession of her. Her hands crept to his shoulders, the nails sinking into his flesh as she anchored herself.

Time stood still.

Kenric knew not how long the kiss went on, only that he finally became aware that he must stop it before he lost control and took her right there on the ground. His hands slipped to her shoulders and gripped them as he tore his mouth from hers.

At once, an emptiness filled him, as if he'd been cut adrift at sea with no companions in sight. He looked into her blue eyes and saw the heat and desire that must be echoed in his own. Her mouth, so tempting, called out for him to return.

He stood and then gripped her elbows, pulling her to her feet. Avelyn swayed and fell against him, her palms flattening against his chest, causing his manhood to stir.

"I am . . . so dizzy," she uttered, sounding confused.

Kenric tightened his grip but pushed her away till he had hold of her an arm's length away.

"Can you walk?" he asked, not knowing where to begin.

"What just happened between us?" she demanded, her voice low but her tone urgent.

He shook his head. "I wish I could say. I . . . I have no words."

"My body is humming—like a lute which has been stroked for a last note that reverberates throughout a still room." Avelyn gazed up at him. "My lips tingle, as does every part of me. These strange feelings . . ." Her voice trailed off.

Kenric never opened up to another soul, never sharing what he thought or felt. But then again, he had never experienced this reaction with any woman—and they had only kissed.

Yet, it was as if he was under her spell as he said, "I feel the same. I am as taut as that lute's strings, yet unknown ripples pour throughout me. I long for you, Avelyn Le Cler. With a depth and breadth that is unfamiliar—yet seemingly has lain dormant within me my entire life."

Her hands reached out and touched his face in wonder. She stroked it gently, then boldly, causing desire to flicker again within him. Kenric lowered his mouth to hers and lost himself in their kiss.

Avelyn leaned against him, her breasts pushing close. He could feel her nipples teasing him through her layers of clothing. He brought a hand to one breast and massaged it, causing her to moan. The sound almost undid him.

Yet, it brought him to his senses—again.

Kenric grasped her wrists and forced her hands from his chest. "We must stop. Now."

She shook her head. "I know. I know," she repeated. "And yet, I want nothing more than to touch you—and to have you touch me."

He took her chin in hand and brushed a soft kiss upon her lips. "I must return you to Lady Merryn. She needs to tend to your ankle."

"Oh." Avelyn glanced down and tried to take a step. "Ouch!"

Kenric bent and placed an arm behind her knees and swept her up close. One of her arms went about his neck. The other rested against his chest, her fingers softly stroking and then teasing as she pulled against the hair there.

"Stop that, wench," he said playfully.

She sighed. "If you insist. Take me to Merryn."

He started back in the direction of the training yard.

"No, she and Alys will have tended to Alaric by now. They have probably returned to the keep."

"Then I will take you there."

Kenric walked more slowly than he usually did, for he did not want to release her from his arms. He grinned down at her like some love-struck fool. That almost caused him to halt in his tracks.

Was he in love with Avelyn Le Cler?

AVELYN CLOSED HER EYES and rested her cheek against the rock-hard chest of Kenric Fairfax.

Was she dreaming?

Nay. Her throbbing ankle told her that she was not abed.

But what had just occurred between her and the prickly knight from Sandbourne?

Actually, he'd only seemed troublesome that first day. She'd come to understand, in the short time she'd known him, that he was a methodical man, one who set his mind to a task and would follow through completely. Michael had charged him to bring her back to Sandbourne—not her and two other females. Avelyn knew her thwarting his plans had aggravated him. Yet, by the second day of their journey, they had begun a conversation that lasted throughout that day and into the next. She found him intelligent and amusing—and very, very handsome.

She didn't consider herself to be shallow like the women who populated the royal court. She shouldn't take Kenric's looks into consideration when thinking about him, but she did. And she couldn't help but think about him all the time. Her thoughts strayed more and more to him during the past few days. And now? After their kisses caused her to burn with desire for his touch, she might never have another coherent thought again throughout her life, be it long or short. Thoughts of Kenric Fairfax would forever linger.

Was that love? Could she possibly be in love with this dark knight?

She had only known him a handful of days.

Yet Elysande and Michael had realized at their very first meeting that they were meant to be together. Raynor and Beatrice had quickly been drawn to one another. And she knew Geoffrey and Merryn had been close companions since childhood. Who knew when their feelings had turned to love?

Excitement filled Avelyn. She wanted—no, needed—to get to know more of this man. She must.

For she wished to spend the rest of her life with him.

But did he feel the same? Was he a man that would even consider marriage? Many knights in service to a liege lord did not, preferring to remain in the barracks and dedicate their lives to protecting the family they served.

Oh, she was getting ahead of herself. Here, she wanted Kenric Fairfax to slip a ring upon her finger and buy a small parcel of land near Sandbourne so they could remain close to Elysande and Michael. She wanted him to make love to her day and night and give her children. She needed to grow old with this man and learn something new about him each day they shared together.

And he had merely kissed her.

What if those kisses did not mean to him what they had to her? Yet Avelyn knew they must have. He had admitted as much—that he felt the same as she had and his body had responded to hers in kind. But did that mean commitment?

Only time would tell.

Avelyn decided, in that moment, that she would not force this knight's hand in any way. She would make no declarations of love. Instead, she would keep her feelings to herself. If he wanted more from her, then he would have to be the one to share that first.

Pressing her cheek closer against his chest, she relished the feel and scent of him. Her fingers longed to run against his skin and play with the dusting of dark hair resting against her palm. Desire caused her to imagine feeling his muscles as they danced under her fingers.

She did none of that, choosing to lie still in his arms.

They reached the keep. Kenric headed up the stairs, carrying her as if she were the lightest of feathers. They entered the great hall and Avelyn spied Merryn.

"There you are. Whatever happened to you, Avelyn?"

As they drew close, she saw Merryn's eyes studying her. It was as if her aunt knew what had gone on between them.

"Lady Avelyn twisted her ankle. 'Tis not broken, but she needs you to tend to it, my lady," Kenric offered, his voice now neutral, holding none of the passion from minutes ago.

"I see." Merryn tilted her head and continued looking at them both. "Take Lady Avelyn up to her chamber, Sir Kenric. I'll meet you there shortly once I've retrieved what I need."

He carried her up the stairs and down the long corridor to the chamber she was sharing with Sela.

"Knock on the door," she commanded him. "Sela may be within and not ready to receive company."

Kenric nodded, a slight blush tinging his cheeks. He knocked, but no response came, so he opened the oak door and crossed into the room. Drawing back the bed curtains, he deposited Avelyn upon the mattress.

"Thank you, my lord," she said demurely.

He stood there, unsure of what to do. Avelyn longed to take his hand, but she had already decided it was up to him to make any intentions known to her, so she refrained from doing so.

It nearly killed her.

The tall knight looked like a lost puppy, unsure of himself in a way he'd probably never experienced. Then he glanced down and picked up the ginger kitten that had scampered over to him and toyed with the toes of his boots.

"Hello, Cattus," he said to the kitten. "Lady Avelyn has injured herself. You must stay with her and keep her company." He placed the kitten in her lap.

At that moment, Merryn entered the room.

"Now that you are here, my lady, I will excuse myself." Kenric turned to go and stopped. "But first, may I ask how Sir Alaric fares?"

"His injury wasn't severe. Alys cleaned the wound and stitched him up in a matter of minutes." Merryn paused. "I'm sure he'd like to visit with you so you can tell him how best to avoid making the same mistake twice."

Avelyn watched Kenric shuffle his feet as a small child might and brought a hand to her mouth to hide her smile.

"Then I'll seek him out, my lady. Good day to you both." He left the chamber, closing the door behind him.

Merryn faced her. "So how long have you been in love with Kenric Fairfax?"

She found herself speechless but recovered quickly. "Why would you ask such a thing? I only met him when he came to London to retrieve me at Michael's command."

Avelyn shifted in the bed, busying herself by petting Cattus. Still, she could sense Merryn's eyes on her.

"I ask because you vanished and I wondered where you'd gone. Then you appear in the arms of a most handsome, worthy knight, looking like a cat that has lapped up a bowl of cream."

She sensed a blush rising on her cheeks but kept her eyes on the kitten.

"And then there are your swollen lips to consider and burned skin where a roughened beard has been rubbed against it numerous times in pleasure."

Her hand crept up to her face. Her fingers touched her lips. Avelyn finally met her aunt's eyes.

"You are most observant, Merryn."

Merryn smiled. "I pride myself on it." Avelyn caught the twinkle in her eyes. "And for spotting a new love that has sprung up."

Avelyn cried, "I had no idea, I swear! I thought him rather arrogant at first, but then he grew on me as we made our way toward Kinwick. Then for some reason, I went charging after him once Alaric had been hurt. And . . . then . . . somehow . . . we were kissing." She shuddered, not in fear, but in pleasure as the memory flooded her.

"I assume that you enjoyed his kiss?"

She fought to keep from smiling and lost that battle. "Oh, very much so. It was as if I truly came alive for the first time in my life. My body buzzed and tingled and felt so unlike it usually does."

Merryn came and sat next to her on the bed. "It's the most wonderful feeling in the world."

"Aye. Exactly. I find it hard to put into words, but I'm not the same person I was when I awoke this morning."

Merryn stroked her hair fondly. "You never will be, Avelyn. Love changes everything about you for the good." She stopped. "Do you think Sir Kenric returns your feelings?"

She bit her lip. "He said as much. Then he abruptly stopped his kisses and became very brusque and formal. He insisted he bring me to you so you could care for my ankle."

Merryn laughed. "Oh, Avelyn. He longed for more, but he realized that you are a lady and not some tavern wench. He had to stop before he carried matters too far."

Avelyn frowned. "I'm not certain I understand you, Merryn."

Her aunt wrapped an arm around her. "First, I shall look at your ankle to see if it swells." She grinned. "And then we will talk of very important matters. I see your lady mother hasn't advised you."

"What should she have taught me that she did not?"

Merryn shook her head. "Ankle first. Then we shall speak woman to woman."

CHAPTER 10

AVELYN SPENT THE REST of the day within the guest chamber. After Merryn examined her ankle, she told her it only had slight swelling. Merryn even said that Avelyn could walk on it starting tomorrow. She would experience a little discomfort, but no real pain should surface. She elevated Avelyn's leg and wrapped it in cold rags to bring down any potential swelling.

Sela brought the noon meal to her and kept Avelyn company as they chatted about what they'd seen that morning during the training exercises. Her friend seemed quite taken with Sir Martin's prowess and Avelyn wondered if a budding romance might occur between the two.

Alys visited after that, bringing Edward with her. Avelyn enjoyed holding the babe while her cousin changed the bandage and then placed a poultice about the ankle for any lingering pain. She was left to nap after that.

She awoke feeling rested but grew bored sitting in the empty chamber. Alys had taken Cattus with her so the kitten could play with Hal instead of being confined to the bedchamber. Avelyn wanted to get up and walk around but feared Merryn would catch her at it and scold her for not waiting till tomorrow.

A sudden knock at the door had her happy that a new visitor had arrived.

"Come," she called out, ready to have a conversation with whomever might appear.

It surprised her when her uncle entered, bearing a tray with the evening meal. But it wasn't all that surprised her. As he closed the door and came closer to the bed, Avelyn sat up, plumping the pillows behind her.

"I can tell by the look on your face that Merryn spoke with you," she began.

He set the tray on the table beside the bed and shrugged. "That's the way between husband and wife. Sometimes, we don't even need words between us. We know each other's mind and what is in our hearts." Geoffrey waited a moment and then said, "Tell me about Kenric Fairfax."

"Actually, I would ask the same of you," Avelyn replied. "I know you met him previously at Sandbourne."

"I did."

"What is he like?"

Geoffrey retrieved a nearby chair and brought it close to the bed. He sat and thought a moment. "I visited Sandbourne with Hal in tow. Merryn was too heavy with child to accompany me. It was only a few weeks before Edward's birth. In fact, I took Hal with me because she needed a break from him and his wild ways."

Avelyn laughed. "I know what you mean. He's the dearest boy in the world, but he can be a handful."

"Michael shared with me how pleased he was with several of his new knights and one in particular. Kenric Fairfax had arrived and told him that he searched for a liege lord to serve. That he had heard the Earl of Sandbourne was a respected and respectable man who rebuilt the force of soldiers at the estate since he had recently come into the title. Fairfax said he wanted a chance to come to Sandbourne and be a part of everything."

"Did Michael say where this knight came from? Or anything of Sir Kenric's past?" Avelyn couldn't help but think of the missing spurs and wondered why Kenric no longer wore them—or if he ever had.

"He only revealed that Fairfax was from the far north and that he preferred to settle in the south."

"I know I enjoy the milder winters here after growing up in the north," Avelyn said. "I can't blame him for that although I detect the south in his accent. Mayhap he was born here but went to foster in the north."

"That could be the case," her uncle agreed. "At any rate, I watched him spar with the other soldiers. Physically, he's an imposing man. He is quick with a sword and accurate with an array of other weapons. I asked to face him and we engaged one-on-one."

Avelyn drew in a quick breath.

"Do not, under any circumstances, reveal that to Merryn," Geoffrey warned.

She grinned. "I'll hold that piece of information over you, Uncle. Mayhap you can bribe me to keep quiet about it. But go on."

He gave her a mock scowl, but she knew 'twas all in fun. "Fairfax bested me. Not by much, but he is as seasoned and talented a knight as I have ever seen, and I've fought many excellent warriors in the past."

"Elysande wrote to me that Michael trusted Kenric."

Geoffrey nodded. "That would be true or Kenric never would've been charged to lead the escort party that brought you from London. But enough of my talk. What do you know of him, Niece?"

Avelyn considered a moment. "He is set in his ways. Stubborn. I didn't want to like him after we first met but, somehow, I came around." She paused. "He is intelligent and a capable leader. He seems of good character."

"And?"

She sighed, knowing she could keep nothing from him. "I find him the most handsome man I have laid eyes upon. If he were at court? He would have to swat the ladies away like a horse's tail does with flies. They would give him no peace until he married." She snorted. "And even after he took his vows, there would be women that still chased him."

"Merryn says you have feelings for this man."

A calm descended upon Avelyn as she heard his words. "I do. A part of me believes that fate has sealed our destiny. From the moment we kissed, I have felt as one with him."

Geoffrey grinned. "So you found that enjoyable?"

She felt the heat in her cheeks. "Quite so."

"Have you ever been kissed before?"

"Uncle!"

He lifted his hands, palms up, as if in surrender. "I know you have been at court, so I thought it only fair to ask."

Avelyn twisted her hands nervously in her lap. "Aye. A few courtiers have stolen a kiss from me, but not for any great length. They were . . ." She hesitated, finding it hard to put into words how bland those kisses had been and how unaffected she was by them.

"Nothing like Sir Kenric's kiss," Geoffrey finished.

She met his eyes. "Nay. They weren't."

Her uncle leaned closer. "Did it feel as if the very earth moved under your feet? That your glow could light the night sky brighter than the stars from the heavens above?"

"How poetic," she declared.

"'Tis how I feel every time I touch Merryn." He gazed at her steadily. "I would hope this for you, as well."

Avelyn nodded. "Aye, it's so."

He sat back. "Good. As your uncle—and with your father gone—I'm responsible for you and your welfare. I know I asked the queen to look for a suitable match for you, yet you found one on your own. I think she will understand."

"But I don't know how Kenric would feel about wedding me," she protested. "And in truth, I know so little about him. He may not be of a marrying mind."

Geoffrey gave her a long look. "If he feels as you do, he won't be able to stop from pledging himself to you. He'll move heaven and earth in order to commit to you." He paused. "If this is what you want, Avelyn, then you have my blessing."

He leaned over and kissed her cheek.

"We can keep this between us for now," Geoffrey said. "But I'll write to Michael and tell him that you have my blessing. I trust he'll look out for your interests while you are at Sandbourne this summer."

Avelyn hugged him tightly. Hope filled her that, by summer's end,

Sir Kenric Fairfax would declare his intentions toward her.

More importantly, she longed to hear from his lips that he loved her.

AVELYN FINISHED THE MEAL that her uncle had brought and rested the tray on the table next to the bed. Before she had time to be bored, Alys arrived.

"I've returned to look at your ankle," her young cousin said.

She removed the poultice and unwrapped the bandage. She studied the ankle, her touch light. Alys rewrapped it with fresh, cold rags that she pulled from her basket.

"The swelling is minimal, so you'll be able to walk on it tomorrow with just a few twinges. You were lucky, Avelyn. It could've been much worse. I've tended to sprains where the swelling caused the joint to balloon up and bring much pain. I have ordered people to bed for a week."

"Then I'm glad it was only a small hole I stepped into and only a slight twist I suffered," Avelyn teased. "Else you would keep me here a sennight and practice your skills upon me."

Alys swept up the tray and excused herself as Sela entered the chamber.

"I wondered where you had gone."

Her friend sat down on the bed next to her. "I had a busy day. Thank goodness it wasn't atop a horse. My poor rump is still sore from being in the saddle for so long. But I did walk a good deal and saw quite a bit of Kinwick. The de Montforts have a lovely estate."

"Did you enjoy seeing it with Sir Martin?" Avelyn asked. She watched as Sela blushed prettily.

"He accompanied me, but several others from Sandbourne and Kinwick came along with us. I met many people and they were ever so friendly. You were right, Avelyn. Country life is much different from that in London."

"I hope you'll enjoy your time at Sandbourne, Sela."

"I'm certain I will. Oh, I came to tell you that Tilda has made up a bed for me in the chamber across the hall. Merryn wanted to be sure that you received a proper night of rest. I admitted to her that I can be a restless sleeper, so you'll be alone tonight."

"Merryn does have a tendency to fuss."

"I like her a great deal. She is full of spirit and life." Sela kissed Avelyn's forehead. "I'll bid you a good evening and return to the great hall."

"Would Sir Martin be awaiting you there?" she teased.

Sela's brows arched. "Mayhap he does." She giggled and climbed down from the bed. "I'll see you soon, Avelyn."

After her friend left, she felt at loose ends. She wasn't ready to retire for the night, but she didn't expect any more visitors. Then a gentle rap sounded at the door.

Something told her that Kenric Fairfax stood on the other side.

She called for him to enter. He stepped in, a concerned look on his face.

The man took her breath away.

She'd never thought a man to be beautiful, but everything about Kenric spoke to that. Avelyn wanted to run her fingers through his dark, curly locks and stare into those hazel eyes for an eternity. More than anything, she wished to press her body against his, sculpted with muscle.

And kiss him. Oh, Sweet Jesu, she longed to touch her mouth to his and never come up for air.

"My lady, I came to see how you fare."

She swallowed and found her voice. "I'm doing well. Alys just left and said that I may get on my feet tomorrow."

"That's good news. Lady Merryn says we can leave as planned. We'll ride all day tomorrow, so you won't have to strain yourself. Then we should arrive at Sandbourne by the noon meal the day after. Your ankle should be much stronger by then."

"Thank you for letting me know."

An awkward silence loomed between them after she spoke. Avelyn had no idea what to say. Then, as she started to speak, Kenric did so at the same time. They both stopped and laughed before they fell silent again.

She wanted him to stay but didn't think he'd take the initiative—so Avelyn took matters into her own hands.

"Would you mind bringing Uncle Geoffrey's chess set upstairs so that we might play a game or two? It can be found in the steward's room, where the records of the estate are kept and managed."

Kenric asked, "Are you certain I should do so?" His hazel eyes twinkled at her. "After all, I must uphold my code of chivalry, which is to always honor women. I wouldn't wish to embarrass you."

Avelyn sensed the flirtation in his tone. "You think to best me at chess?"

He shrugged. "You are but a woman." He gave her a charming smile that caused her pulse to quicken.

She found her eyelashes fluttering instinctively. "I possess just as much ability to think and reason as a man," she told him, a smile playing about her lips. "I demand you retrieve the set at once—then I can prove it to you."

"If you insist." Kenric left the room.

Nervousness built within her as she waited for his return. When the door swung open a few minutes later, it startled her when Merryn came in.

"I stopped by to be sure that you were settled for the night. Geoffrey told me that he spoke with you." Her aunt gave Avelyn a contrite look. "I hope you don't feel as if I betrayed a confidence by sharing what I knew about your feelings for Sir Kenric. I only wanted to make Geoffrey aware of the situation. He is the head of the family and must give his approval if there's to be any match."

Avelyn took her aunt's hand. "I understand. I'm not upset. In fact, he was rather sweet about it. Oh, Merryn, he is so in love with you."

Her aunt's face grew dreamy. "Even after all these years, our love is strong. I cannot imagine myself with another man. Geoffrey is—and always will be—the one for me."

At that moment, Kenric returned. "I'm sorry to interrupt."

"Nay, stay," Merryn told him, "I was about to leave." She smiled. "I see that you're going to play chess."

Avelyn snorted. "*He* thinks women haven't the skill to do so. Much less win."

Merryn cocked an eyebrow. "Then you don't know the de Montfort women, Sir Kenric. Avelyn's half de Montfort. 'Twill be enough to bury you," she promised. She gave the knight a sweet smile. "I bid you a good evening." Merryn swept from the room and closed the door behind her.

Avelyn's anticipation grew as he set up the game pieces. She intended to win.

Not only the game—or the match—but Kenric's heart.

CHAPTER 11

KENRIC FOUND HIMSELF stunned when Avelyn Le Cler beat him soundly in their first game. It happened quickly, as if he experienced a surprise attack by the enemy that left him decimated. He struggled but clawed his way to victory in the second game. Though the noblewoman proved a cunning opponent, when he saw the disappointment in her eyes, he thought to give her an out.

"Mayhap your injury contributed to your loss, my lady."

Her jaw fell open and then snapped shut. "A slightly twisted ankle has nothing to do with my thinking." She eyed him for a moment, much as a cat might before it pounced upon a helpless mouse. "A final game, my lord, to see who'll take the match?"

"Nay." He sat back from the gaming board. "We can reengage in play at Sandbourne."

Her grin told him that he had been caught.

"You wish to think about my strategy and plan a way to try and win." She laughed, a teasing light shining in her eyes. "You think, despite your talk of honoring ladies with your code of chivalry, to embarrass me in front of your home troops in the great hall, where you will have men rooting for you."

Avelyn picked up her queen and toyed with it. "I accept your challenge. It will give me time to give thought to your chess play, as well." Her eyes now sparkled with mischief. "You should fear me, my lord. I won't go easy on you, no matter what witnesses stand present at your defeat."

He crossed his arms. "I fear I won't find an easy victory, for I now see you have a keen mind." He paused. "I underestimated you, Lady Avelyn."

In more ways than one...

Kenric decided to change the subject. "I like Sandbourne very much. I think you will enjoy your stay there with your sister this summer."

"I'm looking forward to our arrival. But why are you there? What caused you to enter into service with Michael?"

He rubbed his chin. "I heard that the earl had come into his title and assembled a new group of men under his leadership at Sandbourne. I decided to seek him out. He has a noteworthy reputation as a warrior and is a fine man, both moral and just."

"So you served no other liege lord before him?" she asked, curiosity lighting her delicate features. "I know some knights become restless in a single place and choose to hire out their services as they travel about England. Does that describe you, my lord?"

Kenric shrugged, not wishing to reveal anything about his time fostering with Lord Forwin.

Or what had happened with the nobleman's daughter.

"I'm happy at Sandbourne and plan to remain as long as the earl wishes my presence there, but I did roam about before then."

"Where?" she asked eagerly.

"Far from here," he said brusquely, wanting to close the topic from discussion.

"I am from the north," she told him. "I grew up in the harsh cold and snow. When my father died, the king had Mother bring us south with her to Hopeston Castle where she wed again. My stepfather passed away suddenly last summer and Mother is charged with keeping Hopeston for now."

"Truly?" The thought of a woman solely in charge of a castle puzzled him. He knew it occurred in times of war when the lord would be away, but for an unmarried woman to have total control baffled him. "The king has left the castle and its people in her care?" he asked, hoping to clarify Avelyn's meaning.

"Aye. Mother is a formidable woman." Her lips turned up into a small smile. "Merryn told you before—de Montfort women are most capable, no matter what task they take on. But what of the women in your family? Your mother? Have you sisters? Tell me what Sir Kenric was like as a small boy."

His body tensed at the mention of his childhood. He wondered how much to share with her.

"I have no sisters, so I have no experience around women."

"But you did have a mother. What is she like? Are you much like her?"

He tried to relax his clenched jaw and said, "Aye, I have a mother. But as a second born son, she lavished her attention upon my brother. As the heir to Shadowfaire, Roland rightly received all her time and interest."

"What?" she asked, sounding aghast. "That's ridiculous! All children need both love and attention from their parents, no matter what their place is in the birth order."

Kenric stiffened at her words.

"I'm sorry," she rushed to apologize. "I sound as if I stand in judgment of your lady mother." Avelyn paused. "Mayhap I am—and I find her lacking."

"I tend to agree with you," he said lightly, "for we never spent time together. She was devoted to my brother and his needs. Roland was a sickly boy. She nurtured him. Read to him. Coddled him. She had no time for a younger son."

Her eyes narrowed. "Hmm. And what of your father?"

"My father was a great warrior," Kenric said with pride. "He taught me all he knew. How to ride. Shoot. Hunt. Fight."

"All the important things," she observed.

"Aye," he agreed, glad Avelyn understood what truly counted. But he saw the odd look that lingered on her face.

"But did he love you?" she asked softly.

Her question puzzled him. He'd never thought of love in terms of his father. He feared the man. Respected him. But love?

"I suppose," Kenric said, but he heard the hesitation in his voice as the words hung in the air.

"You have no other brothers?"

"None."

Avelyn fiddled with the chess piece still in her hand. "It makes me sad that you lived such a lonely existence."

He'd never admitted to himself how lonely he had been. It seemed he'd spent his entire life with no one to depend upon but himself.

"I did spend a great deal of time on my own, but it helped to toughen me up. I wasn't an easy child and was often punished—whether I was guilty or not."

It shamed him to admit it to her. He'd never voiced this thought aloud. It startled him that this noblewoman could draw such information so easily from him.

"What do you mean?"

Kenric decided to open up and tell her the truth. It might be cleansing.

"My brother tended to be a mischievous child," he began and then decided he would not censor his words. "Actually, Roland could be quite cruel at times. Abusing animals. Breaking items without provocation. I was often blamed for his actions."

Avelyn twisted the queen so tightly that he saw her knuckles go white. "So he lied."

The truth lay in the open. This beautiful woman, short of stature but wise in years, gave him the courage to speak about the unspeakable.

"Yes. Often. And when he didn't, Gussalen stepped up to lay blame at my doorstep."

"Who is she?"

Just uttering her name brought distaste to him. "My mother's old nurse. Gussalen was with her at birth and came to Shadowfaire when she married my father." He thought a moment. "She would do anything for my mother. Roland, too. He favors our mother, while I look much as my father did."

Her brow creased. "You're telling me that this Gussalen blamed you for your brother's wrongdoing. You were punished for his poor actions simply because he was the elder and preferred by your mother." Avelyn set down the queen. "Oh, Kenric."

He heard the anguish in her voice even as she took his hand in both her small ones. Tears swam in her blue eyes.

"My heart hurts so for you. What a harsh upbringing you had."

She pulled his hand to her and tenderly brushed her lips on it. His heart sped up, pounding rapidly at the sweet gesture.

This woman saw him for who he was, like no other before had. He told her things he'd never admitted to another soul, becoming transparent before her.

His eyes met hers as Avelyn said, "I can tell you have a good heart, Kenric Fairfax. I'm sorry your mother and brother did not recognize it. And despite their ill will and lack of attention, you have become a fine man. A knight of not only physical strength—but strength of character. I know it was a lonely road, but you've made the journey to honor all on your own."

She pressed warm lips to his hand once more. Kenric brushed aside the tear that spilled down her cheek with his free one.

"I'm glad you've found happiness at Sandbourne," Avelyn said. "I hope you'll remain there . . . and find even more."

LORD GEOFFREY AND LADY MERRYN came to see them off, accompanied by young Alys. Kenric couldn't help but notice how close the lord and lady of Kinwick seemed to be. They stood arm in arm, not only physically close, but each had a glow about them that he had seen present only one other time—on Lord Michael and Lady Elysande's faces. It was like their love was on display for all the world to see, without regret.

"I hope you have a pleasant trip as you complete your journey to Sandbourne," Lady Merryn told him. Her eyes twinkled as she said, "And I hope that you manage to win a game or two of chess in the future."

Lord Geoffrey shook his hand. "Thank you for bringing my daughter safely home from London."

"She was no trouble, my lord," Kenric said, surprised that he felt that way. Alys de Montfort had proven to be a true delight, both on the road and after their arrival at Kinwick.

Geoffrey sighed. "Alys is my easy one. Ancel, too. But young Hal?" He shook his head as the small boy ran wildly about the bailey chasing Cattus, who was to remain at Kinwick. "Hal is a big bundle of rambunctious boy. And I fear tiny Edward, he of the mighty lungs, will learn at his brother's feet to be the same."

Merryn swatted her husband playfully. "You exaggerate, Husband. And while you believe Hal is a terror, I fear you should keep your eye on Alys. I've heard daughters put the gray in their father's head of hair."

"She is already lovely, Merryn," said Avelyn. "A miniature version of you. Alys will grow into quite a beauty." She turned to Geoffrey. "Then Uncle will find himself beating the men away that flock to her. A whirlwind such as Hal will be nothing compared to the problems Alys may stir up—though none of her own making."

Geoffrey snorted. "Let these would-be suitors try to surround my daughter. She is a de Montfort. She has her mother's fair looks, my keen intelligence, and Raynor has taught her to defend herself. She won't be swayed by pretty words." He turned and looked to where Alys said her goodbyes to Sela. "Mark my words, the man she lets through will be the one for her."

Avelyn kissed Geoffrey's cheek and then Merryn's. "I hope to see you both very soon."

"Now that Edward is a bit older, we'll certainly come to Sandbourne," Merryn assured her. "We'll wait for news that Elysande has given birth and then visit shortly thereafter." She embraced Avelyn. "Give her and Michael our love."

"And the same to my sister, Mary," Geoffrey said. "We look forward to seeing her, as well. Godspeed to you."

Kenric mounted Firefall and then reached to draw Avelyn up with him. Martin did the same with Lady Sela. They gave a final wave as Kenric spurred his horse on.

They traveled several hours without incident, stopping once around the noon hour to eat some bread and cheese that Lady Merryn thoughtfully provided. The respite served to also allow the riders to stretch their legs before they climbed back into the saddle.

As they rode on, Kenric sensed his stomach clenching as they neared Shadowfaire's lands. It was the reason he hadn't wanted to stop at Kinwick. The road they'd taken from Sandbourne to London had not crossed this way, but the path from Kinwick back to Sandbourne would. If he tried to avoid it, he knew his men might question why they went so far out of their way to reach home. He was determined never to set foot at Shadowfaire again—especially after the last time he'd seen Roland and his mother when they attended his knighthood ceremony. The memories surrounding those events should remain pushed into the farthest recesses of his mind, never to be recollected.

Kenric tried to bring himself to enjoy his present circumstances. It was a lovely day in May with plenty of sunshine and a soft breeze from the south. Plus, he had a beautiful woman in his arms. Avelyn fit perfectly against him and he enjoyed the feel of her near him. He inhaled the subtle scent of vanilla that always clung to her, knowing he would never smell it again without thinking of her.

He wondered about their budding friendship and how she had wormed from him things he had never spoken of with others. His thoughts drifted to their heated kisses, which caused his manhood to stir a bit. Kenric had never once thought of settling down with a single woman when so many fair maids lived scattered throughout the land. Besides, he'd dedicated himself to being a knight. Yet he now toyed with the thought of always remaining in one place.

With this woman by his side—and in his bed.

Kenric would have lazily stayed with such thoughts if he hadn't spied the scout he'd sent out galloping toward them at breakneck speed. He motioned for the escort party to pull up and await the soldier's arrival.

The man came to a halt beside him. "My lord, riders approach who know you. They were looking for you," he said, out of breath.

Who? Why?

A sick feeling rippled throughout Kenric. It had to do with Shadowfaire.

He looked into the distance and saw two men on horseback heading their way. As they approached, he recognized Sir Jervis. The knight had been close to his father's age and someone Walter Fairfax trusted implicitly.

They pulled up alongside him with Jervis giving a friendly wave.

"Sir Kenric. We are happy to meet up with you. 'Tis Gib with me."

He exchanged a brief nod with Gib. And then Jervis said, "We knew not where to look for you. Gib and I have been throughout the north and were returning home. 'Tis fate to have you cross our paths."

"Why was I needed? Did Lord Roland send you for me?"

Jervis looked downcast. "Your lady mother is dying, my lord, and wishes to see you one last time."

Kenric felt Avelyn's quick intake of breath since his arm pressed against her. He found it hard to believe his mother had requested his presence on her deathbed. He gripped Avelyn more closely.

Before he could reply, she asked, "Are we far from Shadowfaire?"

"Nay, my lady," Jervis said. "You are but an hour's ride from the keep."

Avelyn turned and told him, "We must go to her."

He frowned. "I will see you safely to Sandbourne first. I can leave once—"

"Nay," she interrupted, her tone firm. "Time could be of the essence. We should accompany you there. It's only a short delay. You can send a rider ahead to let Elysande and Michael know about our change in plans. I insist." Her sky blue eyes implored him as much as her words.

"Very well," he reluctantly agreed. Kenric knew Avelyn had a stubborn streak and he didn't wish to argue with her in front of all of these men. He motioned a soldier over and told him to ride to Lord Michael with the news.

They followed Jervis and Gib back to the estate. Only as they rode near did Kenric realize he had not asked about Roland and wondered how his twin fared. Roland had always been so close to their mother. Her death would devastate him.

They reached the gates of Shadowfaire. Jervis signaled for them to be opened and the escort party rode through to the keep. When they reached it, Kenric dismounted and brought Avelyn to the ground, as did Martin with Lady Sela.

Jervis issued orders. "Gib, take these men and their horses to the stables. Have them rubbed down and fed. And then have the men set up to stay the night in the soldiers' quarters. Once that's done, bring them to the great hall, for the evening meal will follow soon after."

Martin remounted and turned his horse to accompany the group that now rode toward the stables.

Jervis led them up the stairs and they entered the keep. The hallway seemed dim after the bright light they left behind. A cold penetrated Kenric. Not a physical one, though the keep was always cool within, but he'd never sensed any warmth in this place.

The knight stopped a servant and whispered a few words. The woman shot off to do his bidding. "Ladies, a chamber will be prepared for you to wash and rest in before the evening meal."

Just then, Kenric spied Gussalen. The old woman carried a tray with a bowl. He assumed it to be soup that she would try and feed to his mother.

Gussalen caught sight of him and stopped in her tracks. A long look passed between them. He sensed Avelyn step closer to him and put a hand on his forearm. The servant lowered her eyes and continued on her way.

"Gussalen?" Avelyn whispered.

He nodded, not wishing to say the old woman's name, so great was his contempt for her.

The servant Jervis spoke to returned and led them upstairs to a chamber, assuring that hot water would be delivered soon. Sela entered the room.

Avelyn stopped and faced Kenric. "Would you like me to go with you to see your mother?"

Kenric longed for her to accompany him, but he needed to do this on his own.

"Nay. I will look in on her and then locate my brother. I will see you later."

He turned and allowed Jervis to lead him down the corridor to a chamber that had been Roland's as a boy. It reminded him again that his brother was now earl and slept in the solar.

"I know not how the lady fares, my lord, since we were returning from our journey of the past month. I am sorry."

Kenric only nodded. No words came. His throat was thick with emotion. Steeling himself, he pushed the door open and entered.

CHAPTER 12

Kenric paused, allowing his eyes to adjust to the dim light of the chamber. He pushed the door behind him closed. Gussalen hovered over the bed and he walked toward her.

Then he caught sight of his mother. Gray streaks ran through her golden hair. Her pale skin, flush with fever, glistened with sweat. Labored breathing let him know that her time on earth drew to a close.

Gussalen's head whipped around. "You!" she hissed. She dropped the wet cloth she held. Her hands balled into fists, ready to attack.

"Sir Jervis informed me that Mother requested my presence."

Her sneer told Kenric what she thought of him. "She did. In a weak moment," the servant admitted grudgingly. "I doubt she really wanted you back at Shadowfaire. You haven't been missed—by anyone."

"Mayhap Mother wished to apologize to me for her neglect." Kenric didn't bother to keep the bitterness from his tone.

"She was a good mother . . . to the one who needed mothering." Gussalen glared at him. "You never wanted her fussing over you. You were your father's boy, from your looks to your speech to your actions. You didn't spare a moment to be kind to my sweet lady as a good son should."

His eyes widened in surprise. "Do you truly believe I didn't need her? That I didn't long for any sign of kindness from her?" He shook his head. "What I would have given for a single loving word or gesture from her. To have her stroke my hair. Cradle me in her arms. For her to tell me stories. Ask about my day."

Kenric snorted in disgust. "She never gave me a second thought once I came out of her womb because her every waking moment revolved around Roland."

Gussalen gave him a sly smile. "He *was* the firstborn, you know. 'Twas only fitting he receive the attention due an heir. Especially since he was frail from the moment of his birth."

He shook his head. "I'll grant you that Roland did need special attention due to his poor health, but I was also her son. She owed it to me to be a true mother and not toss me aside."

The servant crossed her arms. "She owed you nothing. You were so large, you almost tore her apart as she gave birth to you. She could never have another child after you."

Kenric hadn't known that. Guilt swept through him for something he'd had no control over.

"And you were your father's boy, through and through. He took you under his wing. Walter Fairfax spent more than enough time with his second born son, teaching him the ways of being a man."

He couldn't argue with that. His father had taught him well. So why did he feel as if neither parent had done their duty by him?

Kenric shook off the sadness enveloping him. "I want to speak to her. Alone."

Gussalen shrugged. "If you must." She stepped away from the bed and marched across the room.

He watched the servant slip out the door before he turned back toward the bed. He drew a chair over and sat in it, his hands in his lap as he studied the woman lying there, a total stranger to him—as she had always been.

She'd become skin and bones since he last saw her. Always a slender woman, she now seemed no bigger round than a twig. Her sunken cheeks only emphasized the wrinkles about her eyes and mouth. A pang of pity trickled through him at her gaunt appearance. Once, Lady Juliana Fairfax had been a great beauty. Now, she'd faded into nothingness.

Kenric reached out to place a hand over hers. Her skin burned with fever. He wondered how long she had left.

Suddenly, her eyes flew open, the pale blue burning brightly. A brief smile tugged at the corners of her mouth. Hope filled him that, though she had such little time left, they might reconcile the ill will between them.

"You came," she rasped.

"Aye." He did not reveal that he appeared at her bedside as an accident of fate.

"I thought . . ." She paused and swallowed, her eyes closing. Then they opened with determination to continue on. "I thought you . . . might not."

"I would honor your request to attend you, Mother."

Her lips pursed. Rarely had he addressed her, much less by that title.

"I am . . . glad . . . you came."

Kenric gave her hand a gentle squeeze. "So I am." Although he could not forget the years of neglect, he would sweep it aside and treasure these last few moments with her.

"Had to tell . . . you . . ." Her voice trailed off.

He sat patiently, knowing it took much effort for her to speak.

She sighed. "How much . . . I . . . hate you."

He stilled at the words. Had he misheard her? Was the fever causing her to ramble?

Then he watched the smile touch her cracked lips. He'd seen that smile many times. When he tried to climb into her lap as she held Roland and she pushed him aside. When he stood watching her fuss over his twin and she would glance in his direction to make sure he saw he was left out. When she smoothed his brother's hair and told him how much she loved him. She always wore a secret, triumphant smile as she punished her second born child with deliberation.

Her words now cut him to the bone. Kenric felt her imaginary knife twist in his heart in a final, fatal blow. He thought he'd gone beyond feeling such hurt, but it wounded him even more deeply now—because he finally realized that she'd done it with malice. Every time she'd fussed over Roland in his presence, it had been to hurt him on purpose.

Why?

She must have seen that question in his eyes.

"You are your father," she rasped. "I . . . hated him. So I . . . hated you. I told him when he lay dying. How . . . I always . . . loathed him. He laughed." She paused, her gaze now piercing. "I will not . . . have . . . the pleasure . . . of seeing you die."

"So you summoned me to your deathbed to tell me how much you despise me," Kenric said, his voice flat.

"Aye." Her whispered word wounded him more than any physical blow ever had.

Kenric removed his hand from hers and stood. He wanted to rage at her as he looked down at the shriveled husk, but his sense of knightly vows would not allow him to disparage her. Without a word, he turned and hurried from the bedchamber.

As he closed the door behind him and stepped into the corridor, Kenric was dismayed to see Gussalen lurking there, waiting for him.

She cackled with glee. "So she was able to speak to you. And I know what she said, Kenric Fairfax. That she loathed you. Hated everything about you because you were the image of the husband who beat her and humiliated her. If she could, she would have tossed you from the wall walk the day you were born and watched your tiny bones shatter on the cobblestones below. Thank the Christ she had one perfect son who loved her and that she could love—for you could never be the child of her heart."

He looked down at the servant. In a dispassionate tone, he said, "Go spew your venom elsewhere, Woman. I care not what you or my lady mother say. I came from a sense of knightly obligation. My heart is made of stone when it comes to Lady Juliana. She might have given birth to me, but I raised myself."

Kenric turned and strode down the hallway, away from the solar.

Avelyn waited till Sela fell asleep. Her friend had tired easily on their journey from London, not used to being in the saddle for so many hours. The most strenuous thing Sela did was dance and she usually stopped after a song or two had played. Avelyn had allowed Sela to talk for a bit as they washed the dust of the road from their hands and face with the hot water that had arrived. Then she encouraged Sela to lie down and rest before they ventured down for the upcoming meal.

She needed to be with Kenric. She knew he had told her he would go alone to see his mother, but she saw the look in his eyes. Kenric Fairfax might be the largest man she'd ever seen and a valiant knight, but he was a human with a heavy heart. Besides, he had shared things of his childhood with her that she was certain he'd never told anyone before.

Avelyn cared deeply for this man, more than anyone in the world. It wasn't only the kisses they'd shared but some connection that linked them together. She wanted to be by his side and support him in such a time of sorrow. She tiptoed to the door, but Sela slept on. Avelyn slipped out and started down the corridor. She had no idea which chamber Lady Juliana might be in.

Before Avelyn could lightly rap on the first door she approached, it opened. A somber priest stepped out, a frown creasing his brow. By his countenance, she wondered if death had already occurred.

"'Tis a sad day, my lady," he said to her, his brown eyes swimming in sorrow. "I have offered Lady Juliana extreme unction. Mayhap, you could go and sit with the lady as her time draws to a close."

"Certainly. Thank you, Father."

He moved past her and headed down the dimly lit corridor.

Avelyn took a deep breath and entered the room. She saw Gussalen, the old servant they'd seen downstairs. Kenric had confirmed the woman's identity. The sight of the retainer angered Avelyn, knowing what she did to Kenric when he was only a boy. The woman hovered over Lady Juliana, hunched as a crone.

Avelyn moved toward the bed on the far side of the room and

watched Gussalen stroking her patient's hand with affection.

"Ah, my lady. We have spent every day of your life together. You are like my own child." Her voice cracked. "Even after all these years, I am sorry that you were forced to marry The Brute."

The Brute?

"I did something awful, my sweet Juliana, but something I know you would have approved of. We were always of a like mind and so I never had need to tell you of my actions."

Avelyn started to make her presence known, but she wondered about the confession this servant was about to make and decided to hold her tongue.

"The Brute raped me many years ago. Before you birthed your twin boys."

Avelyn's stomach lurched hearing this declaration. Kenric's father had raped this woman?

"And his son looked just like him. From birth. I knew—we knew—he would grow to become a man as his father before him. 'Twas why I did what I did." Gussalen tenderly kissed her mistress' hand.

What had the servant done? Avelyn wondered if she should stop this rambling.

Lady Juliana's eyes fluttered open. Her face was aflame with the fever. Avelyn saw that her eyes glittered with it, too. Then she closed them again.

Gussalen took a rag and dipped it into a bowl of water. She wrung it out and bathed the face of her charge.

"You do . . . love me so," Juliana murmured, barely loud enough for Avelyn to catch.

She hated to interrupt this moment between them because it was so intimate. Avelyn turned to go.

"I must admit what I did, my lady. How I fooled The Brute—all for you."

Curiosity stopped Avelyn. She fought it, knowing she should leave.

"He never knew. Neither did you. But Roland is not your firstborn."

Avelyn stopped in her tracks. She muffled the gasp that threatened to escape her lips and pivoted.

"He chased women all up and down England, even here within Shadowfaire, before your very eyes. He beat you senseless, time and again. Because he could." Gussalen paused. "And he raped me and who knows how many others.

"So I sought vengeance... *and it was mine!*"

A soft moan came from the bed. The servant stroked her lady's hair fondly. "Remember the pain of childbirth? Mayhap you blocked it out. But I remember. You gave birth to a boy that nearly tore you asunder, the very image of The Brute."

Avelyn realized Gussalen spoke of Kenric.

"I almost smothered him. 'Twould have been easy to do so and wrap the cord around his neck." She sighed. "But I came up with a better plan. I knew you carried two babes. I let the younger lord rule over the first. The one who favored you, dearest Juliana. I let The Brute think his firstborn was a weak runt." Wicked laugher filled the room.

Chills ran along Avelyn's spine.

"I let the one who was The Brute's mirror image suffer. He gained no wealth or lands upon his father's death. He remained subservient to his brother." Gussalen chuckled. "The Brute died... never know this."

Avelyn's nails dug into her palms. Her heart broke for Kenric. Shuttered aside as a second son, one not meant to inherit, merely because he came out of his mother's womb resembling his father.

A weak whimper came from the bed. "I... cannot... breathe."

Gussalen cupped Juliana's face in her wrinkled hands. "I am here, my lady. I have always been here. And I will be till the very end."

Juliana shuddered and lay still. Gussalen ran a hand to her lady's throat, feeling for life. "Sweet peace, indeed, my lovely." She reached up and kissed the dead woman's brow.

Avelyn could stay quiet no more now that Kenric's mother had passed. She stepped up and, keeping her voice low, she said, "You played God Almighty with Kenric's life."

Gussalen turned, an evil grin twisted upon her face. "You think I didn't know you were there? You, the court beauty in your fine garments, who loves The Brute's offspring? Why, that little performance was all for you, my lady."

She took a step back, shocked. "I . . . don't understand."

The old woman guffawed. "You empty-headed ass. I saw from the moment you touched his arm that you loved The Brute's son. I did everything in my power to hurt The Brute while he was alive and I did the same to his cur. I would do it all over again, just to spite the fiend who married my sweet lady. Her father loved her, but he gave her to a man with vast holdings and a pretty title. Thank the Christ the old lord never knew how her husband treated her in private."

"But . . . but you had no right . . ."

"*I had every right!* He tortured her. Juliana was miserable. My lady feared him. Then hated him. And though she wasn't the child of my womb, she was mine in every other way. I was the first to suckle her. I am with her now, at the last."

Avelyn shook her head in fury. "But you wronged Kenric. He was an innocent babe and you stole his birthright."

"He looked like The Brute," Gussalen hissed. "I knew if he became the heir, he would be just like his father. My lady loved Roland from the moment she saw his fair hair and blue eyes. The other one?" She snorted. "She felt about the child as I did."

"You must tell Kenric. Now," Avelyn demanded. "Cleanse your soul. Make it right with Kenric. And God."

Gussalen laughed hysterically. "Oh, I shall burn in Hell for what I did—and The Brute will be there beside me in the flames of damnation. There's no forgiveness for my actions. Even if I tried to tell him, The Brute's son would most likely kill me with his bare hands!"

She paused. "Would you wish my spilt blood on his conscience?"

Avelyn knew Kenric would be in a rage when he discovered what had happened on the day of his birth, but she believed this old woman must tell him the truth.

"You owe it to him, for Kenric is nothing like his monstrous father. Nothing. If anything, Kenric Fairfax is the best man I know. You are right—I have been at court. While there, I met every kind of man there is. Some are just like this brute you describe, but Kenric is not the man his father was."

"You are wrong," the old woman said, fire in her eyes. "You care for him. 'Tis why you defend him now."

"I am not wrong," Avelyn insisted. "Kenric is everything a perfect knight should be. He is brave and courteous and holds the respect of every man and woman he meets. Kenric is as much his mother's child as he is his father's. From Lady Juliana, he received his kind heart and compassionate nature. He deserves what you robbed him of. You are obligated to return him to his rightful place."

The servant spat at Avelyn's feet. "I owe him *nothing*," she roared. "You lie—about everything. That one looks just like The Brute. I have no doubt that he's exactly as The Brute was. No—worse."

Before Avelyn could change the old woman's mind, Gussalen withdrew a dagger from her pocket and waved it wildly about.

"You love him so much? *You* tell him. For I will be in Hell with his father."

With that, Gussalen brought the knife to her throat and quickly slashed it across the tender skin. Blood spurted bright red as the woman crumpled to the floor.

Avelyn leapt back in horror and then stood frozen, watching the life drain from the twitching body on the floor.

She couldn't comprehend such vehement hate.

Then a calm descended over her. She realized she must never tell Kenric. For who would believe such a wild tale? It was as if the old woman had cursed her by sharing the truth, knowing that Avelyn could do nothing with it. Kenric must never know about the wicked deception of a crazed servant that had played out for more than a score. Avelyn could only hope that Kenric would assume the title of earl and become master of the vast property and all its wealth one day. With his brother's frailty, it could happen sooner than later.

He'd already suffered so much in his life, never being loved by his mother and mistreated by his brother. Why should she add to his pain when she had no proof? Her words would only bring a world of hurt to him—and change nothing.

Avelyn smoothed her skirts and took a cleansing breath. She would find Kenric and tell him of his mother's passing. Once they returned to this chamber, they could discover Gussalen's body and think her gone mad. She would have killed herself, being so distraught over her mistress' death.

It would be a secret she must always keep. Avelyn turned and exited the room.

CHAPTER 13

Kenric moved down the hallway, his heart racing in fury. He could not understand the cruelty of his mother and her pet servant. They had both set out from the moment of his birth to look upon him with contempt and distaste. While he understood, in the grand scheme of things, that Roland would always come first, being the heir, he couldn't fathom the depth of hatred these two women held for him.

He approached the solar with trepidation, wondering what mood he might find his brother in. Roland's temper proved mercurial. With his beloved mother near death, Kenric could only imagine how quickly his twin's mood might swing. Since the two of them had parted on ill terms after Roland suffered a broken arm at Longshire, they hadn't seen one another. That, too, could factor into how his brother received him.

The solar had always seemed like a fortress to Kenric. Rarely was he welcomed within it since it proved the domain of his mother. His father preferred drinking and playing dice in the great hall with his men to spending time upstairs with his wife and children. The few occasions the family had been in the solar together, Kenric could sense the tension between the adults.

He pushed the door open. The empty room sat in silence, an air of disuse about it. Kenric stepped inside and gazed upon it in sadness. It was in direct contrast to the solar at Sandbourne. Twice he'd been invited to it at Lord Michael's request. If walls could talk, he knew they would tell of happy times within it. Lady Elysande had been gracious and welcoming. Her open adoration of her husband filled the solar with a palpable joy. Kenric could only imagine how that would grow once their child—and subsequent children—arrived.

It made him long for a family of his own. After his own lonely childhood, he would lavish attention upon a wife and children. He would care for them and treat them with gentle respect. But most of all, he would love them, whether they were boys or girls. His children would have confidence from the beginning, due to the innate love he would shower upon them.

And when Kenric thought of children, he pictured no one but Avelyn Le Cler as their mother. The woman's beauty proved not only physical, but her heart and soul spoke of it, too.

Yet, he had nothing to offer the bewitching noblewoman, being a penniless knight in service to another. Avelyn deserved a man who could gift her with everything she desired, from a noble title and lands to jewels and garments in luxurious materials. He could provide none of this for her.

Kenric ached at the thought, but he realized he must put aside the romantic feelings that he held for her. Mayhap, they could continue the budding friendship they'd begun, but he resolved not to encourage her in any manner. Avelyn, with her looks and lineage, was destined for great fortune. He would not stand in her way, no matter how much he yearned to be with her.

He spied the door to the bedchamber ajar and made his way to it. As he entered, he saw Roland propped up in the bed with several pillows behind him, his eyes closed. A woman unknown to him sat at his brother's bedside. Her delicate profile spoke of her fine looks.

As he approached, Kenric cleared his throat to make his presence known since he didn't want to startle her.

She turned her head toward him. He saw how lovely she was, with ivory skin and warm, brown eyes filled with intelligence as she gave him a questioning glance. By the cut of her gown, he saw this was no servant but a noblewoman. He deduced his brother had married since he had last seen him years ago.

"I am Kenric Fairfax, my lady," he said softly so he wouldn't disturb Roland's sleep. "Brother to Roland."

She rewarded him with a sweet smile. "I am Doria, wife to the earl."

"I didn't know he had married."

A shadow crossed her face. "We wed almost two years ago. Roland told me he tried to locate you then so that you could attend our wedding."

"I'm sorry I missed it. And that we are meeting under such sad circumstances now." Kenric looked to the bed. "Is he terribly ill?"

"Roland caught the same fever your mother has, but he's improved in the past few days."

"While she has not."

Doria nodded. "We know that Lady Juliana will soon leave us." She gave him a hopeful glance. "But I know Roland would be happy for you to stay. At least for a while."

Kenric shook his head. "Nay, I cannot. I am in service to Lord Michael Devereux of Sandbourne. I travel now with my men from London, escorting his sister-in-law and her friend back to the estate. I only stopped in briefly to see my mother."

Disappointment turned her mouth down. "Then at least stay for the evening meal and leave tomorrow."

"I would like that."

"Kenric?"

He turned to the voice that came from the bed and saw his brother's eyes were open. Kenric idly wondered how much of their conversation Roland might have heard. In the old days, Roland famously eavesdropped on everyone from stable hands to their father's discussions with his most trusted knights.

"Hello, Brother."

"I see Jervis and Gib found you. Were you up north still?"

"Nay. I haven't been there for some time. As of now, I reside at Sandbourne, which is another five or six hours' ride from here. My liege lord is Lord Michael Devereux."

"So you were practically in our back yard. I wish I would have known."

Kenric didn't like Roland's accusatory tone. Instead, he said, "I must congratulate you on your marriage. Lady Doria and I were just becoming acquainted."

Roland's eyes flicked to his wife and back. "My wife is a true treasure."

Once again, Kenric knew some hidden meaning lay behind his brother's words.

"I'm sorry you've been ill, but your lady wife seems to be taking fine care of you."

"She is a most attentive caregiver." Roland frowned. "Have you seen Mother?"

"I came here from her bedside. She is near death, I'm afraid."

His twin nodded. "She has wasted away. Frankly, I'm surprised she's lasted this long."

Roland's cavalier attitude about their mother startled Kenric. "Are you not sorry that she will soon die?" he asked his brother. "The two of you have always been so close."

Roland chuckled. "That always stuck in your craw, didn't it, Kenric? We both know how much Mother worshipped the ground I walked upon—and how she despised the fact that you even existed."

Kenric stiffened at his twin's words. Behind him, he heard Lady Doria gasp.

"Oh, Mother loved only me. We both know that, Kenric. And we share in the knowledge that Father only saw you. Though I was his firstborn, the one who would claim the title and rule the family lands, Father only had eyes for you, his little warrior child."

Roland pushed himself up to a sitting position, his blazing eyes not holding back the rage.

"Father liked you best. Oh, I doubt he loved you. I doubt he could love anyone other than himself. But he saw himself in you, Brother. He taught you how to be a man. How to hunt and fish and swing a sword. How to outthink an opponent and catch him in an unguarded moment. Father crafted you in his own image. Kenric, the perfect knight, who was Walter Fairfax made over. Kenric, the perfect son, who never complained about his mother's neglect, much less that she loathed her own child.

"You may have claimed all of Father's attention, but I had Mother all to myself. And we laughed about how much we both detested you." Roland chuckled. "We still laugh about it to this day." He fell back against the pillows, spent, his anger subsiding as his eyes fell shut.

Kenric longed to lash out at Roland, but he kept silent. He would not lower himself to reply to his brother's foul words. It didn't matter. What Roland spoke of was in the past. Soon, Kenric would be gone from this place. He planned never to return.

Roland rubbed his eyes wearily and said, "Wife, bring me some soup and a little of the bread. Make sure it's from the center and very soft."

"Aye." Doria stood, her gaze sympathetic as she met Kenric's eyes. "May I escort you downstairs, my lord? It's time for the evening meal. I am sure your men are already present for it. We must also make sure the ladies you escort to Sandbourne join you, as well."

Kenric realized she was with child. He had not noticed before due to the cut of her *cotehardie*. While he'd always known that Shadowfaire belonged to Roland, knowing that his brother's child would soon come into the world reaffirmed his decision not to pursue any kind of relationship with Avelyn Le Cler.

"Kenric?"

He turned and saw Avelyn standing in the doorway, the color drained from her face. Kenric wondered how much of Roland's tirade Avelyn might have heard, then he realized there was more to it as her features crumpled.

"What's wrong?" he asked.

"It's your mother. The priest recited the last rites and she has now passed. I thought you should know."

"Thank you, my lady." He thought hearing of her death would erase the vast void inside him, but he still felt nothing. "Lady Avelyn, may I introduce to you my brother, Lord Roland? And his wife, Lady Doria."

Avelyn composed herself and came closer to greet the couple. "I'm sorry for your loss."

"I'm still hungry, Wife," Roland complained, ignoring Avelyn's sympathetic comment.

Doria, her eyes brimming with tears, bit her lip. Kenric felt she held back the words she longed to say. "I will return with a light meal for you soon, my lord." She looked at Kenric and Avelyn. "If you will come with me?"

Doria led the way from the room. They left the bedchamber and the solar and moved into the corridor before she gave up a heavy sigh.

"I must apologize for my husband. He is in ill health. I know he feels great sorrow at the loss of his mother."

"I know Roland well," Kenric said, his eyes meeting hers. He saw the flicker of understanding in them. "You must see to his needs. I'll find the priest and Gussalen. She'll want to attend my mother and prepare her for burial tomorrow."

"Thank you, Sir Kenric," Doria said. "I hope you will stay for the funeral mass."

It was the last thing he wished to do, but he said, "I will, my lady."

Doria excused herself and hurried down the corridor.

He looked to Avelyn. "Were you with her at the end?"

"Aye. I came in search of you." She placed a hand upon his arm. Her warm fingers comforted him. "I didn't want you to face her alone and sought you out."

Kenric touched her shoulder. "You are a good friend to me, my lady."

He caught the shift in her body language. "We are friends?"

"I would like to think so."

He saw that his answer didn't please her, but he didn't want to get into a deeper conversation at this point.

"We should go find Gussalen and then the priest. I hope you approve of us staying for the funeral mass. We can set out for

Sandbourne after it ends."

"Gussalen was with Lady Juliana when I left," Avelyn said. "I'm sure she's still there."

They walked down the hallway and paused before his mother's bedchamber door. "Why don't you go to Lady Sela and attend the evening meal downstairs? I'll handle everything here."

Avelyn hesitated a moment. "If you insist."

"Go," he encouraged.

She bid him farewell and returned to the chamber next door, giving him an encouraging smile before she entered it. Kenric turned and opened the door before him.

A nightmare welcomed him. His eyes fell first to the bed, spattered in blood. Then he spied the still form on the floor and rushed to it.

Gussalen lay in a large pool of blood, a baselard next to her lifeless body.

Kenric realized that the blood from the bed must have come from the old servant, driven mad with grief at having lost the only person she loved. Once again, he felt nothing as he looked upon her body and then that of his lady mother in the bed. It was as if he looked upon his fallen enemy on the battlefield. He felt no victory in these deaths. No sorrow. No glee. No sense of loss.

Only emptiness. And if he was being honest with himself?

Mayhap a small twinge of relief.

AVELYN TRIED HER BEST to remain attentive at Lady Juliana's funeral mass, but her worries for Kenric pushed all else from her mind.

He should be the Earl of Shadowfaire, not the brother who snapped at his poor wife, treating her no better than a servant. Roland Fairfax hadn't seemed to care one whit that his mother had died. She saw no grief on his face, only impatience at not having been fed. Normally, she would excuse someone who had been ill. It was no fun to lay abed in poor health. Look at her—she had twisted her ankle and only stayed in bed for part of one day, and that had nearly driven her mad. She understood adding illness on top of that might cause someone to misspeak, but Lord Roland had seemed unaffected by the news regarding his mother.

She did like Lady Doria very much. Last night, she learned from her that Doria had lost her first babe a few months after finding herself with child shortly after her wedding. This time, she was over six months along and being very careful, trying not to overtax herself.

But Avelyn knew that Doria should not be the lady of the castle. Lord Roland was no lord at all. Kenric should be the titled nobleman of Shadowfaire.

And yet, she couldn't tell him. She had no proof. Nothing to back up her claim.

Yesterday, when he declared them to be only friends, she'd understood immediately, despite the tender kisses they had shared. She knew Kenric believed that he had nothing to offer her and wanted them to put aside their feelings for one another. Avelyn understood the logic behind his reasoning, but she totally disagreed with it. She didn't care if they lived in a tiny cottage or a grand manor. She only knew she must be with him. Marriage to Kenric Fairfax would be the adventure of her life—and she refused to miss out on a single minute of it.

If she told him what Gussalen had revealed before she killed herself, Kenric would think Avelyn lied in order for him to possess a castle and name worthy of her. Even if he somehow chose to believe her, what options did he have? He could march in and tell his brother what a dead woman had revealed. Not even to him, but to Avelyn, someone the old woman had only just met.

Roland Fairfax would either fall out of his bed in laughter or order his twin off the grounds of Shadowfaire, banning him from ever returning.

She hadn't realized when Kenric told her he was the second born son that he was a twin. And now, Avelyn knew of the switch the crazy, obsessed servant had made on the very day of the boys' birth.

A wave of helplessness almost brought her to her knees.

She could hope that Roland would die, though she feared that would be a grievous sin staining her soul. If he did, by some miracle, Kenric wouldn't instantly assume the mantle as the new lord of Shadowfaire.

For Lady Doria could give birth to a male child. If so, *he* would be named the heir.

And then Kenric would never receive his birthright.

Avelyn's nails dug into the palms of her hands. That old witch had accomplished everything she wanted. She'd kept Kenric from his deserved position of power and wealth when his father died. She'd also found a way to torment the woman who loved him—and couldn't tell him the truth she had learned.

What should she do?

Avelyn had prayed for an answer last night, but God hadn't cooperated by providing a timely response.

If she was at Kinwick, she would share what she knew with her uncle. Geoffrey de Montfort was a rational man and very wise for his years. She clung to the thought that he and Merryn would visit Sandbourne in a month or more, after Elysande gave birth. If she hadn't figured out a solution to this problem by then, she would tell her uncle what she'd discovered and hope he would create a plan of action to help raise Kenric to his full position.

But the knowledge would eat away at her till then.

CHAPTER 14

AVELYN HATED THAT the journey to Sandbourne had almost come to an end. She thought back to when they left London only a short time ago. Her first conversation with Kenric Fairfax had led her to believe she would dread the time spent on the road with him.

How quickly things had changed.

The man she now rode with had proven to be confident and intelligent. More importantly, he had somehow stolen her heart. Avelyn only wished he'd stolen a few more kisses.

She took a deep breath, causing her to press against his massive chest. In response, his arm tightened slightly about her waist. A frisson of pleasure shot through her as she inhaled his masculine scent, mixed with a hint of his leather saddle and Firefall, smells she also associated with him.

A smile came to her face. Elysande would tease her unmercifully if she knew how much her sister now enjoyed the scent of a horse. Well, at least this horse. Avelyn still wasn't overly fond of horses in general, but she'd become comfortable atop Firefall—thanks to riding him while enveloped by his master's arms.

They would arrive at Sandbourne soon, so this physical closeness would come to an end. Avelyn would have to dream up a few more ways she could find herself entwined in Kenric's arms once they arrived. She burned for his kiss. Already, it had been too long since she tasted him.

The green forest opened wide. Avelyn sat up in anticipation as she spied their destination.

"Are you happy that we're almost there?" asked Kenric, his voice low in her ear, adding to her thrill.

"Aye. I've missed Elysande more than I imagined possible. We'd never been separated a single day before she wed Michael. She came here to Sandbourne and I left to go to court to serve the queen."

"So it will be a happy reunion between sisters."

"Indeed."

They arrived at the gates, which opened in time for them to ride through without stopping. Avelyn's heart beat faster as they wove through the outer and then the inner bailey and came to stop at the keep. She glimpsed her mother standing with Sir Charles, a longtime retainer at Sandbourne and remembered how Michael shared that the knight entertained him with stories when he was a boy. Avelyn was glad her mother had already arrived so they would be able to spend more time together. Standing next to Sir Charles was Lady Orella, Michael's mother, whom Avelyn had met last summer.

Then she caught sight of Elysande and gave her a wave. Her sister waved back, as did Michael, who had his arm about his wife.

Kenric pulled Firefall up and dismounted. He reached for her waist and brought her to the ground. Avelyn quickly thanked him and raced toward her sister, who appeared as round and large as a barrel.

"Elysande!" she cried as she started to hug her and then stepped back. "I don't know how to embrace you."

Michael laughed. "I tell her there's simply more of her to love." He kissed his wife's cheek.

"Come here," her sister ordered.

She obeyed and wrapped her arms about Elysande as best she could. "Oh!" Avelyn pulled back. "Was that the babe? I felt it kick from inside you."

Elysande laughed. "The little one knows the joy I feel in having you here."

"Does it . . . hurt?"

"Nay," Elysande reassured her. "It does get a bit uncomfortable at times." She laughed. "And the babe keeps me awake at odd hours of the night. Michael, too."

The earl agreed. "I have been fast asleep, minding my own business, my wife in my arms, when I'm punched and nearly fly off the bed." He grinned as he stroked his wife's rounded belly. "I believe it's a boy. A big, powerful boy who will be a strong warrior and cut down all enemies of the king."

Elysande shook her head. "What if I carry a strong girl child? One who knows her own mind and will always get her way."

Michael lifted his wife's hand to his lips and kissed it tenderly. "You mean a female just like her mother?"

She swatted him playfully. "Whether a boy or girl, this babe definitely has a mind of its own." She smiled at her sister. "But I'm ever so glad to have you at Sandbourne." Elysande looked over Avelyn's shoulder. "My thanks, Sir Kenric, for retrieving Avelyn and delivering her to me safely."

"And what about me?" her mother demanded. "I, too, have missed my daughter. Come here, child."

Avelyn flung herself into her mother's arms, closing her eyes to relish the feel of the familiar embrace before withdrawing. "I believe I missed you far more than you missed me, Lady Mother. You've been busy managing Hopeston, no doubt, and had little time to think of me. But I must introduce you to my friend who has accompanied me on this visit."

She turned and motioned Sela over.

"I brought my closest friend at court home for the summer," Avelyn told them. "Lady Sela Runford, may I introduce you to my family and Lord Michael's mother?" She went through all their names.

Sela gave the group that surrounded her a warm smile. "I feel I know you all very well, for Avelyn has spoken of each of you frequently. I hope you don't mind that I accompanied her back to Sandbourne instead of attending the queen on her summer progress."

"We're delighted to host you, Lady Sela," Elysande said. "Any friend to my sister is a friend to us all. But do come inside. We held the noon meal until you arrived since we knew you'd be hungry."

Avelyn linked her arm through Sela's and followed Elysande and Michael inside the keep. She almost giggled watching her older sister waddle along, her feet turned slightly outward. Avelyn glanced over her shoulder and saw that Kenric and the rest of the escort party had departed. They probably would take their horses to the Sandbourne stables and then join them for the noon meal.

Instead of going to the great hall, their small party went up to the solar. Avelyn hid her disappointment, wishing she could have seen Kenric while they dined, but she understood why Elysande would direct them to the family quarters for their reunion.

"I only had one chamber prepared," Elysande apologized. "I didn't know Lady Sela would be joining us."

"It was a last minute decision, my lady," Sela said. "Avelyn had given me an open invitation to come visit her this summer. I pestered my father, one of the king's advisers, until he granted me permission, and then the queen followed suit. Since Avelyn's escort party had arrived, I thought it would be convenient if I accompanied them."

"And I apologize that I totally forgot to mention your joining Avelyn when Sir Kenric's soldier delivered the message that the escort party, plus one, would be delayed a day. The road to and from London can be dangerous," Michael noted. "I'm glad you returned with Avelyn under Sir Kenric's supervision."

"Oh, he's quite an impressive knight," Sela purred.

Avelyn realized that her friend still showed interest in Kenric—though she often showed interest in various men, including Sir Martin. Avelyn would have to get Sela alone and tell her that she would prefer that Sela not pursue any attachment with Kenric Fairfax. Usually, she told her friend everything, but they'd spent time away from each other when she injured her ankle. They had much to catch up on—including the fact that Avelyn had kissed Sir Kenric and found it very much to her liking.

"Don't worry about having the servants prepare another chamber, Elysande. Sela and I are used to sharing quarters."

Michael laughed. "So you can gossip together, I suppose."

Avelyn felt the blush rise on her cheeks. "Mayhap we'll do just that, my lord."

Elysande provided a large meal for them. Avelyn ate till she thought her sides would burst, but her sister ate even more.

"So you eat for two now?" she teased.

"I'm ravenous these days. The first few months, I couldn't keep a bite down. I would swallow it and it threatened to come back up almost immediately."

"I was the same way with you, Elysande," their mother shared. "With Avelyn, I didn't experience such a problem."

"And yet here I am, the tall one, while my younger sister is so dainty."

Lady Orella laughed. "I couldn't eat hardly anything for weeks when I carried Michael, but I certainly made up for it once my nausea subsided. He came out quite large."

Avelyn shuddered. "All of these stories. It makes me wonder what I will be like when I am with child."

"Let's find you a husband first, my dear," her mother said, patting her hand.

She wanted to tell her that she already had but held her tongue.

"So how do you fare at Hopeston?" she asked. Avelyn turned to Sela and reminded, "Mother lost her second husband, Lord Holger, last summer. The king has allowed her to remain at Hopeston and manage the estate for the time being."

Her mother cleared her throat. "I suppose now is as good a time as any to tell you." She took Avelyn's hands in hers. "Elysande already knows, but I wanted to tell you that I'm to wed again for a third—and what I hope shall be final—time."

"Truly? Where will the king send you? And to whom?"

A sweet smile lit her mother's face. "It's my choice this time. Unlike before." She paused. "Do you remember Sir Charles?"

Avelyn nodded. "Aye. I saw him standing near you when we arrived today." Then it dawned on her. "You're to wed Sir Charles? Then does that mean you'll remain at Sandbourne?"

"I will. Michael has been kind enough to allow us use of the manor house, so we'll make our home there."

She gave her mother's hands an affectionate squeeze. "He's a very fine knight, Mother. He was so protective of you when we were accosted by that wicked Lord Ingram who thought to kidnap Elysande and make her his wife."

"What?" Sela blurted out, surprise on her face. "You haven't told me this tale, Avelyn."

Avelyn shook her head. "You'll have plenty of time to hear it." She glanced back at her mother. "I'm most pleased for you, Mother."

"As am I."

Michael interjected, "Sir Charles has been here many years. He and Sir Thirkell told me stories of the Knights of the Round Table when I was a small boy. He's promised to continue that tradition and tell my children the same tales." He raised his goblet. "To Lady Mary and her upcoming marriage. May you live a long and fruitful life together with Sir Charles here at Sandbourne."

Those gathered lifted their cups in acknowledgement and drank.

"Does this mean you'll marry soon?" Avelyn asked.

"Aye," her mother said. "The king has already appointed a new custodian for Hopeston and awarded its accompanying title to a deserving knight. I brought all of my personal possessions with me and will remain at Sandbourne from now on."

Avelyn smiled broadly. "So when is the wedding?"

HER MOTHER INSISTED that Avelyn and Sela rest that afternoon after their days on the road. In truth, Avelyn had no need to nap. They'd broken up the journey from London with their stay at Kinwick and then their brief stop at Shadowfaire, sleeping in a soft bed both places as opposed to the hard ground out on the road.

Still, she knew Sela was exhausted. As a delicate, court flower, her friend wasn't used to strenuous activity. Elysande, too, made it a habit to rest in the afternoons since she tired easily these days. Avelyn had played the dutiful daughter and retired to the chamber prepared for her, which she would share with Sela.

They lay on the bed now with the curtains drawn about them. Sela snored softly while Avelyn remained wide-eyed. All she could think about was Kenric Fairfax.

She knew she would glimpse him at the evening meal but didn't know if she would have an opportunity to speak with him after it ended. As a family member, she would be seated upon the dais, while Kenric would be at a table with the group of soldiers that guarded Sandbourne. He might not even attend the meal if he'd been assigned duty on the wall walk or in another area of the keep.

That would be the first problem to address—finding a way to talk with him. As a valued member of Sandbourne's guard, Kenric would be involved in daily training exercises, as well as patrol the estate and be scheduled to various duty stations. In short, his time wasn't his own but what the captain of the guard made of it. That meant access to him might be limited to meals he attended in the great hall.

Avelyn decided the best way to find time alone with Kenric would be through Elysande. She would confide in her sister that she wanted to learn to ride. She could explain how she'd felt comfortable with Sir Kenric Fairfax and his horse and believed he'd be a good teacher for her. Naturally, Elysande would be thrilled that her sister finally had realized how wonderful horses were and would, no doubt, encourage Avelyn's interest in riding. Elysande had a passion for horseflesh and knew as much about them as any man did.

Satisfied with her plan of action, Avelyn let her thoughts meander. She imagined Kenric taking her out in the meadow to ride and laughing with him. They'd take a respite from their lessons to snack on fruit and cheese. And somewhere along the way, she planned for kissing to be involved. By the Christ, she wanted more than anything to kiss that man again and feel his tongue mate with hers. She pined to taste his essence and stroke his broad chest and muscled arms.

Avelyn gave a sigh of contentment at the thought.

"Are you awake?" Sela asked.

"Aye."

Her friend rolled onto her side and braced her elbow so that her head could rest in her hand. "I'm feeling refreshed. I like your sister very much. And Lord Michael is dashing. I wish I could find such a handsome man to be so taken with me."

"He does love her a great deal," Avelyn agreed. "Elysande feels the same about Michael. They're definitely a love match."

"The men of Sandbourne are certainly interesting. Some are even more attractive than those at court," Sela said.

"I know you seem taken with Sir Martin."

Sela nodded. "I do like him. And Sir Alaric at Kinwick. But I'm most fascinated by Sir Kenric."

Avelyn's stomach lurched at the turn the conversation had taken. "Sela, I wish to speak to you about something regarding Sir Kenric."

Sela pushed herself to a sitting position. "What about him? Has he confided in you? Has he said something about me?' She fanned herself with her fingers. "Oh, I didn't think he'd even noticed me."

"Nay, that's not what I meant."

Her friend frowned. "I don't understand."

Avelyn also sat up and took Sela's hands in hers. "I've discovered that I have feelings for Sir Kenric. Romantic feelings." She paused to let her words sink in.

Hurt filled Sela's face. "But I told you first I found him most handsome and desirable. You thought him arrogant, Avelyn."

She tamped down her frustration. "And I told you that due to your family's position at court, you needed a husband with wealth and vast lands. Sir Kenric has neither."

Sela's bottom lip thrust out in a pout. "But he might have them. Shadowfaire is a huge estate. He only has the one brother. He could become the earl one day. Anything is possible." She flounced off the bed and began pacing the room.

"I thought you were my friend, Avelyn."

"You know that I am, Sela."

"And I shared with you my interest in Kenric Fairfax."

"And you admitted moments ago of your interest in other knights, as well."

Sela stopped pacing. "Even so, you shouldn't have set your cap for him when you knew I felt myself attracted to him. 'Twas most unfair of you. Even cruel."

Avelyn stood and approached her friend. She placed her hands upon Sela's shoulders.

"I didn't feel your regard for him was more than a passing fancy, in truth. And I spent some time with him. Alone."

Sela's eyes narrowed. "What did you do? While you were *alone*?"

She did not like Sela's tone. Avelyn dropped her hands to her sides. "We shared a few kisses."

"You *kissed* him? You don't kiss anyone—at least at court. Oh, I know a few courtiers have stolen kisses from you, but you've never pursued a man."

"This just... happened." Avelyn took her friend's hands again. "Sela, it felt so right. Like nothing I have ever experienced. 'Twas as Elysande and Merryn told me. I knew from the moment his lips touched mine that I would never wish for another man to do the same. Only Kenric."

Sela huffed and pulled away. "First, you steal away the man I'm interested in. And now you believe, after a few kisses, that you're in love with him?"

Avelyn stood her ground. "I do. I didn't deliberately set out to win Kenric's heart. In fact, it was he who won mine."

Sela stomped her foot. "I thought you were my closest friend, much as a sister would be. I thought we held a bond between us."

"I am," she insisted. "That's why I wished to share this with you now. I want you to enjoy your time at Sandbourne this summer—and that includes the company of the many men here. But I felt you should know—"

"That Kenric Fairfax is *your* property. Oh, I understand quite well." Sela placed fisted hands on her waist. "I see that I'm only beginning to know the true Avelyn Le Cler. You think you're nothing like the women at court, with their devious schemes.

"You are exactly like them. No—worse!"

With that, Sela marched from the chamber.

CHAPTER 15

"SELA, YOU MUST rise. It's time for morning mass."

Avelyn continued to dress as stony silence blanketed the room. Sela remained facing away from her, the bedclothes pulled up past her ears.

She came to a decision. "I'll make excuses for you this time only," she warned. "I'll say that you're overly tired and unused to travel. But Sela, you must rise tomorrow in time to attend mass and then break your fast. It's expected of everyone at Sandbourne. Country folk rise early."

"I am *not* country folk," Sela muttered from underneath the covers, contempt dripping from her words.

"True, but you are in the country now. We do not keep court hours."

"Mayhap I made a mistake by undertaking this sudden trip."

Avelyn waited a moment and then replied, "You might have."

Sela tossed the bedclothes away and sat up, fire in her eyes. "That's exactly what you want—for me to return to London."

"Nay, I wish for you to stay. Let's put this misunderstanding behind us."

Her friend leapt from the bed. "This is no misunderstanding, Avelyn. You want me gone, the better to sink your claws into Kenric Fairfax. Well, I won't make that easy for you. I intend to stay at Sandbourne all summer and be your shadow. You'll never have a spare moment with him, I guarantee you that."

Sela sniffed haughtily and climbed back into bed. "Make my excuses for now. I will see you later." She rolled over, again facing away from Avelyn as she yanked the covers over her head.

"As you wish."

Avelyn finished dressing in silence and left the bedchamber. She wanted to slam the door behind her but wouldn't sink to Sela's level.

Why had her friend turned on her so quickly? True, Sela had remarked on Kenric's good looks. But beyond that, she hadn't mentioned him again. In fact, she'd pursued other knights, flirting with them all the way from London until their arrival at Sandbourne. That she could be so out of sorts bothered Avelyn.

She hurried to the chapel and slipped in moments before mass began. As the priest droned on in Latin, she thought back to her arrival at court. None of the other women had been overly friendly except Sela. Most of the queen's ladies-in-waiting were older, married women, and Avelyn had little in common with them. Sela had warmed to her from the beginning.

But she remembered a few whispers about her friend and how Agnes, the chief lady-in-waiting to the queen, had told Avelyn to guard herself around those she didn't know. Agnes had glanced directly at Sela, sitting across the room strumming a lute, as she warned Avelyn. Was this what Agnes had hinted at—Sela's temper and jealousy?

The two women had experienced no conflicts between them from the time Avelyn arrived at court in early September until now. They'd shared meals and walks, along with long conversations where they spoke their mind about others at court. True, sometimes Avelyn caught the occasional glance from another lady-in-waiting that seemed disapproving in nature, but she hadn't believed she did anything wrong to deserve it. Besides, when no one except Sela reached out to her in friendship, Avelyn had gradually drifted away from the other women.

Had that been a mistake?

She wondered if Sela had spats with other women at court. Sela hadn't seemed close to anyone else over the last several months and had spent all her free time with Avelyn. She wondered if Sela had been friendless before she turned up and, if so—was it of her own making? Had Sela alienated the other women for some reason?

It seemed ridiculous that they would quarrel over a man. Sela had introduced her to dozens of men at court. They'd all seemed friendly with Sela and accepted Avelyn simply because Sela had brought them together.

Then why all this trouble over Kenric Fairfax?

Mass ended and she returned to the great hall to break her fast. Elysande inquired about Sela's absence. She dutifully told her sister that her friend was overtaxed by their journey and had wished to rest. She did ask Elysande if she could speak to her and Michael in private. After they ate, the three returned to the solar.

Michael helped his wife ease into a chair, slipping a pillow behind her back. She gave him a loving glance. Avelyn felt a pang of jealousy at their closeness.

"So what do you wish to speak to us about, Avelyn?" Michael asked.

"I have several things to discuss with you. The first I would have asked of Mother, but now that she isn't returning to Hopeston, I must address the issue with you."

"Go on."

"I've been unhappy at court," she began, then decided to be totally honest. "Miserable, in fact."

Elysande gave a cry of distress and reached for her hand. "What's wrong? Your letters sounded so cheerful."

"There are some things I do enjoy. I like waiting on the queen. She is a wise, caring woman and she is kind to me. I also enjoy the music and dancing."

"But?" Michael nudged.

"Overall, it's a superficial place. None of the women and few of the men care to read or discuss much of anything unless it involves improving their position at court. The ladies-in-waiting, other than Sela and Alys and me, are all married. And some even have children, which they seem to ignore. These women took no notice of me nor extended any sign of friendship. They gossip all day long about the most inane matters and, even though they're married, many of them flirt with courtiers that aren't their husbands—or worse."

Elysande's hand tightened on hers. "They are truly that shallow?"

She nodded. "I thought country life was boring, but court life is tedious. I long to stay busy with fruitful activities. Work in the garden. Cook. Weave tapestries. Nurse the sick." Avelyn's eyes welled with tears. "Please, do not make me go back."

"I wouldn't let you return to that den of snakes," Michael declared. "I assume you'd thought you might return to live at Hopeston?"

"Aye, but with Mother marrying and moving to the manor house with Sir Charles, I don't want to be in their way."

"You'll reside at Sandbourne with us," Michael declared.

Avelyn couldn't keep the smile from her face. "I promise to be helpful, Michael. I can assist with the new babe."

He laughed. "You are family, Avelyn, and always welcomed." He glanced to his wife. "Elysande has been miserable without your company. Oh, she says she loves me—"

"And I do," Elysande interrupted. "But Michael is gone many hours each day, training with his men or riding about the estate, solving all kinds of problems. I would love to have you live here with us." She paused. "But what about Uncle Geoffrey? He'd asked the queen to find you a husband."

"I spoke to him and Merryn when we stopped at Kinwick," Avelyn revealed. "He said that he is head of the de Montfort household and I am his charge. He promised to speak to the queen and tell her I wish to remain in the country while he finds a suitable match for me."

"I'm happy to hear this," her sister said. "It's nice to know we've settled the matter so easily."

"I have more to speak to you about."

Michael's eyebrow shot up. "This sounds intriguing. Please, continue."

Avelyn twisted her hands in her lap, not sure how to address the next issue.

"Go ahead," Elysande urged.

"Uncle Geoffrey doesn't really need to locate a husband for me. I've already found the perfect man."

Michael rubbed his chin in thought. "If you didn't form any attachment with any man while at court, then I don't understand."

"I have you to thank, Michael, for sending him my way. It's Sir Kenric."

"What about him?" he asked, his brows knitting together.

"He is the man I speak of. The man I wish to wed."

"Kenric Fairfax?" boomed Michael. "But you haven't even known the man for a week!"

Avelyn steeled herself. "Nevertheless, I have strong feelings for him and I believe those feelings are returned."

"I cannot begin to see how—"

Elysande reached for her husband's hand, entwining her fingers with his. "It does sound familiar, my love."

His jaw dropped. Then understanding lit his eyes. "You mean like us?" He shook his head. "Nay, 'twas much different for us."

"Was it?" Elysande asked, giving him a knowing smile.

The look on her sister's face let Avelyn know Elysande would support her in this endeavor. She breathed a small sigh of relief. Michael might take a little convincing, but Elysande already had him wrapped around her finger.

Michael huffed. "I feel protective of Avelyn."

"And you sent Sir Kenric to London to retrieve her because you knew how important she is to me," Elysande said. "You told me yourself what a steadfast soldier Sir Kenric is. How you could think of no better knight to bring Avelyn back to Sandbourne. You expressly told me how much you trusted him."

"I did say those things. But I thought of him as a protector to Avelyn as he escorted her on the road. *Not* as a future husband."

Elysande gave him a pointed look. "Is there something wrong with Kenric Fairfax? If so, you wouldn't have him on Sandbourne grounds in the first place. You've surrounded us with the best of the best,

Husband, and if that is the case," she said gently, "then he should be fit to marry my sister. After all, I want the best for her."

"True," Michael grudgingly admitted. He turned to Avelyn, a grin spreading across his face. "It happens quickly, doesn't it?"

She bit her lip and nodded. "More quickly than I could have imagined. One minute, I thought Kenric Fairfax was the most arrogant man I'd met. And the next?" She could not hide her smile. "He seemed like the only man in the world for me."

"Then I will need to speak with him. Lord Geoffrey, too, of course."

Avelyn groaned. "We do have a slight problem. Sir Kenric seems to be wedded to his duty as a knight and tells me he is not in the market for a wife."

"He rejects my sister?" Elysande said angrily.

"I wouldn't put it so strongly," Avelyn said.

Michael spoke up. "He wants you but doesn't know quite yet that he does. He must reconcile his mind with his heart."

"You do understand," she said.

He lifted Elysande's hand to his lips and pressed a fervent kiss against her fingers. "Oh, I certainly do."

Her sister giggled. "For now, we'll let things remain as they are." Elysande's eyes lit with mischief. "But I'm sure we can think of a few ways to help matters along."

"I've considered that," Avelyn said. "I've decided that I want to learn to ride."

Joy filled Elysande's face. "You do? I'm thrilled to hear that."

"You know I've always been reluctant around horses, but Kenric's mount, Firefall, was actually quite sweet."

"That giant beast?" Michael questioned.

"The very one. And I felt comfortable riding him. With Kenric, of course."

"Of course," Elysande agreed. She thought a moment. "Then I believe that Sir Kenric needs to give you riding lessons. You can excuse him from training in the afternoons, Husband," she suggested to

Michael. "That will give them a couple of hours together each day."

"I have a favor to ask," Avelyn said. "I may need you to find things for Sela to do during my riding lessons." She began wringing her hands again. "Though Sela is a natural flirt and had only mentioned once in passing that she found Kenric handsome, when I told her of the attraction between us, she grew quite upset. In fact, she's pouting in bed right now. I fear she'll interrupt my time with him and throw herself in his path at every opportunity."

"Hmm, that would be awkward. Do you want her to return to London?" asked Elysande.

"Nay, for she truly looked forward to her visit here. I think it's just a petty quarrel between friends. I know we can resolve it."

"Then I'll think of ways to keep Lady Sela Runford occupied," guaranteed Elysande.

Michael stood. "I leave such devious matters in your capable hands, Wife." He bent and kissed her cheek. "I'm off to train with my men."

Avelyn started to speak, but he raised a hand.

"And I will let Sir Kenric know that he's to be your tutor in riding, starting this afternoon." Michael laughed as he exited the chamber.

Avelyn looked back at her sister, who had a mischievous look in her eyes.

"So, dearest Avelyn. Now that Michael is gone, we can speak of the most important matter of all."

She frowned. "I've shared the deepest matters pressing on my heart."

Elysande smiled. "Tell me about how you feel when Kenric Fairfax kisses you."

Avelyn burst out laughing.

CHAPTER 16

Kenric wolfed down his noon meal, glad to be back into a routine at Sandbourne. The morning's training exercises had gone well. He'd worked with a young soldier who, though naturally left-handed, wished to learn to fight with his sword in his right hand. It would take many hours, but he thought the man possessed a strong work ethic and good attitude, which would be half of the battle of learning swordplay with a new hand.

He glanced up again to the dais, empty except for Lord Michael. None of the family's women had arrived for the meal in the great hall. Kenric supposed they chose to dine together in the solar and catch up on their news. He should be relieved by not having to keep his glance away from Avelyn Le Cler's fine figure, but her absence actually made him restless.

Kenric had thrust the beauty from his mind that morning, though he was finding it harder to do as time passed. Avelyn drew his eyes when she was in his presence, much as a magnet did. When she was gone, his thoughts constantly turned to her.

And nights?

Falling asleep proved to be an arduous task. Where once he'd been a man who dropped quickly into sleep, nowadays his thoughts lingered on the image he conjured up in his mind. Kenric longed to take Avelyn into his arms again and feel his lips upon hers. He desired her ample breasts pressing into his chest.

He slammed a hand down on the table in frustration. Reaching for his ale, he downed what remained in the cup in a single swallow. He refused to meet the eyes of those soldiers seated around him, for he feared he would appear as a love-struck fool.

Kenric glanced around the table and saw that most of the trenchers were bare and the seats around him empty. He stood and stepped away from the trestle table as a servant came and began to clear the remnants away.

"Sir Kenric—a word?"

Glancing over his shoulder, he saw Lord Michael beckoning him. He headed to meet him.

"You wish to speak with me, my lord?"

Michael Devereux hesitated. The very action was so unlike his liege lord that Kenric took a small step back. Then the nobleman nodded to himself as if he came to some decision.

"Lady Elysande has need of you this afternoon. Report to her in the solar. She will elaborate upon your duties."

"Aye, my lord."

Kenric strode from the great hall, certain that the countess needed something regarding her beloved horses. He had never seen anyone—man or woman—as horse mad as Elysande Devereux. It wouldn't have surprised him if she gave birth to a horse and proclaimed it the most splendid creature on earth. As her time to deliver drew near, she'd asked Kenric to be her eyes and ears in the stables since she wasn't there as often. Now that he'd been back at Sandbourne for a day, she probably wanted a detailed report from him regarding the state of the stables.

He reached the solar and knocked. He entered when commanded and found Lady Mary and Lady Orella on their feet, making their goodbyes. Both noblewomen gave him a smile as they exited. Kenric closed the door behind them and presented himself to the countess.

"Lord Michael said that you had need of me this afternoon, my lady. How may I be of service?"

Her lips pursed as if she were secretly amused. "Please, have a seat, Sir Kenric."

He did as requested and waited.

"I hope you're keeping an eye on all of the horses for me as I asked," she began. "It's hard for me to spend as much time with them as I would like."

"Every horse is doing well since my return, my lady, save for one. Sir Martin's horse was found to have a pebble in the crevice of its hoof when we arrived. The stone's been removed. Martin and the groomsmen will keep a watch on it."

"See that they do." She thought a moment. "If it remains tender after tomorrow, I'll inspect it myself and decide what should be done."

"Very well."

She quickly inhaled a breath of air and shifted in her chair. Stroking her belly, she said, "This one can kick as strong as any horse I have met."

Kenric watched as her *cotehardie* moved, the material poking out as if someone hid under it and nudged it playfully. He'd never noticed this about a woman due to give birth and stared in fascination.

"The babe can put on quite a show at times," she said, as her gown jumped again. "When awake, it can kick until I'm weary. But we have other matters to discuss."

"I am at your service, my lady."

"I wish for you to teach my sister how to ride a horse."

This time he felt as if *he* had been kicked.

"You . . . wish me to teach . . . Lady Avelyn? To ride?"

"I do," she said, nodding firmly. "I believe everyone in the country should know how to do so. Avelyn has expressed little interest. Until now." Her eyes gleamed. Kenric wondered if she suspected—or knew—of what had passed between him and Avelyn.

"She is a tiny thing and horses are incredibly large beasts. I think she's always been intimidated by their size. But Avelyn admitted to me that she has become fond of your horse."

"Firefall? She . . . *likes* Firefall?"

Lady Elysande smiled. "She does, indeed. She said the horse was well behaved and that she trusted him when she sat atop him. And she trusts you, as well. Avelyn thinks you're a fine horseman, my lord. So when she expressed interest in finally learning how to ride, I thought you would be the perfect tutor for her."

"But it could take many hours—"

She waved his words away. "I'm not concerned with how long it takes, only that she's taught correctly and feels comfortable. I agree that you're the one who could teach her how enjoyable riding is. Naturally, you'll be excused from training this afternoon to begin your lessons together at once."

She gripped the arms of her chair and pushed herself against them in order to rise. "I think that Starlight would be the perfect mount for her. She has a sweet temperament and her mouth is not overly sensitive. Do you agree?"

Kenric rose. "Starlight is an excellent choice for a beginner, my lady."

"We can see how Avelyn fares today. Report back to me regarding her progress. 'Tis one thing to ride in front of you on the way back from London and quite another to sit astride and learn to control a horse. She may be very sore by tomorrow. So we'll see if you need to work with her each day or every other day."

He started to protest, not wishing to miss the time training with his friends, then caught himself. Why should he speak up and prevent the one thing he wanted more than anything in the world?

Time alone with Avelyn Le Cler.

Kenric wanted it desperately, but he didn't think any good would come of it. Still, it would give him the perfect excuse to spend part of his day with the woman who haunted his dreams and drove him to distraction. Besides, she'd be returning to London at summer's end. Why not enjoy her company till then?

"I'd be honored to tutor Lady Avelyn in riding," he said.

"Excellent. I thought you'd say as much." The countess gave him a long look. "My sister means the world to me. She is my closest friend, as well as my kin. I'm trusting her well-being with you, Sir Kenric."

"I won't disappoint you, Lady Elysande. I promise she will become a confident rider."

The noblewoman smiled. "She's confident in many things, my lord. Avelyn awaits you in the stables."

He bowed his head and made his way from the solar and out of the keep. The blood roared in his ears with each step he took that brought him closer to the stables. To be alone with Avelyn seemed like manna from heaven and Kenric swore not to waste a moment of it.

Entering the stables, he greeted a groomsman as he made his way to Starlight's stall. Avelyn stood stroking the horse between her ears, outlining the white star that rested there against the black of her coat. One glance told Kenric that the groom had almost finished readying the horse.

"Greetings, my lady."

"And to you, my lord."

She dropped her hand and faced him. Kenric saw that she wore one of the riding gowns that Lady Elysande favored when she rode. It was cut so the sleeves were tight against the arms and wrists, but the skirts ballooned out in order to give freedom to ride astride. He glanced down and saw the *cotehardie* dragged the ground by several inches.

Avelyn caught him doing so and laughed. "This is something Elysande gave me to wear. She said my hands will be most important and that I needed to be able to see them. I had to hem the sleeves since they dipped below my fingers. I didn't have time to cut off and hem the gown to my height, though." She smiled. "I fear I'm a strict seamstress and couldn't have abided a poor job."

She gripped the *cotehardie* and lifted it. "It won't matter once I'm seated atop Starlight. Elysande said if my feet are in the stirrups properly, my gown hanging over my feet won't matter. But after today's lesson, I'll retreat to my room and make sure it doesn't drag the ground when we ride the next time." Avelyn laughed. "It was cumbersome making my way from the keep to the stables without tripping over it."

"Your sister is right. Once atop the horse, you'll be fine."

The groom opened the stall door and led the horse past them.

They turned and followed him, though Avelyn struggled with the gown. They reached the open area just outside the stables and the stableman handed Kenric Starlight's reins.

"Normally, I would teach you to saddle your own horse, but I fear you're too small to lift the heavy saddle. In the future, though, you'll be the one to lead Starlight outside." He grinned. "Once you're properly attired."

"Must we always come outside for me to mount her?"

"That's a good question. A horse can become frightened and try to bolt if you climb on in a confined area."

"So if I lead her myself, we can both become used to each other."

"Aye. I'll also teach you to check the girth before you mount, but we'll save that, too." He handed her the reins. "Take these in your left hand. Gather them with a tuft of the mane."

She did so and reached with her right hand to turn the stirrup.

"Good. That's the next step. Now hold here on the back of the saddle with your right hand so that you're steady. Place your left foot in the stirrup. Let the ball of your foot rest comfortably on the bottom. Your right leg is balancing your weight now."

Avelyn did as instructed.

"I'll help you, but I want you to spring forward as I lift you."

"And toss my leg over," she added.

He nodded. "The last thing is to ease down. Don't drop your weight heavily, for you might startle your horse. Think of yourself as a feather, floating down from the sky to land in the saddle. Ready?"

With a push, she took off. She weighed very little, so lifting her caused no problem. Avelyn threw her leg over and came down gently, settling in nicely.

"Perfect. Starlight could not have asked for a better mount from you."

She grinned. Kenric could tell she was pleased with herself.

"Keep holding the reins gently and leave a bit of the mane in your hands. That will tell Starlight that you know you are the one in charge."

"And what will you be doing?" He heard a bit of nervousness in her voice.

"I'm going to adjust your stirrups. Don't look down while I do so. In fact, never look down. If you do, you can't see where you're going. And with your head down and bent, 'twill stiffen your spine. Any stiffness in your body makes it more difficult for Starlight to carry you."

"'Tis good to know."

He saw her gaze steadily to the front and quickly adjusted the stirrups. "And as far as where you look? Keep your chin up and your eyes forward."

Kenric let her sit a few minutes to grow comfortable atop Starlight and also allow the horse to become used to a new rider.

Then he said, "Close your eyes."

"Oh!" Her eyes went wide at his command. She bit her bottom lip then squeezed her eyes tightly shut.

"No," he said gently. "Relax. Just accustom yourself to Starlight."

Avelyn did as he asked. He allowed her to stay that way for a while.

"Now, with your eyes closed, I want you to think on this. When in the saddle, you should be able to draw a straight line. Start at your ear. Move it down to your shoulder. Then to your hip. And finally, your heel. Can you see it?"

She nodded. "I can. I can feel it," she said eagerly.

"Open your eyes. Next time, I'll take you out riding Firefall, so you can see my example. You want to keep your shoulders even and your back upright and straight."

He studied her. "Very good. Never round your shoulders, especially on a long ride, for you'll regret it the next day."

Kenric thought a moment. "I can't see your toes because of your gown. Point them toward the sky."

"Why?"

"If you keep your heels down and toes up, that absorbs some of the shock of the ride."

"And keeps my feet from slipping," she noted. "I can already tell I'm more anchored by doing so."

"Good. Now release Starlight's mane, but keep the reins in your hand." He reached and moved her hands closer to her body. "Keep them here, in front of the pommel. They must remain steady. If not, you'll jab Starlight's mouth with the bit."

"Oh, I wouldn't want to hurt her."

"Then stay aware of your hands at all times."

"I will," Avelyn promised.

"Let's work on how to hold the reins. Let go a moment." Kenric took the reins. "Now make a fist with both hands. That's right. Pass through the reins with your wrists sideways. Thumbs on top. Smallest finger on the outside."

"Like this?"

He nodded. "And remember that Starlight will bob her head up and down as she walks. You must accommodate her movement by readjusting constantly."

"How do I do that?" she asked, curiosity written across her face.

"Allow your arms to hang down at your sides, then they can swing subtly, back and forth. Just don't let the reins slide through your fingers. Once we give her a chance to trot, she'll lift her head slightly. You'll have to balance and adjust again as she moves."

Avelyn shook her head. "You've already told me a half-dozen things to do and we haven't even moved a step forward. How will I ever remember all of this?"

"With practice," he said glibly and found his insides flutter as her sweet laughter sounded through the open air. He wished he could bottle it so that he could take it out and drink deeply from it.

"I think you're ready for me to lead you about," he told her. "I won't take the reins unless I sense you're in trouble."

Kenric saw a bit of doubt in her eyes, but she gave him a brave nod. He took a few steps away from her and said, "Follow me."

Though he wanted to turn and make sure Avelyn was fine, he wanted her to believe in herself. She already had much to remember.

If he constantly glanced over his shoulder, she would start focusing on him and not what she had just learned. So he walked at a leisurely pace through the inner bailey. His ears told him that Starlight followed as he started, stopped, and moved in different directions.

It also surprised him that she hummed softly. Kenric had no idea why she did so.

After some minutes, he led them back to the front of the stables. Finally turning to face her, he saw the glee on her face.

"I did it!" she proclaimed. "All by myself."

"What did you learn as you followed me?"

Avelyn thought a moment. "That I can't clench my body. I had to let my legs dangle from my hips. She was very sensitive to any movement from me."

"Good. What else?"

"To always listen to my sister. At least where horses are concerned."

Kenric cocked his head. "I'm confused, my lady."

She laughed. "Elysande said you would tell me many things and that I would have a tendency to concentrate so hard that I might hold my breath. She said that would confuse Starlight because it would make me tense. So she told me to hum a tune under my breath. I could still concentrate on what needed to be done, but I'd be more relaxed as I focused."

Kenric grinned. "Lady Elysande is a wise woman when it comes to horses." He paused. "Have you had enough for one day?"

"No," she said. "I want to go round the bailey another time."

"I'll admit that you're a quick learner. I'll lead you around again if you think you're up to the challenge," he tossed out.

He took off again, this time his stride longer and his pace quicker, wanting to provide her an opportunity to push herself. He increased his speed until he trotted along. Kenric threw a glance over his shoulder, wanting to check on her.

The sight that greeted him almost stopped him in his tracks.

Avelyn's cheeks were flushed. Her sky blue eyes sparkled with pleasure. Wisps of honey blond hair had escaped her braid and curled about her face. Kenric wanted nothing more than to pull her from her horse and kiss her till the sun set.

"Don't stop," she called, making her way to pass him.

He fell in next to the horse and stayed with it until Avelyn brought them to a halt back at the stables. He signaled a groom to come and take the horse. She handed the reins to the man.

"Last lesson for today," Kenric said. "Grip the mane as before and bring your leg over toward me. I'll catch your waist, but you can slide your body along Starlight's left side till you touch the ground. Ready?"

"Aye." She did as instructed. His hands captured her small waist and eased her to the ground. He didn't want to release her but, already, she tugged away from him.

"Good girl," she cooed to Starlight. Avelyn reached into her pocket and removed an apple. She placed it in her palm and brought it to the horse, who took it. Avelyn leaned over and pressed a kiss along Starlight's neck.

Kenric felt a stab of jealousy and shook his head. How could he be jealous of a horse?

She called a farewell as the groom led the horse away and turned to him, her eyes bright.

"I could tighten my legs slightly, and she knew to go faster," Avelyn said, excitement lacing her words. "Oh, I wish I'd known how much fun riding is. No wonder Elysande enjoys it so much."

Avelyn let out a satisfied breath and smiled up at him. "You are a most wonderful teacher, my lord. I cannot wait for our next lesson." She lifted the long skirts that puddled on the ground and headed toward the keep.

Kenric would count the minutes till that occurred.

CHAPTER 17

AVELYN FLOATED BACK to the keep, happy how her first riding lesson had turned out—and even happier for the time she'd spent with Kenric.

She fought hard to listen to his instructions at the beginning since it was exciting simply being near him again, having his full attention. She'd enjoyed being near enough to inhale his familiar scent. He'd seemed pleased at her progress and she desperately wanted his approval.

Avelyn tripped over the too-long *cotehardie* as she reached the last few steps that led into the keep. She found herself sprawled on the stone steps, her palms and one cheek scraped. Picking herself up, she brushed the dust from her hands. When they stung, she turned them over and saw the bottom half of each hand red.

Lifting her skirts high again, she entered the structure and gingerly made her way up to the solar. She discovered Elysande sitting in a chair, a pillow behind her back, embroidery in her lap.

"Oh, dear," her sister murmured, a frown creasing her brow. "How many spills did you take?" She started to rise, but Avelyn motioned for her to stay seated.

"None," she said triumphantly. "I had a most successful lesson with a dedicated tutor and I didn't hold my breath even once. I learned how to mount. The proper way to hold the reins. Where to place my feet to anchor myself. I know now to look where I'm going and not down at my horse or the ground." She chuckled. "That proved to be my downfall in years past. No one ever told me to focus on what lay ahead."

"I'm sorry. It must've come naturally to me. I would never have thought to tell you that. I just assumed everyone looked straight ahead." Elysande paused. "If your time with Sir Kenric went so well, then why are you in such a sorry state?"

Avelyn turned her palms face up and studied them. "Carelessness. I tripped over the extra material at the hem of my garment as I returned from the stables. I threw out my hands to catch myself."

"You scraped them badly. And your poor cheek is quite red and already swelling." Elysande set her sewing aside. "Fetch the basin of water and some soap from the bedchamber. And bring me the small box in the chest under the window. Merryn gifted me with it after I married Michael at Kinwick. It has several salves that can help heal your wounds and reduce the pain."

Avelyn retrieved the items and allowed her sister to bathe her face and hands before applying the ointment.

"Mmm . . . it tingles some, but it's a pleasant feeling."

"It works wonders. Merryn is knowledgeable about these things. Take the jar with you and use it several times over the next few days."

Avelyn slipped it into her pocket. "You know how I love to garden. I wonder if I could learn some things about herbs from Merryn."

"She'd be happy to share her knowledge with you. So would Alys. That child has a natural gift when it comes to herbs and their healing properties."

She sat in a chair next to Elysande. "That's certainly true. Courtiers constantly hunted for Alys, asking for various remedies from her. Even the king and queen call on her upon occasion when they have need of a headache powder or something to aid them in sleep."

"So, it sounds as if Sir Kenric showed you quite a bit."

Avelyn smiled, noticing how her sister steered the conversation back to Kenric. "He did and he's very patient. After he told me more than I thought I could remember, he began walking about the bailey. I was to follow him on Starlight."

"How do you like her?"

"Oh, she's a lovely horse. Very calm and gentle."

"I thought she would be the mount for you. And you remembered to give her the apple?"

"I did, after our lesson. I wanted to leave her with good thoughts about our time together and be eager to see me tomorrow." Avelyn sighed. "Kenric did test me, though. It wasn't all fun and games. He varied his pace and turned in many directions. I learned some by trial and error, but instinct did take over, at times. I know now how to hold a horse back and how to urge it on. At least when walking and at a slow trot. I fear it might become more difficult when the speed picks up."

Elysande nodded thoughtfully. "Still, it seems you accomplished much on this first outing. I'm pleased that you seem eager to try again tomorrow. Is that your newfound love for riding . . . or because you want to spend time with Kenric Fairfax?"

"Both," Avelyn replied. "I truly enjoyed being on horseback today. I felt a certain elation and freedom. I can only imagine what I'll experience when I learn enough control to gallop across the meadow or down a road." She paused. "Spending that much time with Kenric was pleasant because I had his full attention."

"And he had yours, I daresay." Elysande patted her hand. "I'm happy to hear it went well." She yawned. "I'm sorry. I get so sleepy nowadays. Mother says my body needs more sleep than usual, thanks to the growing babe."

Avelyn rose. "Then why don't you lie down until we dine?"

"I think that's an excellent idea," Elysande agreed.

She helped her sister to her bedchamber, removing her slippers and lifting her *cotehardie* away. It surprised her how large Elysande's belly had grown.

"Are you certain is doesn't hurt?" she asked, staring in fascination.

"Nay. It's more of an inconvenience. And I do lose sleep, at times, when the babe decides to kick during the wee hours of the morning. The two of us do not always sleep at the same time."

Avelyn pulled the bed curtains and slipped from the room. She returned to her own bedchamber, relieved to see that Sela was absent from it. Deciding to change from her clothes and wash some of the scent of Starlight away, she stripped down to her smock and used the vanilla-scented soap she was fond of, lathering it up to wash her arms, neck, and chest. She rinsed the soap away and dried herself.

Remaining in her smock, Avelyn retrieved her sewing kit. Taking Elysande's riding *cotehardie*, she cut off the length of her index finger all around its bottom and dampened the bottom of the garment before she began to hem it. She combined a fell and running stitch for durability. She wanted to finish it so that she could wear it again for tomorrow's lesson with Kenric.

Over an hour passed before she completed her task. Sewing had always been a favorite pastime for her and she'd been proficient in it from the time she was younger than Alys. Now that she'd arrived at Sandbourne, she would make a few things for the coming babe.

Avelyn decided to go through her sewing box in order to see what yarn she had that could be turned into a cap for her future niece or nephew. She also wanted to make her mother a new headdress to wear for her wedding to Sir Charles. They could look over the scarves Avelyn possessed and discuss what colors her mother might choose. She would retrieve them now and show them to her mother after the evening meal.

Avelyn draped the finished *cotehardie* over the back of the chair she sat in and went to her trunk. Rummaging through it, she pulled out a few scarves as possibilities. Then she remembered that Sela had borrowed one of peacock blue that would look lovely against her mother's hair and bring out the blue in her eyes.

She hesitated a moment, wondering if she should go into Sela's trunk. Before their spat, Avelyn would have thought nothing of it—but now with harsh feelings between them, she was unsure. Still, it would only take a moment to find it. Her friend could be careless with items and probably didn't even remember that Avelyn had loaned the scarf to her. She could find it and reclaim it, with Sela being none the wiser.

Opening the trunk that sat next to hers, Sela's usual haphazard mess greeted Avelyn. She pushed aside a few items and spied the blue of the scarf that she'd loaned out. As she lifted it, the material caught on something and a handkerchief came out with it.

One she recognized as belonging to Queen Philippa.

Avelyn dropped her scarf atop her trunk and fingered the yellow handkerchief. As she inspected the silk, an uneasy feeling grew in the pit of her stomach.

Why would Sela have the queen's missing handkerchief in her possession?

"What are you doing?"

Avelyn turned and saw Sela had slipped into the room. She sensed her cheeks burning with guilt as her friend confronted her.

"Have you been going through my things? Prying inside my trunk?" Sela marched toward her and yanked the handkerchief away. She retreated to the other side of the bed and plopped down, her bottom lip sticking out in a pout.

"I was—"

"You were meddling in my privacy, Avelyn. I didn't think you'd stoop so low."

She remained calm. Losing her temper would only add fuel to Sela's growing fire.

"I remembered that I had loaned you a scarf. I didn't think you'd mind if I fetched it from your trunk. We've always been open with one another. But I apologize that I invaded your private space. I promise that it won't happen again."

"I should hope not." Sela stroked the yellow silk lovingly. "It's just like the one the queen has," she said. "Father knew how I admired it and he gifted this to me."

"He did? I haven't ever seen you carry it."

Sela sniffed. "I was waiting for the right occasion. So many people admire what the queen wears. They copy her sense of fashion at every turn." She laughed. "I thought, mayhap, I would sew it into the neckline of one of my gowns. Or even use it in a headdress."

Avelyn wanted to believe that Sela told the truth. She had no reason to lie.

Yet why did Avelyn feel that was exactly what her friend now did?

CHAPTER 18

Avelyn left the great hall after the noon meal to ready herself for her afternoon ride. Elysande had passed along another of her specially cut *cotehardies* for riding. After making adjustments to it, Avelyn alternated between wearing the two gowns.

She entered the empty bedchamber, glad that Sela had asked for her own room two weeks ago. Avelyn knew it was because of the incident over the scarf, but Sela had told Elysande that she wasn't from hardy stock and that she'd need to rest frequently throughout the day. Elysande had arranged for Sela to move into the room directly across the hall from Avelyn. She didn't pursue why the change was being made nor did her sister ask about the cool relations between the two women.

Avelyn still took her friend around the estate. Sela joined in some activities, but she never volunteered in household tasks such as candle making. When Avelyn made time to work in the garden or try out new dishes in the kitchens, Sela made herself scarce. They did see each other at meals and both stayed in the great hall in the evening, where they listened to music or stories and danced every now and then. Avelyn doubted anyone realized how strained matters were between them.

As she changed into new clothing, she reflected on how Sela kept apart from most of the women at court, though she knew them all and had introduced Avelyn to dozens of them upon her arrival. Thinking back, she realized how Sela latched on to her and dominated much of her spare time. Avelyn hadn't questioned having a new, dear friend to show her about the Palace of Westminster.

Then she considered how Alys reacted when she noticed Avelyn growing close to Sela. Her young cousin had made it known she was not fond of Sela Runford or her father, but Avelyn hadn't paid much attention. Alys, though she had a generous nature, sometimes took an instant dislike to someone and never hid her feelings. Any time Sela came to their shared bedchamber to gossip, Alys had usually made herself scarce. Avelyn determined the next time she saw her cousin she would ask about it.

Of course, it wouldn't matter in the long run. Avelyn had determined not to return to court at the end of the summer. She supposed she would have to go back to collect the belongings she'd left behind and possibly speak to the queen about her decision, but that would be a stay of short duration. Sela could return with her and Uncle Geoffrey at that time. He'd taken Avelyn and Alys to London last September. She assumed he would do the same again when autumn arrived.

After that, she doubted she would ever hear from Sela Runford again. It was a shame, for the young woman had made life at court more pleasant.

Avelyn finished dressing and went to the stables, her routine since the riding lessons with Kenric commenced. At every session, the knight quizzed her over what she'd previously learned and always praised her for having the correct answers. She desperately wanted to show him that she was no empty-headed court fool.

He already awaited her at Starlight's stall. The horse turned her head and whinnied as Avelyn approached. She stroked the velvet nose and murmured a few endearments.

"I told you that you wouldn't have to prepare your horse to ride, but I thought you might enjoy learning how to groom her," Kenric said.

"I'd like to try. Elysande says that's one of her favorite things to do with her horses."

He opened the stall door. "Come in. And remember—"

"Not to stand behind her. I know."

Kenric reached for the brush and handed it to Avelyn. It proved heavier than she thought it would be. He picked up another brush and went to stand on Starlight's right side. He motioned for her to take a spot on the left.

"Always start with the neck."

He began stroking the horse. Avelyn imitated his moves, gliding the brush smoothly against the animal's coat.

Kenric continued the grooming lesson. "You'll move back from the neck all the way to her hindquarters. Be careful, though, round the belly and stifle."

She'd never heard that term before. "Stifle?"

He laughed. "I forget that you're still a novice." He pointed. "Here. It's this joint, above the hock in her hind leg. The stifle in a horse is as a knee is to people."

She gently ran the brush under Starlight's belly. "Like this?"

He watched her a moment. "Aye. Some horses are sensitive in their belly or stifle. And some can be ticklish in either spot."

"Truly? I'm ticklish on my feet and belly. My father used to tickle me both places when I was young. I would laugh myself silly." She continued easing the brush slowly and softly. "And would you be ticklish, my lord?" she asked, looking up briefly at him before returning her attention to her task.

For a moment, Avelyn physically felt the charged air about them.

Kenric grew still. "I don't know, my lady. No one has ever tickled me."

Avelyn's arm fell to her side. "No one's ever tickled you? I find that hard to believe." She began brushing Starlight's side again and then brought the brush up to run along her back.

"Nay. My father was not one to play games with his sons." A shadow crossed his face. "My mother did with Roland. But never me."

Her heart twisted with the sadness she heard in his words. She placed a hand atop his.

Kenric paused the brushstroke, staring at their joined hands. "If I ever had children, I would tickle them," he said softly. "I would do as

Lord Geoffrey does with Hal. Swing them about. Let them ride on my shoulders." He paused. "I would be a very different father than the one I had."

He cleared his throat and Avelyn took that as a sign. She removed her hand from his and continued grooming Starlight. She bent to run the brush down the horse's leg and started to sit in order to reach the leg better.

"Nay," he warned. "You must kneel, my lady. Never sit. If for any reason something startled your horse, you might be trampled before you could react."

"But Starlight knows me by now," she argued.

"She does—but what if a stranger appeared at her stall door, one she felt menaced by? Or even something as small as a bee flying by and landing upon her, even stinging her, might cause her to react unpredictably."

"I hadn't thought of that," she admitted.

He grinned. "That's why you have a most excellent tutor to inform you of such situations. Now, let's tackle the last areas—face, mane, and tail."

Avelyn stood, listening attentively.

"A horse's face can also be its most sensitive. That's one of the reasons we start grooming at the neck and stroke all the way along the body. It gives time for the animal to adjust to being touched. Once you're ready to curry the face, you switch to a brush with much softer bristles. Use a gentle, slow motion. And not as much pressure as you exerted along the flanks. If she starts, back away and then approach her slowly once more. Some horses don't tolerate having their face touched overly much, so be aware of their mood."

Kenric handed her a different brush. "You try."

She did as he asked, moving slowly and with a lighter touch than before. Starlight accepted what she did and nickered softly, seeming to enjoy being pampered in this fashion.

"Nicely done, my lady," Kenric praised. "You have a true feel for animals."

"My father always did. I thought only Elysande took after him in that regard. Mayhap I was mistaken."

He gave her a sudden smile that flipped her stomach upside down. She'd fallen off a horse once, many years ago, when her father tried to teach her to ride when she was young. Her stomach had behaved in a similar fashion, causing her to feel nauseated and dizzy at the same time. Yet, in this case, the sensation didn't sicken her at all. It only made her feel giddy as her heart pounded louder and faster. Avelyn feared Kenric would hear it.

Instead, she looked away to scratch Starlight between her eyes and asked, "So what of her mane and tail?"

"Those are more complicated. I think you've learned enough about grooming today and you can show off that knowledge to your sister. Let's move on to the riding portion of your lesson."

Avelyn handed him the brush. He replaced the ones they had used on the shelf behind him and then had her step out from the stall while he readied the horse for her. Out of habit, she reached for the reins from him and led Starlight from the stables into the warm sunshine of the early June afternoon. After she checked the girth, Kenric helped her to mount and adjusted the stirrups before he returned for Firefall.

Avelyn soaked up the rays, feeling self-assured atop Starlight. She hadn't thought that possible only a few weeks ago. Kenric had done an excellent job in giving her the confidence to ride.

He returned and set the pace. She'd learned a trot was between a walk and a run, and she pressed her legs slightly inward to allow Starlight to fall in behind Firefall at this gait. They rode through the inner and outer baileys at this moderately fast pace. Avelyn took pride in how she held her reins correctly, with a light touch but a firm grasp. She'd also learned how to move with her horse when the speed picked up and how to pay attention to Starlight's head and make the proper adjustments.

They rode through the open gates and out to the meadow where they'd come every day to practice small circles and increased speeds. Kenric whirled Firefall around, so Avelyn closed her fists on the reins and sat back in the saddle, letting Starlight know to stop.

"Your alignment is good," he told her. "I believe it's become second nature for you."

She laughed. "I know my posture is much better—even when I'm out of the saddle and walking on the ground. I used to wonder why Elysande always stood perfectly straight at all times while I seemed to slouch. Now I know that it's a carryover from riding."

"Would you like to test yourself?"

Avelyn nodded, licking her lips nervously. She knew they'd been building up to a full, all-out gallop. Subconsciously, she began humming to calm her nerves as she lowered her heels some for more support and balance.

Kenric let out a cry and turned Firefall quickly, galloping away. She urged Starlight on and set off after him.

They rode at this pace several minutes, riding the entire length of the meadow and looping around to do it again. Finally, he slowed Firefall to a trot and then a walk. Avelyn rode up beside him as they continued to let their horses cool down. She ceased the tune she'd been humming.

"It looks like rain will hit at any moment," he said as thunder rumbled low.

She looked around, having been unaware that darkening clouds had blown in. "I didn't realize. I was concentrating so hard on keeping up with you and doing everything you've taught me."

"I should've noticed sooner," he apologized. "I'm afraid we'll be caught in a downpour."

"I don't mind," she said. "I'd rather have stayed out here the entire time and finished our lesson." She grinned. "I feel exhilarated. Riding that fast is liberating."

The first drops of rain began to pelt them.

"Follow me," Kenric said, taking off as the clouds began emptying themselves.

Avelyn followed as he made his way toward the forest at the edge of the meadow. The rain quickly started coming down in sheets.

Flashes of lightning caused her to tense, but she remembered how attuned Starlight would be if she did so. She forced herself to relax as she raced across the meadow.

Kenric slowed as he entered the grove of trees. She did likewise, keeping her horse to a walk as they went more deeply into the woods.

"The trees are thick here and should provide us some shelter." Kenric dismounted and looped his reins around a low branch. He came and helped her down before securing Starlight's reins. The two horses bent to munch on the grass beneath them.

"You're soaked, my lady. Again, I'm sorry for not being more mindful."

Avelyn shrugged. "It's only a bit of water, my lord. I'm not a fragile flower that washes away."

"Not the way you rode Starlight today. I feel the need for your lessons have drawn to an end. You know everything I can teach you at this point. It will only be a matter of practice in order to make your knowledge become instinct."

She knew his words to be true and wondered if he was eager to be rid of her so he could return to the training yard in the afternoons. A splat of cold rain hit her forehead and ran down her nose, causing her to shiver.

"You're cold." Kenric moved closer to her.

Then he did what Avelyn had wished for during many sleepless nights. He wrapped his arms about her, drawing her into his broad chest. The warmth that enveloped her made her feel as if she had been gone to some distant land and had now returned home.

Home. Kenric's arms felt like home. Her cheek nestled against his chest. Her arms wrapped about his torso and she could hear his beating heart.

This was where she should stay—always.

He must have sensed it, too. His arms tightened about her and his large hands began to stroke her back. The most wonderful tingling filled her.

Avelyn looked up and saw the flame of desire burning hot in his hazel eyes. She willed his mouth to come to her—and it did.

The minute his lips touched hers, a searing fire lit between them. The kiss never had time to start gently, for the spark pushed them past a slow beginning. Kenric's tongue thrust into her mouth, almost picking a fight with hers. They warred with one another, first one having the advantage and then the other. His hands roamed up and down her back, dropping below her waist, cupping her buttocks and pulling her closer.

She clung to his gypon then found her hands sliding up, brushing his neck, touching his face. Her fingers stroked the stubble before pushing into his thick, dark hair. A low growl came from within him, as deep and powerful as the thunder that echoed about them. Avelyn locked her hands around Kenric's neck and pulled down.

Without thought, she hitched herself up, wrapping her legs around him. He twirled around and she found her back pressed against a wide tree as they devoured one another. Her nether region pulsated in a primordial beat. Avelyn couldn't remember the last time she'd taken a breath. She was consumed by the immense heat this man emitted as she brought her arms together behind his neck, nuzzling as close as she could.

He broke their kiss. They both panted, out of breath, then he moved to her ear where his tongue did wonderful things that made her shiver in delight. Hot lips trailed from there to her cheek and under her jaw before sliding down the column of her throat. She reveled in the feel of the rough stubble burning a path against her skin. His mouth went lower, now grazing the top of her breasts, causing a quick intake of breath. The drum that pounded within her demanded something. She knew not what—only that he could provide it.

His manhood now pressed hard against her. Something in her wanted to meet it. She lifted up against it and then leaned back into the tree, only to move toward it again. His member called out to her. She must heed the call before she fell to pieces.

He moaned again as his lips returned to hers. She echoed the sound as her breasts seemed to swell against his chest.

Then, somehow, she found herself alone, the heat gone as she sagged against the tree for support. Kenric had released her and took a step back, his gaze intense, changing his hazel eyes to a vivid green.

"I want you," he said, his voice rough and low.

Avelyn nodded, words impossible to form.

He took her hand, drawing it to his mouth. His lips brushed against her knuckles, causing her knees to go weak.

Kenric cupped her face gently with his other hand. "But I have learned that I can't always have what I want. It's a hard lesson a man must learn."

"Then why—"

His fingers touched her mouth, burning her, silencing her.

"You are destined to be a great lady someday, Avelyn Le Cler. You'll marry a powerful man who will treasure you and give you everything you deserve. I would not spoil you for him merely to satisfy my own desire," he said softly, his hand squeezing hers.

Kenric released her hand and took a step back. "I will always remember you as you are in this moment. Your hair coming undone and damp. Your lips bruised with my kiss. Your cheeks flushed with desire. You are the most beautiful woman who walks this earth, Avelyn. I pray the Most Holy God brings the right man into your life. That you will wed and be happy together. Even come to love one another."

He turned and went to their horses, where he loosened the reins and brought them back to where she stood, dazed, not comprehending his words.

Then anger boiled inside her. She saw red as she looked up at him.

"How dare you tease me!" she spit out. "Make me want you. Make me fall in love with you . . . and then cast me aside for some nonexistent, future husband. I hope you burn in the fires of Hell, Kenric Fairfax."

Avelyn drew her arm back and slapped him as hard as she could. She saw the stunned look upon his face. Before he could react, she jammed her foot into Starlight's stirrup and tossed her leg over, snatching up the reins as she rode away in the rain.

CHAPTER 19

KENRIC FROZE A MOMENT, the sting of Avelyn's slap spreading deep shame through him. He hadn't meant to tease her, nor did he want to take advantage of her. It was why he finally put a stop to their kisses.

But she had spoken of love . . .

She told him she wanted him. By the way her body had responded, he knew that to be true.

But love?

Avelyn was young and inexperienced and knew nothing about love—if it even existed. True, she had been at court and exposed to all manner of men there. She was an incandescent beauty, so he knew men had fallen at her feet. Had she not been attracted to any of them?

Or . . . had she felt what he had that stirred between them?

For Kenric knew in his soul that he did love Avelyn Le Cler. Loved her as he never had another. Loved her as he never would any woman again. She had stolen his heart. He was no longer a rational knight with a steady hand and thoughts only toward soldiering. Instead, he was a lovesick fool who would have done anything to win her heart in return. Yet, though he wanted it, he could never claim it. She was much too good for him and deserved far better than he could ever provide for her.

Yet, she said she had fallen in love with him . . .

Then he realized the rain still came down and that Avelyn had dashed away, an inexperienced rider on slick soil. She could already be lying injured, thrown from her horse—or worse.

Kenric leapt onto Firefall's back and took off, the horse's hooves thundering more loudly than the storm. He saw Avelyn ahead of him in the distance, riding at breakneck speed.

"Oh, God in Heaven, protect her," he murmured under his breath. He, who never prayed, because it never had done any good. Yet he repeated this mantra over and over as he urged Firefall on, trying to catch up with her.

She reached the open gates of Sandbourne and sailed through them without a backward glance. At least she was off the slick grass of the meadow, but the gravel and mud within the castle walls could prove just as menacing. Kenric pushed his horse harder.

He caught up to her as she reached the stables. Avelyn slung her leg over and slid down Starlight's side. Kenric knew from experience that anger drove her, providing a physical energy that surged through her body. He dismounted and dropped his reins, racing toward her.

Avelyn turned and dug her heels into the ground, glaring up at him. Kenric halted in front of her, unsure what to say now that he stood before her.

"I made it back fine, my lord." Her eyes narrowed. "And you are right. I believe our lessons have come to an end. I'll continue to put into practice what I've learned. I plan to ride every day that I can so that the knowledge will remain at my fingertips."

She gave him a mocking curtsey. "Thank you for doing such a splendid job. I rode Starlight today with no fear." She paused. "I will never fear a horse again. In fact, they quite have my heart now. They're loyal beasts, much like a dog, and give their affection freely. Without cause. Without any expectation."

"Avelyn, I'm . . . sorry that I've . . . hurt your feelings," he stammered.

"Sorry?" She barked out a harsh laugh. "I'm sure you've said that to many women, many times." She looked him up and down. "You're an excellent tutor and an even better kisser, Kenric Fairfax. But you've received your last kiss from me. I will take my tattered heart elsewhere. Mayhap to a nunnery, for I have no plans to give it to any man."

Her words shocked him. "My lady, 'twould be a waste of your intelligence and beauty to lock yourself away in a convent. You will feel differently, given time, once you return to court at summer's end and make a great marriage."

An odd look crossed her face, then she said, "'Tis no concern of yours. I bid you a good day, my lord."

She walked away from him in the rain, her clothes clinging to her sweet curves. Locks of her honeyed hair escaped the braid and swirled about her.

It seemed as if a fist closed around Kenric's heart and squeezed unmercifully as he watched her depart, a pain as physical as any wound he'd ever experienced. He tried to let loose of the hurt as he grabbed the reins of both horses and took them into the shelter of the stables, returning each animal to its stall and removing the riding gear. He tended first to Starlight, rubbing her down and feeding her oats, and then cared for Firefall.

When he finished, Kenric collapsed onto the straw, reluctant to see anyone in his foul mood. He sat, sulking as a child, wishing he could change things between him and Avelyn. But he knew it was best in the long run to have a clean break between them. He would do his best to avoid her for the remainder of her time at Sandbourne. If Lord Michael asked him to be part of her escort party when she returned to London, he would beg off. As things stood, Avelyn would probably request that Kenric not be among those who accompanied her back to court.

He reached over and toyed with a bit of straw, wondering how long he could stay with Firefall before being missed. Then he heard voices, faint at first, but eventually they grew stronger as they came his way. From where he sat in the stall, he heard a couple of men shuffle by. Then the stall across opened, where Starlight was housed.

"Only this one and one more left to muck out," said one.

"Should have done it 'fore Sir Kenric brought 'em home."

"Lady Avelyn looked all out of sorts."

"She did, indeed."

He heard the familiar scraping sound of tools as the men went to work.

"She's a fair one, the lady, with those blue eyes and sweet smile."

A snort. "You think? I suppose you didn't hear what I did."

"What? Don't hold out on me."

A pause. "I heard Lady Avelyn was in a bit o' trouble in London."

"Trouble? What kind o' trouble?"

A laugh. "She seems to have a hard time with the truth. Tellin' it, that is."

"Huh. You'd never know it by lookin' at her sweet face."

"I know. And I also heard she may be a pincher."

"The lady . . . she's a thief?"

"Aye. 'Tis what I heard some of the soldiers talkin' 'bout. A few of the ones that done brought her here to Sandbourne."

"Wonder if the master knows."

"Like he'd care. 'Tis his beloved wife's sister. The countess has the earl wrapped about her finger, she does. And if she wants her sister here, then here she'll be and stay for as long as she likes."

Kenric bolted to his feet. He found it hard to believe the overheard conversation. Avelyn . . . a thief? And a liar? That was as far from the truth as he could imagine.

But he hadn't known her for long—and did not know the woman who had lived at the royal court in London. Mayhap, his first impression of her when he arrived to escort her back to Sandbourne was correct.

He slipped from the stall. The two stable men were oblivious as he exited. As he hurried away, Kenric wondered exactly which soldiers had been gossiping about Avelyn—and where they'd heard it from.

AVELYN STORMED INTO the keep, her temper hot and her nerves frayed. She rounded a corner and crashed into Lady Orella.

"Oh, my apologies, my lady. I was in a hurry and wasn't watching where I went."

Michael's mother still seemed an enigma to Avelyn. She remembered meeting the woman at the Convent of the Blessed Sisters, where Orella was known as Sister Shiloh. Even now at Sandbourne, Orella seemed to glide along the corridors gracefully, a sense of peace about her. Still an ethereal beauty, she seemed to watch from afar the events that unfolded around her.

The noblewoman studied her with equal parts of kindness and interest on her features. "You seemed troubled, my dear. May I invite you to my chamber? We could speak there."

Avelyn believed being around Lady Orella might do her some good. Her anger still hummed just below the surface. If anyone could calm her, it would be this former nun.

"I would appreciate that, my lady."

"Call me Orella, my dear." She slipped her arm through Avelyn's and led her upstairs to her large bedchamber, asking a servant to bring fresh clothes. Orella helped her from her wet clothes and helped Avelyn dress again before guiding her to two chairs in the corner.

Once seated, Orella asked, "May I offer you some wine?"

"Please."

Just being in this woman's presence helped cool Avelyn's wrath. She sipped the wine given to her, letting it warm a path to her belly.

They sat in easy silence for several minutes before Orella asked, "What troubles you, Avelyn?"

She set down her goblet. "I've only shared this with four others—Geoffrey and Merryn while I was at Kinwick and then Elysande and Michael when I arrived here. I'm desperately in love with Sir Kenric Fairfax."

She omitted that the knight had dismissed her feelings. Avelyn believed it was because he thought she wanted a husband with lands and a title, and he had nothing to offer. Little did Kenric know that he was the Earl of Shadowfaire. And she couldn't think how to tell him so that he would believe her.

"You haven't spoken of this affection with your mother?"

"Nay. Once I found that Mother was to wed Sir Charles, I wanted her to enjoy the time leading up to her wedding."

"She adores the headdress you made for the occasion," revealed Orella. "She's boasted how talented you are with a needle and thread."

"Thank you, though apparently not talented enough to convince Kenric of my feelings for him." She related the situation over the next few minutes, ending with, "And so he still believes I am to return to London, where I'll magically find a worthy man who'll lavish upon me gifts beyond compare."

She stood and began pacing. "But the most worthy man I know is right before me," Avelyn insisted. "I've never been one to care for material goods." She threw her hands in the air. "Why can't Kenric see that we are meant to be together?"

"I understand your frustration," Orella said, "but no man reacts well to it, especially coming from a woman." She paused, a faraway look in her eyes. "I found myself in an impossible marriage to a man I could never respect or like—much less try to love. He was filled with anger and built a wall around himself composed of it. If I lost my temper and reacted to him in such a manner?" She shuddered. "It was a most unpleasant experience."

Avelyn went and knelt by her side. She took the older woman's hands in hers and said, "I know you suffered greatly during your marriage and were banished to a convent."

Orella squeezed her hands with affection. "Going to the Convent of the Blessed Sisters was the best thing that ever happened to me. Except for giving birth to Michael," she amended. "The sisters taught me how to quell my rage over the injustice I had suffered. They led me to a path of peace and acceptance."

"You're so wise, my lady. Do you have any advice for me in this matter of the heart?"

Orella cupped Avelyn's face tenderly. "Your sweet temperament and angelic face will be more than enough." She kissed Avelyn's cheek. "I'd advise you to be kind to Sir Kenric. As if nothing upsetting had occurred between you."

Avelyn frowned. "Truly?"

"Some would tell you to play games with him. Ignore him and then seek him out. That is the common practice of those at court. Aye, I did spend some time in London and know of what I speak. But you are not a court person, my dear."

"Nay," she said softly. "Growing up, I thought I would enjoy the excitement and change from the drudgery of living in the country. Having lived in London only a short while, I now realize how much I believe in a life spent helping others, not one of empty gossip and political intrigue and only caring about my appearance and befriending those who can benefit me in some manner."

"Like your friend, Lady Sela?"

She cast her eyes downward. "I'm not sure if Sela was ever my friend. It's been awkward having her at Sandbourne since we fell out. We've avoided one another." Avelyn looked up and laughed. "And what did we argue over that caused our rift?"

"Sir Kenric Fairfax?" Orella asked and chuckled.

"Exactly," she confirmed. "But our estrangement helped me to put our friendship into perspective. Even if I was returning to the royal court at the end of summer, I don't think we would remain close."

The noblewoman said, "You asked for my advice with Sir Kenric. I would tell you to be yourself. That's what attracted him to you in the first place. Mark my words. He'll regret his actions and come around. I have faith that this will occur. I will pray for the outcome you seek with this knight."

"Coming from you, it means a great deal," Avelyn told her.

"I spent many years where all I did was pray," Orella said. "And I'm very good at it."

A knock sounded at the door. Avelyn rose to answer it.

Her mother stood waiting when she opened the door. "I was looking for you, Avelyn. When I couldn't find you, I thought I'd stop and visit with Orella."

"We have been talking of your wedding, Mary, and the lovely headdress your daughter created for you," Orella called out as she motioned Lady Mary in.

Avelyn loved the radiant smile that graced her mother's face, glad her mother had found happiness with a man she obviously loved. The fact that her mother would also be able to remain at Sandbourne to be near her first grandchild only added to the joy.

"I'm most eager to become Sir Charles' wife," her mother admitted. "Being with him makes me feel like I was a young girl again."

The three women laughed.

Elysande poked her head inside the open doorway. "I heard all the laughter and wondered what I was missing out on."

"Come in," Orella said. "We are talking of Lady Mary's wedding."

Her sister took a few steps in and stopped abruptly. A hand went to her stomach as a frown crossed her face.

Avelyn rushed over. "Are you all right?"

Elysande shrugged. "The midwife tells me it's nothing. I'm used to faint flutters and kicks from the babe but, in the last week, several times I have felt these aches. The midwife says it's only false labor pains that some women have."

Avelyn led Elysande to a chair and eased her into it.

"I had those pains with Michael a good two weeks before the real ones began," Orella said. "Believe me, when the time comes, you will know the difference."

"I didn't experience any false pains with you, Elysande," Lady Mary said, "but I did just days before Avelyn's birth. They surprised me since I'd never felt them before."

"Each babe is different," Lady Orella proclaimed. "You must put your trust in God—and your midwife," she added wisely.

Avelyn knew that Michael's mother gave good advice to Elysande. She only hoped that Orella's suggestion to her would prove fruitful. She feared Kenric would do something foolish before the stubborn man realized they belonged together.

CHAPTER 20

After mass the next morning, Elysande linked her arm through Avelyn's as they left the chapel. She slowed her gait to match that of her sister, whose belly seemed to have grown even more enormous overnight.

"I'd like to see the progress you've made at riding. Could I come watch today's lesson?"

Avelyn evenly said, "I don't have a lesson today."

Elysande stopped. "What's wrong?"

Her sister had always been in tune to Avelyn's moods.

"Nothing." She didn't want to worry Elysande so near the birth of her child with petty problems.

They started walking slowly again toward the keep.

"I suppose the meadow would be too far for me to go," her sister mused. "Still, it's been more than a week since I went to the stables. I would love to see my sweet Morningstar one more time before the babe comes."

They reached the steep stairs leading up to the keep and began their ascent.

Avelyn asked, "Could you make it down all these stairs and back up again today? I know you do it each morning for mass, but you sound out of breath to me even now. You shouldn't overtire yourself."

Elysande sniffed. "I am with child. Not infirmed." Her mouth set in stubborn determination.

Recognizing her sister's mood and knowing that seeing her horses would improve upon it, she said, "Then let's go after the noon meal to visit the stables. Cook can provide plenty of apples for us."

They reached the top. Elysande paused and took a deep breath before she hugged her sister. "Thank you. I fear it will be the last time. And I know my spirits will be raised."

Avelyn made sure that Elysande ate her fair share and then took her to her chamber to rest. They arranged to have a quiet meal at noon in the solar together before heading out to the stables.

She went to the kitchens and told Cook what she needed. The stout woman handed her a basket and Avelyn held it as Cook filled it with apples.

"The countess always takes plenty with her. She does love spoiling all those horses."

Avelyn thanked her and took the basket to her bedchamber, passing Sela in the hall. Her friend gave her a cool smile but didn't linger.

She and Elysande ate roasted pheasant in the solar, enjoying the time alone as they talked about horses. Avelyn knew that Elysande's life was on the brink of change. Once the child came, everything would be different.

After they finished their meal, Avelyn placed the basket over her arm and led her sister downstairs. People streamed from the great hall, having finished their own noon meal. They stepped aside to let most of the people pass before they ventured outside to tackle the staircase. Elysande held on to her tightly as they gingerly made their way down. Avelyn hoped the apples wouldn't spill out and roll down the stairs.

"May we help you, my lady?" A familiar voice brought her to a halt.

Avelyn looked over her shoulder and found Kenric standing with Sir Ralf. Both men looked concerned.

"Please, my lady, let us assist you," Sir Ralf said.

"I wouldn't want to keep you from the training yard," Elysande told them.

Ralf laughed. "I'm scheduled to fight Martin next. I don't mind keeping him waiting. If I'm a little late, his temper will be riled—and he doesn't concentrate as well when he's angry." He grinned. "I admit that I need any advantage I can get when dueling with Martin."

"And I have a riding lesson with Lady Avelyn now, so I'm not expected in the training yard," Kenric said.

Elysande shot her a look, which Avelyn chose to ignore. She wanted to fire off a retort and contradict Kenric's words. Instead, she smiled sweetly at him, Lady Orella's advice in mind.

"Get on each side of the countess," she told the two men. "She can lean on you better that way."

The men did as instructed, with Avelyn falling in behind them, the basket of treats intact.

When they reached the stables, Sir Ralf excused himself. They wished him luck in his bout with his opponent.

Then Kenric said, "I must compliment your sister, Lady Elysande. In a short time, she's mastered Starlight. She sits well and has a gentle touch with the reins."

Elysande considered his words. "What about when she rides at a faster gait?" she asked. "How does she fare then?"

Avelyn felt Kenric's gaze upon her as she looked across the bailey. She grew warm as he said, "Lady Avelyn has proven herself most adept, my lady. In every circumstance."

"I'm pleased that Avelyn's learned so much from you, Sir Kenric. As you know, riding is one of my greatest pleasures in life," Elysande said. Then a smile crossed her face. "Next to time spent with my husband, of course."

They entered the stables and Elysande stopped at each stall. She spoke to every horse, rewarding them with an apple, asking various stable hands about the horses' health and well-being.

Then they reached Morningstar's stall. The mare poked her head over the stall door, excited to see her mistress. She whinnied and bumped against the door, stretching her neck so that she could nuzzle Elysande's ear. Her sister giggled as she stroked her favorite horse, murmuring endearments to the mare as she fed the horse one apple and then a second.

"Michael has someone ride her daily," Elysande said as she stroked the horse's neck, "but I can't wait till I'm the one on her again." She bid the horse farewell, promising to bring her babe on her next visit so that Morningstar could approve the newest member of the Devereux family.

As Elysande stepped away, she stumbled. Kenric caught her arm and elbow, steadying her.

"I'm sorry. It's one of those silly pains again. They've been coming on and off all morning. I—"

Elysande gasped and hunched over with a low moan. Then a swish sounded. A perplexed look crossed Kenric's face, but Avelyn knew what had occurred.

"My water's broken," her sister announced. Elysande looked around and sighed. "I don't know if I can make it back to the keep."

Avelyn heard the uncertainty in Elysande's voice. "You can't find an empty stall and give birth here," she teased, trying to lighten the mood.

"It was good enough for our Lord Jesus Christ to be born in a stable," Elysande retorted, but Avelyn heard the humor behind her words.

"True enough, but it would not be good enough for Lord Michael's first child," Kenric declared. With that, he swept Elysande up into his arms.

"Oh!" Her sister's eyes grew wide. She looked at Avelyn and said, "Find Mother and Lady Orella and tell them it's time to find the midwife. Michael brought her to the keep a week ago so she would be nearby."

Kenric started off. Elysande called over her shoulder, "And find Michael after that. He would be most upset not to be informed that his child has decided to be born today."

Avelyn lifted her skirts and raced ahead of them. She reached the keep and was happy that the first person she saw was her mother.

Panting heavily, she got out, "The babe comes!"

Lady Mary broke out into a smile. "I'll bring the midwife and find Orella. Go find Michael," she instructed.

Avelyn nodded. As she turned to leave, Kenric entered with Elysande in his arms and quickly strode up the stairs.

Elysande called out cheerily, "Michael should be in the training yard."

Avelyn rushed back outside and to the area where the soldiers spent the majority of their day. She found Michael with a sword in hand, demonstrating moves to a gathered group. Avelyn motioned him over.

He stopped and hurried over, an irritated look upon his face. "I don't wish to be interrupted—"

"It's time!" she cried.

Michael froze. "The babe?"

Avelyn nodded. Then she began to laugh as the Earl of Sandbourne dropped his sword and took off like a comet. She ran behind him, following him all the way up to the solar.

Elysande sat on the bed, her mother and mother-in-law hovering over her as they slipped off her shoes and stockings. Kenric stood awkwardly in the corner.

The midwife shook a finger at Michael as he hurried across the room to his wife. "This is no place for you, my lord." She snapped her fingers at Kenric. "You. Take the earl and be gone. There's women's work to be done here."

Michael glared at the tiny midwife who ordered him about. "I will speak to my wife first."

The two mothers stepped aside. Michael knelt by the bed and took Elysande's hand in his, lowering his lips and pressing a tender kiss to her fingers.

"How are you, my love?" he asked, his voice thick with emotion.

Elysande gave him a beautiful smile. "I'm ready, Husband."

"I know," he said softly.

She grimaced as a birthing pain struck and then asked, "What if the babe is a girl?"

Michael brushed a stray curl from his wife's cheek. "If it's a girl, my fondest wish will come true—to have two beautiful Devereux women in my life." He smiled. "And if you produce a boy, I will love him all the same."

He kissed her fingers again. "Take care, Wife. The next time I see you, you will be a mother. The mother of our child."

Michael rose and looked over at the only other male present. "Sir Kenric, come sit with me in the solar. I could use your company." He glanced over to Avelyn. "Bring me regular reports of what goes on here."

"I will," she promised.

"Enough!" cried the midwife, waving her hands about. "Out, my lords."

KENRIC FOLLOWED LORD MICHAEL from the bedchamber. He didn't want to stay with the nobleman in the man's solar. He had no right. He wasn't a relative or a trusted friend. He merely served the Devereux family.

"Have a seat. I don't know about you, but I'm eager for a glass of wine." Lord Michael poured a healthy amount into silver goblets for each of them and handed him one.

He gripped it and downed a mouthful before taking a seat in a chair next to the fire.

His liege lord sat in one opposite him and sighed. "I don't know how women do it."

"My lord?"

"Have babes. I'm already sick to my stomach and worried out of my mind, yet Elysande has only begun the lengthy, painful process of giving birth to my child." He brought the goblet to his lips and sipped. "Men may flash their swords about and charge into battle without a thought for their safety, but women? They are the ones with a core of steel and full of unimaginable bravery. If we men had to bear children, the population might dry up in a score. Or less."

Kenric didn't know what to say to such bold, unorthodox remarks, so he took another drink of the most excellent wine. He stared into the goblet at the rich color, wishing he could offer comfort to Lord Michael.

"So, you've expressed an interest in Avelyn."

The earl's words came from nowhere and nearly knocked him from his chair.

"Don't look so stunned, Sir Kenric. Avelyn and Elysande are quite close. They would naturally speak of such matters together. I happened to be on hand when they did."

Kenric chose his words carefully. "Lady Avelyn is an intriguing woman, my lord. If I was of a mind to pursue a woman and marry, I'd hope to be lucky enough to wed someone as beautiful and intelligent as she is."

Lord Michael looked at him thoughtfully. "But you aren't interested in marriage or settling down. With Avelyn. Or any other woman."

He took another drink. "Nay, my lord. I decided when I took my knight's vows that I would live a life of service." He leaned forward. "I traveled far and wide and listened carefully when men spoke. When I learned of your reputation, I knew you were the lord I wished to serve. You and your family," he added. "And that includes Lady Avelyn."

"So you believe you can live without her kisses? Continue on without her touch?"

Kenric shot to his feet. "My lord," he sputtered, wine spilling onto the floor.

"Sit back down," the earl instructed. "Mayhap, I spoke out of turn." Michael Devereux rested his cup on a nearby table, his eyes carefully studying Kenric.

Finally, he addressed Kenric again.

"I never expected to find love with a woman," the nobleman confided. "Least of all one as spirited and independent as my Elysande. But I will tell you that my life would be worthless without love in it. Without sharing everything with my wife. My hopes. My dreams. The daily events that take place at Sandbourne."

Devereux sighed, running his hands through his hair. "Elysande is life itself, Kenric. I adore everything about her, even when she pays more attention to her horses than she does to me. I am devoted to making her happy. Our nights—and even many afternoons—are filled with passion," he said, a twinkle in his eye. "I will never be able to get enough of her. I cherish everything about my wife. She is the entire world to me. I would tell you that our bliss goes beyond our love play. Being with Elysande, loving her, has made me a better man."

He paused. "I only know how very dear Avelyn is to the both of us and I wouldn't wish to see her unhappy. In fact, I would want for my sister-in-law all that Elysande and I have found in each other. Avelyn deserves to love—and be loved—as much as her sister is." The earl looked him up and down. "You're as fine a knight as I have ever known, Kenric—and that includes my former liege lord, Geoffrey de Montfort. I would give thanks to our Blessed Lord if Avelyn could be matched with you."

Kenric sat, the goblet propped upon his knee, spilled wine dampening his hand. "You may admire my way with a sword, my lord. My leadership and intelligence. But I have nothing to offer Lady Avelyn beyond my name. My twin brother holds the title and Shadowfaire. And his wife is now with child. I will never be able to give the lady everything she desires."

Kenric paused. "And there is the matter of my lost honor. I never speak of it, but 'tis the reason I no longer wear my spurs."

Devereux assessed him. "I wondered why you did not wear them when you came to Sandbourne. What of it?"

He swallowed, knowing his liege lord asked him out of concern for Avelyn. "An incident occurred on the day I swore my knightly oath. Something too painful for me to share with you, my lord. Only know that because I hurt someone deeply, it changed the course of her life. And mine. Mayhap, one day I'll once again feel worthy enough to attach them. But because of what happened that day, I cannot marry. Ever. No matter how much my heart desires it."

He set the goblet down and ran a hand through his hair. "Lady Avelyn will have no problem finding a husband at court. With her beauty and grace and loving spirit, men will clamor for her hand." He sighed. "I must excuse myself, my lord."

Lord Michael gave him a sympathetic look that ate into Kenric's very soul.

Then a piercing cry came from the other room. The earl leapt to his feet, uncertainty on his face. This nobleman, an unmatched leader of men and expert warrior, looked as if he might come undone at any moment, thanks to his wife being in pain as he stood by helplessly.

"Go," the earl whispered, thrusting his hands behind his back as he started pacing the solar. A low moan came from the bedchamber. "But if Avelyn has crept into your heart, Kenric, she will never leave. And you won't be able to push her out, no matter how hard you may try."

Kenric nodded brusquely and exited the room, knowing Michael Devereux spoke the truth.

CHAPTER 21

"AVELYN, YOU NEED to put David down," Elysande said. "You must change your gown for my churching ceremony."

Avelyn brought her nephew's tiny fist close to her face and rubbed her nose against it. He gurgled, his wide eyes looking at her in adoration. She loved everything about young David Devereux and was fascinated by all that he did.

Elysande came to stand beside her sister and reached her arms out. "Hand him over. He has spit up on your *cotehardie*. Father Tib would be horrified if you came into the chapel smelling like soured milk."

"All right." She kissed the soft cheek of the babe and reluctantly returned him to his mother. "I won't be long."

"Meet us downstairs in the great hall," her mother instructed. "We'll leave from there for the ceremony."

She returned to her bedchamber and quickly removed the soiled *cotehardie*, which had been stained while she burped David. The last three weeks had been the happiest of her life. The birth of David Devereux had taken hours, but Elysande, thankfully, came through it with no problems. Life at Sandbourne now revolved around the needs of the tiny child who was heir to the estate.

Avelyn was glad her nephew took up so much of her time. When not rocking or singing to him, she busied herself making clothes for the babe. It helped keep her mind off Kenric Fairfax. She didn't know how to change the stubborn knight's rejection of her and still hadn't arrived at a way to tell him of his true heritage, so she thrust it aside for now. When Geoffrey and Merryn arrived for their visit tomorrow, she would seek out their advice.

A new *cotehardie* of pale blue now smoothed into place, she hurried downstairs. As she entered the great hall, she saw David resting in the crook of his father's arm. Michael wore an expression of wonder and contentment as he gazed at the tiny infant. Avelyn had known from the way he treated Elysande that Michael was a good husband and he proved on a daily basis that he would also be the best of fathers.

"Go now, sweetheart," Michael told his wife. "David and I will sit here and have a wonderful conversation about you while you're being churched."

"As if he could understand you," Elysande said, stroking her son's head.

Michael grinned. "We men understand each other from an early age. Be careful, Wife, or I will tell him all of your secrets."

She kissed her husband and then her son's forehead. "Be good, you two. And stay out of trouble."

Avelyn joined her mother and Lady Orella as the midwife made her appearance. Now that all of the women who had aided in David's birth had arrived, they could go to the chapel for Elysande's churching. She linked arms with her sister as they walked the short distance to the chapel.

Father Tib awaited them outside the massive oak door and began the ceremony. Elysande hadn't been allowed to enter the chapel after she'd given birth until this churching took place. The priest gave a blessing to Elysande after her recovery from childbirth. Avelyn knew this ceremony was partly a thanksgiving for her sister's survival. So many women died in childbirth and she was grateful both Elysande and David had come through the birth unscathed.

They entered the church. Elysande moved to the altar and knelt. Father Tib blessed her with holy water and said a series of prayers over her. At the end, he had Elysande rise. He then explained to her that she would now be able to attend mass once more and receive the sacraments, as well as partake in all womanly tasks.

The group of women strolled back toward the keep in high spirits.

"Michael will be glad that you can, once more, bake bread," Lady Orella said. "He told me no one bakes a loaf the way you do—filled with plenty of yeast and even more love."

Elysande laughed. "I hope I have time to do so since David keeps me very busy. It's nice to know that Father Tib has purified me and that I can return to things such as preparing food once again."

They ascended the steps and returned to the great hall. Servants pulled trestle tables away from the walls since the workers were returning for their nightly meal. Avelyn noticed Sela coming her way.

The noblewoman had grown even more distant since David's birth. She hadn't participated in it, claiming herself too squeamish. She had only held the babe once, an uncomfortable look on her face. Once he began to wail, she quickly returned him to Elysande's arms. Sela spent much of her time locked away in her bedchamber and Avelyn felt they'd become strangers.

"How did the churching ceremony go?" Sela asked.

"It was simple and short," Avelyn told her. "Now Elysande can resume all her former activities."

"You've spent much of your time with her and David," her friend said.

"It's the reason I wanted to be at Sandbourne this summer. I enjoy being around them. David is a sweet babe and I love holding him."

"Would you be able to make time for us to visit? Mayhap after we dine this evening?"

Avelyn was touched by the request and had hated their estrangement. Though she believed they would never truly be as close as they were while at court, she hoped they would part on good terms. It seemed Sela offered Avelyn an olive branch now and she was most willing to accept it.

"I would, indeed, enjoy sharing time with you this evening," she assured Sela.

They sat together and chatted about the babe and things happening at Sandbourne as they ate. Avelyn shared that Merryn and Geoffrey would be arriving by the noon meal the next day and that

Michael said they were bringing a friend with them who wanted to look over some of Michael's horses for breeding purposes.

"Do you know anything about this friend, other than his interest in horses?" Sela asked.

"Nay. Michael didn't share his name, only that the nobleman would be at Sandbourne a day or two before he returned to his own estates."

At once, she saw the glimmer in Sela's eyes at the prospect of a new male coming to Sandbourne. Avelyn imagined Sela cozying up to this guest. She supposed not much had changed when it came to Sela and her interest in men.

They finished their meal. Avelyn said she wanted to go up and say goodnight to David. "I'll return straight away to your room and can stay as long as you like."

"I'll see you there."

Avelyn excused herself, hoping that they might continue the pleasant conversation that had begun at dinner. She hoped Sela would not pump her for any more information about the guest coming tomorrow and that, instead, they could speak of other things.

Elysande and Michael had taken to dining in the solar several nights a week, enjoying family time together. Her sister could nurse David while they ate. She'd told Avelyn she looked forward to this time alone with her husband and son.

She knocked on the solar's door and Michael answered, ushering her in.

"We're giving David a bath or rather we're attempting to. He's a most slippery boy."

Avelyn laughed. "Wait till he is older. He'll be splashing about so much that you'll wonder who's receiving the bath—David or you!"

She went to the cooing babe, who seemed to enjoy being in the warm water, and kissed his damp head. "I had to come say goodnight to my favorite Devereux," she told him. Knowing how Elysande cherished her family time, she excused herself and made her way toward Sela's bedchamber.

The door was slightly ajar. Avelyn thought Sela must have left it so for her convenience. She pushed it opened without knocking and froze in her tracks.

Sela was kissing a man—a very large, very familiar man.

Avelyn gasped as Kenric pushed Sela away. He turned his head and caught sight of her, a pained expression on his face.

Sela also glanced Avelyn's way. She looked like a cat that had gotten into the cream—utterly satisfied and not remorseful in the least.

Avelyn stumbled back and raced across the hall to her own chamber. She slammed the door behind her and leaned on it for support as her limbs shook. Her insides twisted and she thought she would be sick.

A strong rap sounded behind her head from the other side of the door, startling her.

"Avelyn!" Kenric called out. "Avelyn! Open the door. I beg you. I can explain."

Seeing Kenric Fairfax was the last thing she wanted to do. Her body trembled violently now, his betrayal seeping through her pores.

The pounding continued.

She didn't want Elysande and Michael—or anyone else—to be witnesses to this scene. With reluctance, she opened the door in order to silence him.

Tension coiled around his body as if he would strike at any moment. Avelyn glanced past him and saw that Sela stood in the doorway across the corridor, an amused smile playing about her lips.

"You may enter," she said evenly, not meeting his eye. "I will close the door for a moment if only to give us privacy from . . . her."

Kenric looked over his shoulder and then back. He nodded and stepped into the room. Avelyn shut the door behind him.

"Calm yourself," she said. "I don't want you disturbing my sister and her family. Once you've done so, you need to leave."

"But I must speak to you," he implored.

She brought herself to her full height, using her best posture she had learned from riding, and willed the tremors to cease. "We have nothing to speak about. Take a few deep breaths, my lord—and then leave."

"Avelyn." He wrapped a hand around her upper arm. "It's not what you think."

She looked at his fingers resting on her. Once, she had longed for him to touch her. Now, she felt violated. She shrugged it away and took a step back from him.

He must have realized how upset she was. He didn't make another attempt to touch her. He said quietly, "She asked me for my help. Said that she had something heavy that needed to be brought downstairs." Kenric ran a hand through his thick hair. "I thought . . . I thought . . . it might be her trunk."

Avelyn frowned, not understanding him.

He rushed to explain. "I know something occurred between the two of you. You were thick as thieves when we left London, but there's been a distance between you since we arrived at Sandbourne. Lady Sela has seemed most unhappy."

"And you were trying to cheer her up?" Avelyn regretted the bitter words that slipped out.

"Nay. I thought she'd decided to return to London and that was what she wanted me for. But without warning, she latched on to me. She . . . kissed me."

"And you let her."

Kenric shook his head violently. "I was stunned. I pushed her away. And then," his voice cracked, "I saw you. Avelyn, I have no feelings for this silly woman. I only—"

"I don't care for your tiresome explanation, my lord. It's none of my business. I would ask now for you to leave me in peace."

"Avelyn?"

She gazed into his eyes and what she saw nearly broke her. She turned away, giving him her back. "Please leave, my lord. I would ask that you not address me again."

"Of course, my lady." She heard the control that had now returned to his voice. Once more, Kenric Fairfax was a stoic knight. Avelyn heard the door open. For a long moment, only silence reigned. Then it closed softly.

She spun around, the room now empty, and slumped to floor, hot tears falling down her cheeks.

CHAPTER 22

AVELYN SLEPT LITTLE the night before and almost dozed off during mass the next morning. She pinched herself to stay awake. But being awake meant her thoughts were flooded with images of Kenric. She couldn't rid her mind of the scene she'd stumbled upon. Was he telling the truth? Had Sela Runford lured him to her chamber, all to make Avelyn jealous? Or to hurt her beyond measure?

If so, Sela had been successful—on both accounts.

Avelyn boiled with rage when she thought of her so-called friend's body pressed against Kenric's tall, broad frame, Sela's arms entwined about his neck, her lips greedily pressing against the knight's. If Avelyn had been a cat, Sela would no longer possess her eyes, for Avelyn would have clawed them out.

She held on to the anger—for if she didn't—misery would take hold of her and eat her alive. It filled her with agony, like a physical pain suffered. In her heart, she wanted to believe that Kenric was innocent in the display of affection and that Sela had deliberately thrown herself at him, all to hurt Avelyn.

She dug her nails into her palms, trying to channel the pain somewhere else. If this was the case, Sela must truly despise her. What kind of person was Sela Runford to ingratiate herself with Avelyn again, all for the sole purpose of punishing her? Sela had acted as if she hadn't a care in the world and that they could pick up their friendship where they'd left off. To be able to blithely converse and offer false kindness while Sela plotted against her shocked Avelyn to her very core. She'd never known such wickedness.

Avelyn wished she could ask Elysande to have Michael return Sela to London at once, but she didn't want to offer an explanation for such a request. With company arriving today, Elysande already had a lot on her hands and didn't need more distractions from her duties as a hostess and new mother.

Even if Sela left Sandbourne, Avelyn doubted anything would change between her and Kenric. He seemed to be a lost cause to her. Though she longed for him and wished to shower him with her love and trust, she was coming to realize that nothing would change the knight's mind. Instead, she would have to be the one to change. She'd taken the first step last night by asking him not to speak with her again.

For when he spoke to her, she burned for his touch. She wanted to taste him, hold him, be held by him. So it was better for them to have nothing to do with one another. Avelyn would mend in time. She was stronger than she'd given herself credit for. In time, she supposed she would enter a marriage, hopefully with a man she could respect. Mayhap, in time, her feelings might turn tender toward her husband as the years passed and their children entered the world.

But it would always be Kenric Fairfax that she loved with her heart and soul.

Avelyn passed the morning helping Elysande care for David and making last minute preparations for the de Montfort party's arrival. All too soon, a servant arrived and announced that their guests had been spotted and would arrive in the next few minutes. She accompanied Elysande and Michael, who immediately took David from his mother, as they went to greet the de Montforts. Her mother and Lady Orella joined them.

"Michael is quite smitten with his son," Avelyn told Elysande.

Her sister smiled. "I wouldn't have it any other way."

A party of over two dozen rode into the bailey. Avelyn waved, spying both Geoffrey and Merryn. Geoffrey had Hal seated in front of him and the young boy helped his father hold the reins. Merryn had a bundled Edward nestled against her. She also saw both of the twins, happy that Ancel could come along with Alys for this visit.

Then Avelyn recognized a figure from the royal court in London. Lord Sewell Talbot was a dozen years older than she, with a wife and two children at home in the country. He'd flirted with her outrageously and even tried to steal a kiss upon one occasion after drawing her into a darkened alcove. When Avelyn let it be known that she didn't welcome his advances, he laughed it off—and they'd become quite friendly after that. He shared with her tidbits about various courtiers and had explained some of the politics of the day.

Merryn lifted Edward from the pouch he rode in and handed him to Alys before she made her way directly to Michael. One look from her and he handed David over without a word.

She cooed to the babe and pressed a kiss upon his brow before she looked at Elysande. "He's the most marvelous babe in the world," she proclaimed. "Next to my four darlings, of course."

Elysande laughed. "David is life itself."

As Geoffrey strolled up, Michael added, "He already has everyone at Sandbourne wound about his smallest finger." The two noblemen greeted each other with slaps on the back.

Geoffrey said, "We're happy for your new addition." He then greeted his sister with a kiss and spoke to Lady Orella.

Suddenly, Hal appeared underfoot, dancing about. "Michael, Michael!"

The earl swept him up. "And how are you, my good friend Hal?"

Hal gave Michael a sloppy kiss and then squirmed, ready to be set down.

"Talbot, come over here," Geoffrey ordered.

Avelyn watched the new visitor amble toward them. When he caught sight of her, he made straight to her.

"My lady." He bowed and reached for her hand, placing a brief kiss upon it. "I had no idea you would be here."

"Lady Elysande is my sister, my lord." She turned and held out her hand. "The Earl and Countess of Sandbourne. My mother, Lady Mary, and the earl's mother, Lady Orella. This is Lord Sewell Talbot."

The handsome nobleman greeted them all. "I met Lady Avelyn at court. She broke hearts left and right—including mine," he explained.

"I doubt that, Talbot," Merryn chimed in. "I'm not sure if you even have a heart."

Talbot gave Merryn an anguished look and pretended to stab himself in the heart. "Oh, but you wound me, my lady."

Merryn's brows shot up. "I know you to be an incorrigible flirt. You flit from one woman to another. You have no time for your heart to break."

He flashed a smile. "I'll admit that I tried to win Lady Avelyn's favor but, instead, I won her friendship, a far more valuable gift."

"So you're a part of the royal court?" Elysande asked.

Talbot shrugged. "From time to time. I chose not go on summer progress with them. I'm looking to expand my stables and asked help from my friend, Geoffrey, who has the best knowledge of them." He eyed Elysande with appreciation. "He believes you, my lady, know more about horses than most men and that your husband's stables have some of the finest horseflesh in all of southern England."

Michael placed an arm around his wife's shoulder. "The countess is more than knowledgeable. And one of my knights, Sir Kenric Fairfax, is another you need to speak with about my horses. But come, let's go inside. The noon meal is about to take place." He glanced over to Merryn. "And you'd better return my son to me, my lady. He's not yours for the taking, no matter how much you enjoy babes."

They all laughed and made their way up the staircase, Hal leading the way. Lord Sewell fell into step beside Avelyn, placing her hand upon his arm in order to escort her inside.

"I see the resemblance between you and your sister," he remarked. "It's a pleasant surprise finding you here—especially without your shadow."

"I beg your pardon?"

"You know I mean Lady Sela Runford. It was hard to hold a conversation with you without her hovering nearby."

"Actually, she accompanied me to Sandbourne for the summer,

my lord."

Sewell frowned. "I see."

"But we have grown apart during our time here," Avelyn added.

"Good."

They reached the entrance and filed in. She wondered why Lord Sewell thought her estrangement with Sela a good thing. Determined to find out, she leaned over and asked, "Is there something I should know?"

He gave her a cool smile. "Many things, my lady." He glanced over and scowled. "But we'll speak of them another time."

Avelyn turned and saw Sela hovering at the doors leading into the great hall. She stiffened slightly as Sela came forward.

"What a surprise to see you at Sandbourne, Lord Sewell."

"I felt the same when I heard you were present, Lady Sela."

"You must catch me up on all that's happened at court since we left in May. You must know some gossip which you can share with me." Sela gently wrenched the blond nobleman away from Avelyn and led him into the great hall.

"I see she hasn't changed."

Avelyn turned and saw Alys de Montfort standing behind her, her small brother still in her arms, fast asleep.

"You've never liked Lady Sela, Alys."

Her cousin shrugged. "It doesn't matter. You do."

"Actually, I don't. Not anymore."

Alys' eyes went round, then a smile crossed her face. "It's good to see you, Cousin."

Avelyn held out her hands. "May I?"

Alys handed Edward over.

"My, he's grown heavy since I stopped at Kinwick." She touched the babe's nose. "You are a most precious child, Edward, and you're close in age to your cousin, David," she told him. "The two of you, along with Hal, will have so much fun together."

"Hello, Avelyn."

She turned and saw Ancel. "Oh, my!" she exclaimed, seeing the boy standing next to her. "Ancel, you've grown so tall since I saw you last summer. How do you fare at Winterbourne?"

"The earl is hard to please, but I'm learning much under his tutelage. He allowed me to come home to Kinwick a week early so I could accompany Mother and Father to Sandbourne. He knew I was eager to see Lord Michael and my cousins."

"Well, I'm glad Lord Hardwin was so generous. It's good to see you. Come, both of you, let's go in to dine. Elysande has made all of your favorites."

AFTER THE NOON MEAL, Elysande and Merryn wanted the young children to be put down for a nap. Avelyn assisted in getting David, Edward, and a very fussy, protesting Hal to bed. The two grandmothers decided to stay with the children while the rest decided to walk down to the stables to show Lord Sewell the Sandbourne horses.

Michael had requested that Kenric, Ralf, and Martin accompany them. Avelyn knew all three knights to be expert horsemen and supposed that Michael might have them ride a few of the horses to show off their lines. Sela placed herself between Ralf and Martin on the walk through the bailey, chattering away with an arm linked through both men's arms. Kenric separated himself from the trio, but she saw Geoffrey engage him in conversation.

Avelyn found Lord Sewell at her elbow again and was ready to have her questions answered by him.

"I see Lady Sela never changes," he said. "She always has to be around wherever men gather and become the center of attention."

"I've come to know her better since we've been away from court and have found we aren't suitable companions," Avelyn told him. "Would you now tell me of what you hinted at earlier?"

He steered them away from the large group and slowed his pace till everyone had passed before he fell back in line behind them and continued toward the stables.

"Lady Sela is not your friend," Lord Sewell said bluntly. "I tried to find you and warn you, but you'd already left court when the rumors swirled enough for me to be concerned regarding your reputation."

"My reputation?" Avelyn's stomach lurched.

"Did you ever wonder when you first arrived why she latched on to you? And that she possessed no other friends?"

"I thought her only being friendly. We seemed to have more in common than I did with others."

"I believe that she deliberately isolated you from other women. On purpose."

Her heart began beating faster. "Go on."

"Sela Runford has said many harmful and unfair things about you, my lady. At first, I took no notice of it, for she's an insignificant person at court." He shook his head. "She has been a false friend—smiling to your face and treacherous behind your back."

She gripped his arm tightly as understanding dawned. "I used to feel others stare at me as I passed. They would grow silent when I went by them. I always had an odd feeling that they spoke ill of me, but I thought it was my own insecurities about being new at court that caused me to imagine this."

"Nay, it wasn't your imagination. The rumors grew worse before your departure. Do you know anything about missing items in the queen's chambers?"

Avelyn stopped. "Aye," she said softly. "The queen misplaced a comb. A shawl. A pair of hose. Just before we left, Lady Agnes told us she couldn't find a silk handkerchief that the king had gifted to the queen." A sick feeling washed over Avelyn as she remembered finding one identical to the queen's in Sela's trunk.

"Lady Sela has given the impression that *you* are the one who has taken these items—and more that have gone missing among the other ladies-in-waiting."

Her jaw dropped. "But I would never—"

"I know that, my lady, and I believe most courtiers do, too. But you are fairly new to the palace. You've kept yourself separate from the other women who live there and you're most popular with the men. That causes some women's jealousies to rise."

Avelyn swallowed hard as she blinked away tears. "Have . . . have these rumors . . . have they reached the queen?"

Lord Sewell shook his head. "I think not. For if they had, she would have spoken to you immediately. Queen Philippa is not one to tolerate dishonesty—much less thievery." He gave her a sad smile. "I'm sorry I had to bring this to your attention, my lady, but you deserved to know."

Determination filled her. "I'm glad you did, my lord. I plan to confront Sela. Now."

Avelyn broke away from him. The group had reached the stables and started to file in. She hurried to the front where Sela stood and said, "I must speak to you at once."

Sela cocked her head. "Your tone is sharp, Avelyn. Is something wrong?" she asked sweetly.

"Something is very wrong and you're at the root of it."

Conversation ceased around them. Avelyn saw the puzzled looks as everyone stared at her. She shut out everything around her and focused on the treacherous woman before her.

"I'm going to ask you a direct question, Sela. Actually, more than one. I expect an immediate—and honest—answer."

A red flush sprang up on the noblewoman's pale neck and crawled up her cheeks as her eyes cut over to Lord Sewell and back. Sela brought fisted hands to her waist. "Go ahead. I'm just sorry that your petty jealousy over my relationship with Sir Kenric has caused you to challenge me in such a public way." Sela's voice softened. "Should we not go and speak in private? As friends should?"

"Nay," Avelyn told her. "I want witnesses to hear how deeply you've wronged me." She drew a calming breath and then tossed out her accusation. "Have you spread false rumors about me at the royal court?"

Sela tittered, her eyes darting about. "Why would I speak ill of my closest and dearest friend?"

She narrowed her eyes. "That's exactly what I wish to know. Will I be accused of thievery when I return to court? By the queen herself?"

Avelyn heard the gasps around them but continued. "Have you stolen from the other ladies-in-waiting—*and the queen*—and blamed me for your actions?"

Sela began to sway. Both Ralf and Martin reached out for her, but she slapped their hands away. "Leave me be!" she commanded.

"I asked you a question. I want your answer. Now."

Sela looked about helplessly, her mouth falling open, tears gathering in her eyes. Avelyn saw the moment she gave up, knowing she couldn't weasel her way out with pretty words and flirtatious actions. Sela took a step closer to Avelyn and lashed out in fury.

"I've lived at court my entire life. My father is a favored man who advises the king. I had the attention of any man I chose until *you* arrived. You, with your fresh face and country clothes, interested in everything from history to poetry to music. You were not at court a day until you had the attention of everyone.

"And I hated you for it."

Sela's face had grown redder and her body began to shake. "So I befriended you, the lost and wide-eyed Avelyn Le Cler. You clung to me all while you curried favor with the queen and every eligible man at court. It should have been me they focused on. Me! Not you."

She kicked the dirt at her feet. "So I told a few little lies about you. I didn't think anyone would believe them, but a few of the women did—and passed them on. And then I took a hand mirror from that tyrant, Agnes, who always orders everyone about as if she were the queen and not Philippa. You know what? I enjoyed the feeling it gave me every time I pulled out that mirror and saw myself in it."

"But you took more than a simple mirror," Avelyn accused. "And you blamed me for it."

Sela's eyes blazed in anger. "So what if I did? Each time I felt powerful when I did so. I took a prayer book. A pair of stockings. A few ribbons. Then some letters. When I slipped something into my pockets and no one discovered it, it was exhilarating. Then I saw an opportunity and seized a comb of the queen's."

"And her silk handkerchief," Avelyn said. "The one I found in your trunk not long ago. The one you told me your father gave to you."

Sela laughed. "You mean the one I blamed you for taking?" Then tears welled in her eyes. She shuddered and crossed her arms protectively in front of her. "But . . . I went too far. I . . . I stole a necklace from the queen. The very day you were leaving for Sandbourne. I was so afraid someone would find it in my trunk. So I hurried to your chamber and begged to go to Sandbourne with you."

"Where is the queen's necklace now?" Avelyn demanded.

Sela smirked. "I left it in *your* room. While you and Alys hurried after the page that was leading you to your escort party in the courtyard, I slipped it inside your mattress. I couldn't dare be caught with it."

"So if someone finds it, I will be blamed?"

"Aye!" Sela hissed. "You came to court with nothing, but you have everything. I hated you for it." She paused. "I still hate you."

A calm descended upon Avelyn. "I pity you, Sela. You've been given every opportunity and have squandered it. I gave you my friendship freely and loved you as a sister, but you've betrayed me in the worst way."

Avelyn turned to Michael. His face grim, he nodded. Michael glared at Sela and said, "Return to your chamber in the keep, my lady, and remain inside it. A guard will be posted at your door until you leave Sandbourne tomorrow, never to return."

Lord Sewell spoke up. "If it pleases you, Lady Avelyn, I can see this woman to where the royal court now resides and place her into her father's hands, apprising him of the situation. Lord Runford is an ambitious yet decent man. He will see that the queen's necklace is returned and no blame placed upon your shoulders."

The nobleman looked at Sela with a withering glance. She cringed, dropping her head in shame.

"Knowing her father as I do," Sewell continued, "his punishment will be to banish her to his country estate far in the north. Or, mayhap, marry her to a man old enough to be her grandfather since it's obvious she requires a strong hand and constant supervision. Lady Sela will no longer grace the court with her presence. You will never have to see her there again."

"Thank you, my lord." Avelyn trembled, the anger having rushed from her in a swoop, leaving her physically weak.

Lord Sewell said, "I would only ask that I first conduct my business with Lord Michael, which may take a day or two. But I'm sure Lady Sela can remain out of sight until I prepare to leave with my men."

"We would be most grateful to you for your help in this atrocious matter, Lord Sewell," Michael interjected. He motioned to the two knights nearest Sela. "Take this woman back to the keep. Remain at her chamber door until I send men to relieve you."

"Yes, my lord," Ralf said. He reached for Sela, but she glared at him. Without a backward glance, she marched from the stable, Ralf and Martin on her heels.

Elysande and Merryn rushed to comfort Avelyn. Each hugged her tightly, asking if she was all right. She assured them that she was.

Her eyes met her uncle's as he came to stand next to her. Geoffrey said, "You may not have ridden into battle with your enemy carrying a sword in hand, but you bested that enemy all the same, with courage and dignity. I'm so very proud of you, Avelyn."

She went into Geoffrey's arms. He locked her in a powerful hug, bringing her comfort.

Avelyn looked out at those gathered around, seeing their concern for her. Only Kenric Fairfax stood apart, a grim look upon his face.

He looked as if he could kill at that moment.

CHAPTER 23

KENRIC STOOD GUARD in front of Lady Sela Runford's bedchamber, anger still boiling within him at what he'd learned yesterday. The noblewoman was pure evil, worse than any enemy met in battle. She'd befriended an inexperienced Avelyn Le Cler and betrayed her by weaving vicious lies about her. He wished he could mete out the justice due and strangle the Runford girl with his bare hands—and no one would ever find the body.

He shook off the violent thought. It was unlike him to become emotional. Among the men he knew, he remained cool and rational at all times. But everything about Avelyn stirred his blood. He hurt—because she did.

He wondered what her return to court at summer's end would be like. Whether true or not, Kenric knew Sela's rumors would follow Avelyn. Not all would believe them, considering the source, but enough might to make her a lonely outcast. More than anything, he wished she wouldn't go back to London.

Then he asked himself where she could go. Her mother's marriage today would have Lady Mary and Sir Charles making their home at the manor house on Sandbourne land. Her only sister resided on the estate, as well. If not in London, Avelyn would be here—where he couldn't speak to her because she wished it so.

Kenric realized he had wounded her as much as Sela had—if not more. Mayhap, his penance would be to see her on a daily basis, so close, yet a woman he could never have.

It would be best for her if her family married her off quickly before the untrue rumors spread. With Geoffrey de Montfort's connections, not to mention Avelyn's angelic beauty, it wouldn't be difficult to find a suitor. Yet the thought of another man touching Avelyn's satiny smooth skin, his hand on her bare breast, thrusting his manhood inside her, pleasuring her until she cried out—those thoughts would drive Kenric into madness.

What did he have to look forward to? A miserable existence while the woman he loved married another. He could picture her future visits to Sandbourne, where she would proudly show off her children to her sister and mother. Kenric would see the happiness written across her face.

And it would destroy him.

His gut told him he should go elsewhere, move on and find a new liege lord to serve. If he left this area behind and headed far north, Avelyn Le Cler—and even his remaining family at Shadowfaire—would be buried as the past.

Kenric decided to ask Lord Michael's permission to accompany Lord Sewell and his men when they took Lady Sela to her father. Once the woman had been handed to her father and no longer posed a danger to his beloved, he'd return to Sandbourne and give his notice to Lord Michael. He could start over in a new life. It would be empty of love, but he couldn't stay here and punish himself over and over by seeing Avelyn now or in the future.

A servant arrived with a tray. Kenric unlocked the door and allowed her into the bedchamber, where he saw Lady Sela pacing as a caged animal. She stopped long enough to give him an unpleasant smile. It infuriated him that this woman had used him, kissing him to make Avelyn suffer.

In that moment, an overwhelming urge to protect Avelyn swept over him. Kenric believed that he could protect her like no other—especially from the likes of vipers such as Lady Sela Runford. The strong feeling made him want to throw caution to the wind and do whatever it took to always watch out for Avelyn. But would he ever have a chance to do so? Not if he left Sandbourne behind. He found himself torn as never before, unsure where his future lay, much less with whom.

The servant set the tray down and scurried out. Kenric locked the door again and placed the key in his pocket. His arms returned to his side as he pushed aside all thoughts and left his mind a void.

Eventually, music drifted up the stairs, accompanied by the smell of food that made his mouth water. He supposed, by now, the wedding between Lady Mary and Sir Charles must be over and all gathered in the great hall for the celebration. Kenric was glad he'd offered to stand guard duty today instead of attending the nuptial mass. He didn't want to hear words of love and promises the older couple would make to one another with Avelyn in the same place.

He noticed Martin coming down the corridor and assumed the soldier came to relieve him.

"You've been on your feet for hours," his brother knight said. "Come, go join the celebration."

"I'd just as soon stay here. I'm in no mood for—"

"Go." Martin placed a hand on Kenric's shoulder. "It's obvious you have feelings for the lady and she could certainly use some comfort after yesterday's events."

Kenric frowned. "If you think—"

Martin squeezed his shoulder hard. "It's not what I think. It's important what you think. What you know." The knight gave him an encouraging look. "Look inside your heart, Kenric Fairfax." Martin dropped his hand.

Wordlessly, he handed over the key to Lady Sela's chamber and started down the hall, Martin's words ringing in his ears.

Could he truly have a future with this woman?

It was time to find out.

Kenric went to the great hall. Trestle tables laden with every imaginable food provided a feast for his eyes. His belly growled at the sight. He hadn't eaten all day and decided he should before seeking Avelyn out. It wouldn't do to try and romance the beauty only to be interrupted by a gurgling stomach. Joining a table of fellow knights, he ate only enough to satisfy him. His eyes searched the great hall as he chewed, but he didn't spy her anywhere.

Excusing himself, he wandered aimlessly and then followed the sound of the music. The nuptial celebration had spilled outside into the cool, early July night, with dozens dancing in the moonlight. Kenric saw Lord Geoffrey and Lady Merryn with their two youngest and Lady Elysande and Lord Michael with their infant son. Both couples radiated happiness.

He wanted that for himself and Avelyn.

Like a lightning bolt that struck him from the blue, it came to him that love was what mattered. He might not be able to provide a wealth of material goods for Avelyn Le Cler, but she had told him she loved him. In his heart, he knew she wasn't a woman impressed by money or power. She had bared her deepest feelings to him and he had callously turned her away.

Kenric hoped it wasn't too late for them.

He passed young Alys de Montfort dancing with a fleet-footed Lord Sewell, while Ancel de Montfort partnered a laughing Lady Orella. Sir Charles twirled his new wife about. Even in the older knight's eyes, Kenric saw the love the man showered upon Lady Mary.

But where was Avelyn? His curiosity turned to concern as he actively searched for her. He wondered if she could have returned to her bedchamber since he couldn't locate her.

In a flash, he realized where she would be.

Kenric made his way to the Sandbourne stables, remembering her comment about the faithfulness and affection of dogs and horses. Something told him Avelyn would be with Starlight tonight, seeking comfort in the midst of the happy occasion.

The bright moon made it easy for him to make his way to the stables. He opened the door and glimpsed inside. As he expected, he saw a faint light about halfway down the long row of stalls. As he drew closer, he heard her humming before he reached Starlight's stall. Kenric paused and listened to it, and the melancholy in the tune tugged at his heart.

No longer hesitating, he strode to the stall and looked inside.

Avelyn had her back to him, a brush in her hand as she curried Starlight's side. She hummed softly as she stroked the horse. Desire flooded Kenric at the sight of her. He stepped into the stall and slipped his arms around her waist.

"Oh!" She dropped the brush she held and whipped her head around. Her lips parted as if she wished to speak, but no words came forth.

He yanked her to him, wanting the feel of her body against his. His lips found her throat and nibbled on it. A contented sigh escaped from her and she reached a hand up to stroke his face. He reveled in the touch of her fingers.

Kenric spun her around and caught her waist, spanning it with his hands. Her sky blue eyes went wide as she licked her lips nervously. He needed to taste her, now and always. He crushed her to him as his mouth came down on hers. Plundering, demanding, wanting everything she had to give. Her hands plunged into his hair, kneading his scalp, pulling him nearer as her tongue mated with his.

His hands rode up her ribcage and came to rest just under her full breasts. His thumbs reached out, brushing across her nipples, teasing them through her layers of clothing. She began to moan, her fingers bunching his gypon tightly. He allowed his hands to encircle her breasts and then squeezed them lightly. The perfect globes were meant to fit in them. His mouth touched the top of one breast and he lightly ran his tongue along it as his hand slipped under her skirts.

His fingers found her core dripping, ready for him. Slipping two fingers inside, he stroked her as his other hand pulled away her *cotehardie*. He pushed down her kirtle and chemise until he had freed her breast. His mouth closed on it and suckled her as his fingers moved in and out. Avelyn writhed against him, her breathing fast and shallow. Her head fell back as he increased the speed of his fingers. He sensed the coiled tension building within her.

Suddenly, her body trembled. She gasped, then whimpered, small cries of sweet pleasure sounding as she clutched his gypon, pulling and pushing on it repeatedly as she rode the wave of ecstasy. He grazed his teeth against her erect nipple, causing more shudders. She held on to him as her body began to still.

Then she wept, her breath coming in hitches. Kenric brought his mouth to her cheeks and kissed at the tears.

"Did I hurt you, my love?" he asked, afraid to hear her answer.

"Nay," she whispered. She bit her lip as her eyes searched his. Finally, she said, "that was . . . so beautiful. As if two halves of a whole had been united after many years apart."

Kenric smiled at her words, brushing away more tears with his callused thumbs. "If you think this was meant to be, wait till we join our bodies together, Avelyn, when God Almighty has blessed our union. When we will lie naked, our limbs entwined, and two truly do become one."

"But I thought—"

He placed a finger against her lips. "You always knew. You always believed in the two of us together. I was the fool that thought you needed another man." He kissed her forehead. "I realized that the love between us is rare and that I shouldn't cast it aside."

Sweeping her up into his arms, he told her, "I may not have riches on this earth, but everything I have is yours."

Avelyn rewarded him with a slow smile. "So, you're not merely wedded to being a knight? If I understand your words, you wish us to marry?"

"Aye." He gave her a lingering kiss so that she wouldn't doubt him.

"I do want to marry you, my love. I want you to bear our sons and daughters. I wish to partake in the joy that I see when I look at your sister and Lord Michael together. I want the same happiness that is obvious when your uncle and his wife exchange a tender look. And I would grow old and gray with you. Many years from now, we'll look back on when we were young and our love was new and fragile. We'll laugh, knowing we've weathered many storms in our years together and be fulfilled in a love that has grown stronger over our lifetime."

She cupped his face and gave him a slow, sweet kiss, one full of hope and promise.

Then she drew back, a mischievous grin on her face. "And I'll remind you of how stubborn you once were, pushing aside the love of your life out of pride or whatever manly reason you thought must keep us apart. Not often, mind you, but I'll bring it up just enough to keep you in line."

Kenric laughed. "I will let you—only because I do love you so. It will make our children groan and run and hide when they see their parents turn affectionate with one another."

"We'll laugh when they do so. And we'll hope they'll find the same lasting love for themselves one day."

"I love you, Avelyn Le Cler. I eagerly will do your bidding, now and forever."

He kissed her again, knowing he'd made the right decision by letting his guard down as pride and arrogance flew out the window. They would start afresh this night and love long and strong forevermore.

"Oh!" Avelyn exclaimed.

Kenric looked up to see Starlight butting her head against Avelyn. He put her back on the ground and gave the horse an affectionate pat.

"You need to behave," he chided the horse. "If you do, your mistress and I will brush you till your coat gleams."

He picked up a brush to lavish attention upon the horse and Avelyn did the same. True to his word, when they had finished, Starlight gleamed just as tonight's moon. Kenric replaced the brushes and they left the stall. He wrapped his arms around the woman he loved, resting his chin against the top of her head. They stood that way in contentment for a long time.

Finally, she asked, "So when will you ask Uncle Geoffrey for my hand?"

He gazed down at her, seeing the glow of happiness on her face. "Tonight."

"I love you, Kenric Fairfax."

"I love you more, Avelyn Le Cler." He paused. "But I must share something with you. If you change your mind regarding our plans, I'll understand."

"What could possibly change my mind? I love you, Kenric, with all my heart."

"Have you ever wondered why I don't wear my spurs?"

She nodded. "I noticed. But I would never ask."

"I wish to tell you why." He kept his arms about her, needing her warmth for encouragement. "I fostered far from home, at Lord Forwin's estate. I spent my youth at Longshire, first as a page, then a squire. Finally, I took my vows and became a knight."

"Was your brother, Roland, there with you?" she asked.

"For a while. But his temperament and health weren't suited to such a harsh climate. He returned to Shadowfaire and grew up there."

"Were you lonely without him?"

"Nay. I thrived under Lord Forwin's tutelage. But my closest friend, Hudd, warned me to stay away from Lord Forwin's daughter. Lady Jannet was a beautiful but spoiled child. The day I received my spurs and took my knightly vows, she declared that she loved me and wanted us to wed."

Avelyn looked thoughtful. "Did this take you by surprise?"

"Aye. I had barely spoken to her in all my years at Longshire. I told her I had just become a knight and that my duty was to her father. I didn't wish to marry." He sighed. "She told her father of her desire to wed me. Lord Forwin had already made other plans for Jannet to wed a wealthy earl, not a penniless knight like myself."

"Lady Jannet did not take this announcement well, I suppose."

Kenric grew still. "Nay." The word came out a whisper. "That night, while the celebration went on recognizing my achievement, all those gathered danced under the moonlight, much like tonight."

Avelyn placed a hand against his chest. The gesture comforted him. Kenric forced himself to continue.

"She went up to the parapet. Everyone stopped and stared at her. She said if we couldn't be together, then she wanted to be with no man." His eyes met hers. "Jannet threw herself from that great height, Avelyn. She killed herself. Because of me."

"But it wasn't your fault."

"My head told me so, but my heart spoke otherwise. I knew she was slightly unbalanced, but I felt responsible for her death. I'd only won my spurs and knighthood that morning, and they represented my badge of honor. I hacked them off, believing I'd disgraced myself. My honor had fled. My code of chivalry seemed broken since I had not protected Lady Jannet and the family I was sworn to die for.

"I have kept my spurs as a reminder of my lost honor."

"I'm glad you told me of this, Kenric." Her palm touched his face. "Yet, it doesn't change the way I feel about you. In fact, I love you all the more. I hope you'll reconsider and choose to wear your spurs once more. You have no blame in this matter. You didn't lead Lady Jannet on or give her false expectations. You're innocent of wrongdoing." Avelyn smiled at him. "You are the most honorable man I know."

Kenric touched his lips to hers in a tender kiss. Just having told her of the events from long ago seemed to cleanse his soul. Mayhap Avelyn was right and he should, once again, wear his spurs.

She broke the kiss and placed a hand against his chest. "Before you speak to my uncle, I also have something I need to tell you." She worried her bottom lip and he saw she grew serious.

Kenric released her. "Do you have a secret lover I must send away?" he teased, trying to change her mood. "Or, mayhap, two?"

Avelyn took his hands. "Listen to me. I have something very important to share with you. I didn't know how to before. I thought . . . well, never mind what I thought. You're here now and you must know of this matter, as you told me of what you wanted me to know."

"What worries you so, dearest?"

"Do you remember when we stopped at Shadowfaire on our way from London to Sandbourne?"

"Aye. How could I forget my mother's death?"

She gripped his hands more tightly. "I fear how you will take this news."

A sense of dread filled him. "Tell me, Avelyn. I bared my deepest secret to you."

"You . . . are the Earl of Shadowfaire. Not your brother."

He dropped her hands and took a step back. "What? Are you mad?"

"Roland was not the firstborn son, Kenric. *You* were."

He couldn't comprehend her words. A fog seemed to surround him.

Her words came out in a rush. "Gussalen told me. She was the only one present during your mother's childbirth. She said you were the firstborn and that Roland came out after you. She lied because she hated your father—and you favored him strongly, while Roland looked like Lady Juliana. She denied you your birthright, Kenric, all because she thought you'd be just like your father.

"And then she killed herself right in front of me. Your mother had died mere moments earlier. The truth then died with Gussalen." Avelyn's eyes swam with tears. "We didn't know each other well then. I didn't think you would believe me if I'd told you what I'd learned."

Kenric felt like he was drowning. He heard what Avelyn said, but it seemed a long way off. Rage filled him.

"You use my mother's passing and Gussalen's death to speak such wicked lies? You selfishly want me to wrestle the title and Shadowfaire away from my twin brother and his unborn child, all because you desire that I possess them?"

Avelyn reached out and placed her hand on his arm, but he shrugged it off.

"I thought you'd be happy marrying *me,* even though I had nothing but my name to give. But I can see that's not enough for you. That once you drew me into your web, you wanted more."

He took a step back. "I didn't think you were like other women who hanker after riches, but I've sorely misjudged you, Avelyn Le Cler. For you to tell such outrageous lies just so you could become a countess—and at my brother's expense? Such an untruth would never be believed by anyone, least of all me."

Kenric quaked with anger. "I trusted you. I *loved* you. And I was not enough for you. Mayhap, Lady Sela didn't spread rumors about you. Mayhap, she had proof that you are a liar and a thief." He glared down at her. "I want nothing to do with a woman of your sort, my lady."

"But you must believe me, Kenric," Avelyn cried. "Gussalen did all of this. *You* should be the earl, not your brother."

"I would only become earl if Roland died and his unborn child is a girl." He stared at her. "God forbid that should occur. But if it did, you would be the last woman I would ever want as my countess."

"Kenric!" She moved to touch him again.

"Nay. Stay far away from me—and hold your tongue when it comes to my family. If you continue to repeat such lies, I won't be responsible for what happens."

Kenric strode away, her pitiful cries falling on deaf ears.

CHAPTER 24

Avelyn's world crashed around her. To go from the soaring elation of having Kenric tell her he loved her and wanted to wed her—then for her to tell him the truth regarding his birth and have him twist it in such a way that it drove a permanent wedge between them. Her legs gave way from under her. She pitched to the ground, doubled over as if he'd run his sword through her. Great sobs engulfed her, sweeping away all the good and leaving only heartache.

Shakily, she rose to her feet. She mustn't let anyone see her in such a state, least of all her mother. Lady Mary had looked years younger all day long, joy apparent on her face now that she'd wed a man of her choice. Avelyn would not ruin this day for her.

Instead of blindly running from the stables, Avelyn drew from an inner reserve of strength and slipped out silently. As she headed back to the keep, she skirted the merrymakers, averting her tearstained face. Thankfully, no one called her name.

Reaching her chamber, she spotted her sister emerging from the solar down the corridor. She supposed Elysande had put David to bed. Avelyn ducked inside and shut the door, hoping Elysande hadn't seen her. She ran to her bed and fell upon it, bawling like a lamb that had lost its mother.

A knock sounded at her door. "Avelyn?"

She mashed her fist against her mouth. It was Merryn's voice. She couldn't let her aunt see her in this state.

"Avelyn, are you all right?"

She heard muffled voices outside the door and supposed Elysande had joined Merryn. She'd better answer them.

"I'm unwell," she called. "Please . . . leave me be."

She buried her face into the pillow, trying to let it absorb the wail that erupted without warning.

Then hands stroked her head and back. Avelyn sensed the mattress sink and knew she was no longer alone.

She turned her head and saw Merryn. "Go away," she muttered, burying her face again.

"Does this have to do with Sir Kenric?" Elysande asked from her other side.

Avelyn might as well get the worst over with. Mayhap, they would leave her alone to her tears if she shared with them what had occurred. She pushed up to a sitting position and nodded.

"I made a disastrous mistake. I meddled where I shouldn't have—and now I will pay the price for the rest of my life," she choked out before she dissolved into tears again.

Merryn rose and returned with a cup of wine. She pressed it into Avelyn's hands. With a loving yet stern look upon her face, she said, "Drink this. We three are strong women and can solve anything together, but we need to know what we're up against. Calm yourself. Then speak to us."

Avelyn took the wine and sipped it. The liquid burned a path from her throat to her belly.

"Take deep, even breaths," Elysande instructed.

She did as her sister said. Between that and the wine, the flow of tears stopped.

Only the emptiness remained.

She handed Merryn the cup and rubbed her swollen eyes, not knowing where to begin.

"Is everything all right?"

Avelyn saw her uncle and Michael standing in the doorway. She hadn't realized the chamber door was open. Geoffrey sized up the situation in an instant and ushered Michael inside, closing the door behind them. Both men came over to the bed. Avelyn took another deep breath so that she wouldn't dissolve into tears again.

"We're here to help you, Avelyn. In any way we can," Geoffrey said quietly.

"It will be easier to share this only once," she said. "I'd been waiting for you and Merryn to arrive to help me with a dilemma I faced. I wanted to speak to you about it after Mother's wedding. I didn't want it to be a distraction to her and Sir Charles' happiness."

"Does this involve Kenric Fairfax?" Geoffrey asked.

"Aye."

"I assume your feelings have not changed about him, and that you told Elysande and Michael?"

"She did," Elysande said when Avelyn couldn't find the words to respond. "But something has happened this evening between the two of them." She looked at Avelyn. "Do you think you can share it with us now?"

Avelyn told them how she'd been with Lady Juliana when she passed away and the secret she'd heard Gussalen reveal to her mistress. How Gussalen had claimed a different order of birth for the twins due to her hatred of Walter Fairfax and that Kenric had been mistreated his entire life by his mother and brother.

"He's the rightful Earl of Shadowfaire," she said. "I wanted to discuss this with all of you and come up with a way to tell him, but I ruined it tonight by telling Kenric of his birthright."

"Why did you decide to do so?" Michael asked. "If you'd waited all these weeks?"

"Kenric told me before that he had nothing to offer me and would not allow a future for the two of us together. Something—or someone—changed Kenric's mind, for he sought me out tonight. He proclaimed his love for me and said he wanted us to wed."

Avelyn paused and decided to reveal everything. "Kenric even told me why he didn't wear his spurs as other knights do." She quickly related what had occurred with Lady Jannet at Longshire and saw how affected they all were by the tale.

"He wanted nothing but honesty between us and gave me the

chance to reject him once he shared his story. Since he bared his soul to me, I wanted nothing hidden between us. That's why I told him how Gussalen had wronged him all these years."

Elysande took her sister's hand and pressed it against her cheek in comfort. "Oh, Sir Kenric has suffered. Even more than we can imagine."

"He didn't believe me, Elysande. Kenric accused me of only wanting to be his countess. Of being like all those women at court who want nothing more than a fortune and title when they wed." She wiped a falling tear away. "I told him it wasn't true. That I only loved him but owed it to him to share what I had learned."

"And now he wants nothing to do with you," Geoffrey concluded.

Avelyn nodded. "I told him the truth, a truth that died with Gussalen. I have no way to confirm her words. It was better that he never knew than to hear the truth and reject it. Now he hates me and I'm afraid he'll always doubt himself."

Her tears began again. Elysande and Merryn comforted her while Geoffrey and Michael spoke in hushed tones.

Finally, Avelyn brushed her hands across her cheeks. "I've done him enough damage. I've ruined our chance for happiness together, for he will never trust me again. Mayhap, I should return to court so we won't come into contact with one another here at Sandbourne."

"The news you informed him of hurt him deeply," her uncle said. "He lashed out at you as its bearer. It's best if he has time to think upon what you revealed."

Michael said, "Lord Sewell wishes for Kenric to accompany him to his home in the north. He's most impressed with Kenric's riding skills and way with horses. Sewell asked me if Kenric could return with him to help care for the horses he's purchased during the journey home and to stay on a bit to work with his stablemen regarding training and breeding." He paused. "I think allowing Kenric to go with Lord Sewell would give him time to think. I've done some of my best thinking while on the road."

Geoffrey gave Merryn a sad smile. "Sometimes, separation makes your heart realize what's most important." He clasped her hand and Avelyn saw tears well in both of their eyes. She didn't know of the separation Geoffrey spoke of, but it obviously had impacted him and Merryn greatly.

Avelyn turned back to Michael and nodded.

"I'll tell him tomorrow that he's to travel with Lord Sewell. First, they must take Lady Sela back to her father before they head north with the new horses. That means Kenric will be gone several weeks, Avelyn. Are you sure that's what you want?"

Her gut told her this might be their only chance. "I do. Thank you, Michael."

Elysande gave her an encouraging smile. "Sir Kenric will come to his senses. Whether he decides to challenge his twin for ownership of Shadowfaire or simply remain in service here at Sandbourne, I know your love for him will remain constant."

Merryn gave her a hug. "I know it'll be hard to sleep tonight. I can give you a sleeping draught if you wish."

Avelyn thought how much she would toss and turn, a thousand thoughts closing in on her. "I would like that," she told her aunt. She searched the faces of her loved ones. "Thank each of you for your concern. I'm truly blessed with family."

She only hoped that, one day, she would have a family of her own—with the man she loved.

KENRIC DUNKED HIS HEAD in the trough and pulled it out. Cold water dripped onto his bare chest, rejuvenating him after a long, blistering afternoon clanging swords with Lord Sewell's men. He ran his hands through his wet hair, tired but satisfied at the day's efforts.

He'd come to work with the stable hands and discuss breeding and training techniques to implement in order to improve the current stock. Somehow, he'd managed to move into the training yard and had spent the last few weeks with Lord Sewell's soldiers, teaching them all he knew of dueling and swordplay.

More importantly, he'd used the time to push Sandbourne—and Avelyn Le Cler—far from his mind.

"Sir Kenric? My father wishes to see you at once. You'll find him in the solar."

Kenric turned and saw young Drew Talbot standing nearby. The quiet, sturdy boy had become his shadow over the past few weeks, asking questions day and night. In a way, Drew reminded him of Hal de Montfort, curious about everything. Once Hal began speaking in full sentences, the boy would be much the same as the Talbot lad.

It pained Kenric that he would never have a son like one of these boys. Never have a wife or a home to call his own.

Never have Avelyn Le Cler in his life.

He shook off the depressing thoughts. "I'll change my clothing and report to your father immediately, my little lord," he teased.

Kenric stopped by the barracks and dressed in clean clothes so as to be presentable. He'd seen Lord Sewell only a few times since their arrival. From what he gathered from the other soldiers, the nobleman spent a majority of his time at court and only a few weeks each summer at his country estate in the north.

He arrived at the solar and knocked. A deep voice bid him to enter.

"Ah, Sir Kenric. Would you care to join me in a cup of wine?" asked Lord Sewell, dressed impeccably in midnight blue and gold.

"Aye, my lord. I've been up to thirsty work. Wine would be most appreciated."

Lord Sewell handed Kenric a pewter cup and offered him a chair. They sat and discussed various horses in the stables. The nobleman was especially interested in the additions he'd bought from Lord Michael.

"I appreciate all the knowledge you've shared with my men, Sir Kenric, both in the stables and the training yard. If Lord Michael would allow it, I would wish for you to remain on my estate in my service."

He wondered if that was a possibility. "I've enjoyed my time here, my lord. You have good men under you, especially your captain of the guard."

The nobleman snorted. "Lord Michael would never let me steal you away and I shan't ask him to grant me that. But I have called you here to ask a favor from you."

"Anything, my lord."

"I know it's time you returned to Sandbourne and I would ask that you take my son with you. I've arranged for Drew to foster with Lord Michael. In fact, I may send both my daughters to be under Lady Elysande's tutelage when they come of age. It's time I returned to court, for soon the king and queen will complete their summer progress and be bound for London. I have much to do there in order to prepare for this."

Kenric's desire for answers got the best of him. He ventured, "You knew Lady Avelyn at the royal court, my lord?"

"Of course. She wasn't there long, but we did become friendly. She was unlike many there."

"How so?"

"She had no interest in the trappings and lifestyle. She seemed most uncomfortable with the pomp and rituals. We had conversations over many topics. Politics. Music. History. I quite enjoyed speaking with her. She was like a breath of fresh air."

"How did the other women treat her?" Kenric asked.

Lord Sewell studied him a moment. "You were there that day when Lady Sela revealed her ugly side to all. Are you concerned her falsehoods might hurt Lady Avelyn in some way once she returns to the queen's service?"

Kenric shrugged, not trusting any words that he might speak.

He watched the nobleman pondering the question. "I would say the lady should be fine. I don't think those unfounded rumors will hold water, especially when Lady Sela doesn't return to court to perpetuate them." He gave Kenric a sly grin. "And I can put a word into the right ears. Lady Avelyn should have no problems. If she returns," he added.

Kenric's heartbeat sped up. "Why would she not return?"

"She seemed unhappy during her time in London. She told me once she'd rather tend her garden and care for babes. Lady Avelyn is a nurturing soul and likes to remain busy, not idling her time away listening to gossip. It will be the lucky man who claims her as his wife."

Kenric knew he had to ask. "So you don't think her to be a liar?"

Lord Sewell laughed heartily. "Nothing could be further from the truth. Avelyn Le Cler is honest to a fault. Mark my words, whatever Lady Avelyn says may be taken as seriously as the Gospels themselves."

The nobleman's words landed a blow to Kenric's gut. He'd been blinded so by his hurt at what Avelyn had told him that he blamed her for it. Ignored her words. Pushed them as far away as possible.

But what if she had spoken the truth? That he was the true Earl of Shadowfaire?

He had no way to prove it, but did it matter? If he could have Avelyn—have happiness—why not reach for it? Kenric realized he'd been a fool.

"So . . . are you listening to me, Sir Kenric? I wish you to return to Sandbourne at once with my son. I trust Drew with you as I have no other, for I've seen that you're a most honorable man and how you are in the boy's company."

Kenric drew a deep breath, excitement building within him. "Young Drew is a most delightful child. I would be honored to have the lad ride with me to Sandbourne."

For the first time in weeks, Kenric felt happy. He would be going home—to Avelyn.

If she would have him.

CHAPTER 25

AVELYN HAD MIXED FEELINGS about returning to London and severing her ties at the royal court. Though she knew she wouldn't stay for long, she didn't look forward to her conversation with the queen. Her uncle assured her that he would do the majority of the talking and she would only have to speak if the queen wished to question her. At this point, since she'd fallen out with Kenric, they'd agreed that Geoffrey wouldn't bring up the knight's name as a possible choice of Avelyn's future husband.

She wondered if it was possible to ever get back in Kenric's good graces. Her heart told her that, despite the way things ended when they last saw one another, Kenric still loved her. Though they'd been separated for many weeks, he'd finally returned last evening with young Drew Talbot in tow. Though they had yet to speak, Avelyn dreamed of Kenric putting his harsh words aside so they could return to the way it had once been between them. How she longed for his touch and his kiss and the tenderness he'd shown before she destroyed their future by speaking out of turn.

Avelyn concentrated on the days and weeks ahead. She planned to visit at Kinwick after they spoke with the queen and she gathered her remaining possessions at the palace. Geoffrey said that he and Merryn would always welcome her with open arms, so they would stop first to allow her to visit Kinwick once they left London. Still, she prayed every night to the Blessed Virgin that once she arrived back at Sandbourne, somehow, she and Kenric could reconcile their feelings.

A knock at the door interrupted her thoughts. "Come," she called.

Elysande entered the chamber, a swaddled David in her arms.

Wordlessly, Avelyn held out her arms and her sister handed over the babe. Avelyn brought him close, brushing her lips atop David's head as her finger stroked his sweet cheek.

"I'll miss you while I'm gone, little one," she told the sleeping babe.

"You will have one of your own soon," Elysande assured her. "I hope our children can grow up near one another and be as close as siblings."

"I'll need to find a husband first before a babe is the result," Avelyn said, making light of things.

Her sister put an arm about Avelyn. "Everything will go well in London. I'm certain of it. You can visit with Merryn and then return to Sandbourne. I believe a certain knight will miss you during your absence. I caught him glancing at you several times during the evening meal."

"You think Kenric will ever change his mind?" she asked wistfully, doubting it but hoping nonetheless.

"He would be a fool to try and keep apart from you," Elysande insisted, "though I may have to take a broom to him to beat some sense into his thick skull."

She chuckled at the thought of her sister chasing Kenric round the great hall, swatting him with a broom.

"It's time for you to go. I came to say goodbye here since I'm about to feed David."

Avelyn kissed her nephew's cheek and handed him back to his mother. "Then I will also say farewell. Take care of this little one and watch after Mother."

Elysande laughed. "I daresay Sir Charles is doing a splendid job of that."

Young David began to stir. "Godspeed, Avelyn. Good luck with the queen." Her sister left as the babe started to fuss.

She glanced about the chamber. Her trunk and the bulk of her clothes would remain here. They would drop off some items when they called at Kinwick in order to retrieve Alys as they made their way back to London. With a sigh, Avelyn stepped from the room and closed the door behind her.

Michael and Lady Orella awaited her downstairs. Both wished her a safe journey as they walked her outside the keep and began the long descent down the steps. She spied Uncle Geoffrey and Ancel and waved at them. They both mounted their horses.

Then Avelyn's feet faltered. Michael quickly grabbed on to her arm as she stumbled, preventing her from tumbling down the steep staircase.

"Are you all right?" he asked before his eyes turned to where she stared.

Kenric Fairfax had begun mounting the stairs. He reached them and Avelyn caught sight of a rolled parchment in his hand.

"I'm sorry to interrupt, my lord," he said, his eyes fastened on Michael's. "I ask that I be allowed to accompany the escort party."

She saw Michael glance down and knew he saw the parchment Kenric clutched tightly in his hand.

"Have you news from your brother?"

Kenric shook his head. "Nay, from Lady Doria, his wife. She said Roland is seriously ill and not expected to live. She would have me come and be with my brother at the end."

"Then you must go," Michael agreed. "Stay as long as you wish. Send word if you have need of anything."

"My sister-in-law also made an odd request in her missive." Kenric glanced to Avelyn. "She asked that Lady Avelyn come, as well. That she had something important to speak to her about."

Avelyn bit her lip in confusion. Why should Doria Fairfax have need of her? They had only met briefly.

"Avelyn?" Michael asked.

"If Lady Doria requests my presence, I'm willing to make a slight detour. Once I have, Uncle Geoffrey can then see me to London and our appointment with the queen."

"We should inform Lord Geoffrey of the change in plans."

Michael and Kenric hurried down the stairs to speak with Geoffrey.

Lady Orella gave her a smile. "Sometimes, our Dear Lord moves in mysterious ways." She gently patted Avelyn on her shoulder. "Make the most of the opportunity, my dear." She excused herself and returned inside the keep.

Avelyn made her way down the remaining steps. The inner bailey hummed with its usual activity, accompanied by the escort party. She counted a dozen de Montfort soldiers and Ancel, her young cousin, sitting tall in his saddle. He waved in greeting.

The men finished speaking as a groom led Firefall over to Kenric. He turned and took the reins and then looked to her.

"Would you care to ride with me, my lady?"

Joy burst in her heart, though Avelyn kept her features schooled and coolly answered, "Thank you, my lord. I will."

He held a hand out to her. She took it and found herself swept up into the saddle, her pulse racing as Kenric secured her against him. Then the lead rider turned and took off, and all the other men followed. Avelyn found herself finally taking a breath.

In Kenric's arms, she felt as if she had come home.

THEY ARRIVED AT SHADOWFAIRE just after noon. Sir Jervis greeted them and made provisions for their horses to be watered and fed and for the soldiers to be brought into the great hall to dine. Geoffrey sent Ancel along with the rest. Avelyn could tell the boy was pleased, being considered one of the men.

"Lady Doria asked that you and Lady Avelyn be brought up to the solar when you arrived, Sir Kenric." Sir Jervis paused. "I'm not sure if she knew others would accompany you."

"I'm Geoffrey de Montfort. Lady Avelyn is my niece and I am escorting her to London for a brief visit."

The older knight smiled. "I do remember Lady Avelyn from her short stay at Shadowfaire. One does not forget such a radiant beauty."

She sensed the heat springing to her cheeks. "I would wish my uncle to remain with me when I speak with Lady Doria. I hope this won't be a problem."

"Nay, my lady," Sir Jervis assured her. "Please, follow me."

They accompanied him to the solar upstairs. The room was empty but, immediately after their arrival, several servants entered bearing trays with food and drink for them.

"I'll leave you to your meal and let Lady Doria know that you've arrived." The knight excused himself.

They ate with little conversation. Avelyn knew Kenric must be worried about his brother. As they finished up, the door opened. Lady Doria had arrived. By a glance, she knew the countess had already given birth. Not only did she appear thinner, but the noblewoman carried a swaddled babe in her arms. But had she delivered a boy or a girl?

The three rose to greet her. Avelyn introduced her uncle and explained why Geoffrey accompanied her.

Then Avelyn asked, "I'm curious, my lady, why you asked me to come today. We exchanged but a few words during my brief visit here. I know Sir Kenric is eager to see his brother and speak to you regarding his condition."

"I believed it was important for you to hear my words today, Lady Avelyn." She glanced from her to Kenric. "What I have to share with Kenric also concerns you."

"But . . . how?"

Doria gave Avelyn a hesitant smile. "It was obvious from your visit here in May that you and Kenric have strong feelings for one another. I saw it in both your eyes."

"My lady?" Kenric sputtered.

She glanced back to her brother-in-law. "I have something of great importance to share with you, Kenric. It concerns your future. I thought Lady Avelyn should hear what I have to say. If you love one another, you will need each other's strength to bear this news together."

Avelyn saw the confusion she experienced mirrored on Kenric's face. She looked to her uncle, but his features gave nothing away.

"Please. Have a seat," Doria said, indicating they move away from the table and come to the furniture surrounding the fireplace.

They followed their hostess' lead and took seats around her as she eased into a chair, the babe asleep in her arms.

"My father died shortly before he signed my betrothal contract. That left my brother as my guardian. And he wasn't fond of the man I was supposed to marry. Instead of carrying out my father's wishes, my brother wanted a heftier bride prize.

"That was how I came to be at Shadowfaire. A reluctant bride, far from home, married to . . . a stranger."

Avelyn could tell by her restrained tone that Doria had most likely had feelings for the man she originally should have married. Her heart went out to the noblewoman for being placed in circumstances beyond her control.

"I discovered that my previously dull life quickly became a nightmare." Doria swallowed. She kept silent for a few moments before she took a calming breath and continued.

"My new husband was sickly. Cruel both in word and deed. He could not . . . perform . . . his husbandly duties and blamed me for this. He beat me accordingly, night after night." Her voice became monotone, as if what she related had happened to someone else.

"The Shadowfaire healer, as she attended me, told me some illness in Lord Roland's childhood caused him not to be able to pleasure me as a man should, much less get me with child. She feared for my life. Because of that, she gave me a potion that caused my belly to swell."

"So that Roland would think you were with child and not touch you," Kenric said softly.

"Aye. He did stop hurting me." She gave a snort. "And he actually began to believe I carried his child, but I knew the charade must end. I quit drinking the potion and told him I had lost the babe."

"But he wasn't satisfied," Kenric said.

Doria shook her head. "He insisted that we have a son. That our child must secure the future of Shadowfaire so that his twin could never gain access to it."

Avelyn watched the shadow cross Kenric's face. Her heart went out to him, knowing the words cut him deeply.

"But how could you have a babe if he could not . . . help you?" she asked.

The noblewoman hesitated. "When I did not grow with child, Roland told me that he would give me to one of his knights. A man taller and broader than Kenric Fairfax, so that our son would be strong and healthy. I was to lie with him till I found myself with child."

Avelyn gasped. Then silence filled the room as Doria gave them time to understand her meaning.

"It was awkward at first, but Sir Heymon proved to be gentle with me and kind." She paused. "We fell in love."

"And then you found yourself with child," Kenric said.

Doria nodded. "We weren't allowed to spend any time alone after that, but I dreamed of becoming Heymon's wife. I fantasized about leaving Shadowfaire behind and raising my child with the man I loved. *His* child. Not the demon spawn of Roland Fairfax, but the sweet babe of the most loving man I know."

The babe began to stir. Doria stood and rocked it from side to side in a slow, steady motion.

"As my belly grew larger, I began to hope that Roland would die from one of his numerous illnesses. I know it was wrong of me to think such wicked thoughts, but I couldn't help myself." She glanced down at the child in her arms. "Two weeks ago, I gave birth to a son, the new heir to Shadowfaire. I would be tied to this place—forever.

"But I don't think I can keep the secret of his birth from others."

Doria reached and gently tugged away the babe's knitted cap. Avelyn saw the bright red hair and green eyes as the boy awakened and gurgled sweetly. Doria had brown hair and brown eyes. She knew Roland to have fair hair and blue eyes, as had Lady Juliana.

"The minute the people see Wymund's hair, they will know who his father is," Doria proclaimed. "I've only seen this shade of hair on

Heymon, nary another soul. They will think me unfaithful to the Earl of Shadowfaire."

She stomped her foot, causing wee Wymund to whimper. "I refuse to live like this. I want to take my son from here and have nothing to do with the vile man lying abed in the next chamber. I want a life with Heymon."

Doria wheeled and faced Kenric. "And my son should never rule at Shadowfaire. For *you*, my lord, are the real heir."

CHAPTER 26

Doria's words stunned Kenric. His sister-in-law confirmed what Avelyn had revealed to him.

He was the heir to Shadowfaire.

"Explain yourself, my lady," he said calmly, though the blood roared in his ears.

She rocked tiny Wymund back and forth as she said, "I discovered it from Roland's ramblings. He talks in his sleep. More than once, he spoke of you as your father's true heir."

Doria began pacing slowly, continuing her rocking motion to keep young Wymund calm. "At first, I thought it no more than mumbled nonsense. Odd dreams Roland might be having. Mayhap, he thought the Earl of Shadowfaire should be a man of strength and courage instead of the sickly coward I'd married." She shrugged. "So I ignored it and never told him what he'd uttered in his sleep."

She returned to the chair since the babe had quieted. "Then he caught that fever that killed your mother, my lord. My husband must have had you on his heart with your recent visit here. As I sat by Roland's bedside, I could understand his mutterings more clearly. He grew quite frantic at one point, sitting up, frightened that you would come and take everything away from him."

Doria stroked the babe's cheek. "When the fever broke and he recovered and grew stronger, I finally asked him about it."

Kenric leaned forward, eager to hear her next words, yet dreading them all the same.

"He laughed till tears streamed down his face. He admitted it was the truth and that Gussalen held a grudge against your father. She was the only one present at the birth and told Walter Fairfax that Roland was the first babe that appeared—when in reality, it had been you."

Shock reverberated through Kenric. His thoughts whirled like a strong wind and he gripped his knees till his knuckles turned white. Finally, he asked, "Did Roland say how long he'd known the truth?"

"Since childhood."

Kenric tried to think back. So many times Roland had lorded over him, a sly look in his eye. This had been a great secret for a young child to keep. His brother proved stronger than Kenric had thought.

One questioned burned within him, though. "Did he say if my mother knew?"

Doria gave him a sad look. "Roland said Gussalen told only him. That no one else knew—not even your lady mother. The birth had been a great strain on her and she was unaware of the order her boys came out." She shuddered. "My husband swore me to secrecy. He said our son would follow him as the next earl. Then the secret would die, with you never being the wiser.

"But I can live like this no longer. Lady Juliana is dead. Gussalen, too. And though she could have verified this abomination, that old witch loved Roland with a passion. If confronted, she never would have betrayed her pet in that manner."

"So Roland knows," Kenric said, still finding Doria's words almost too fantastic to believe.

"He does," his sister-in-law asserted. "It's why I sent for you—and a priest. Roland must confess to God of his crime against you. *You must have your birthright returned to you, my lord. Shadowfaire should be yours.*"

Kenric stood and found his legs unsteady, his hands trembling.

Then Avelyn came to stand by him. She took his hands in hers and gazed into his eyes. Her warmth flooded him, racing through his veins, giving him strength and courage for what lay ahead.

"I'm sorry I doubted you."

She released one of his hands and placed a single finger against his lips. Desire burned in him at her touch.

"Do not apologize. Go now with Lady Doria. Confront your twin and put your demons to rest."

He captured her hand in his, turning it upward and pressing a searing kiss into her palm. He sensed the shiver run through her. Kenric longed to take Avelyn into his arms and kiss her senseless, but Roland awaited them in the next chamber. Kenric gave Avelyn a reassuring smile, but he knew long ago that he had given this woman his heart. He looked over to Lord Geoffrey and saw the nobleman wore a satisfied look.

Doria touched Avelyn's sleeve. "I fear that heated words will be exchanged between these two brothers and I don't want Wymund to be frightened. Would you keep him safe for me while we are gone?"

"It would be my pleasure." She took the sleeping babe into her arms.

Kenric could only stare. Avelyn holding a child looked like the most natural thing in the world. In that moment, he knew he wanted to marry her more than anything. He wanted to spend his life with her and plant his seed deep within her. Kenric longed to see her belly grow and then watch her nurse their child at her breast.

Lord Geoffrey stepped next to him. "It's like being struck by lightning," he murmured.

Kenric slowly nodded. "I see so clearly now, what's been before my eyes all this time. I love your niece, my lord, with my heart and mind and soul. She completes me."

"She has loved you always. Merryn and I knew this from the time you stopped at Kinwick when you escorted her from London. I'm only glad that you realized it before you became an old man," he teased. "Now go. Speak with your brother. No matter what the outcome, you have a strong, intelligent, capable woman who waits for you."

Kenric tore his eyes from Avelyn reluctantly as he watched Doria open the door to the solar. She ushered in the priest that he recognized from his mother's funeral mass.

Doria brought the man over and said, "This is Father John, my lord. I've made my confession to him. He knows that Wymund is Sir Heymon's son and that my husband ordered me to break my marriage vows and lay with another man." She paused. "I have also shared what I learned from Roland regarding your birthright. Father, this is Lord Kenric Fairfax, the Earl of Shadowfaire, and Lord Geoffrey de Montfort of Kinwick, along with his niece, Lady Avelyn."

Kenric nodded at the priest, Doria's words ringing in his ears.

He was the Earl of Shadowfaire.

He could surrender to bitterness—but that would change nothing. Instead, Kenric decided he must live in the present and look to the future. His brother would no longer have power over him.

"You'll be welcomed back to your home, my lord," Father John said. "I've heard from others who live at Shadowfaire and they thought highly of you as a boy. I believe you will make a fine earl for your people."

"Thank you, Father."

"Then shall we make our way to see Lord Roland?" Father John led the way with Doria and Kenric following him.

Before he crossed into the bedchamber, Kenric looked over his shoulder. Avelyn gave him a brilliant smile that filled him with confidence.

The room smelled of death. A few candles burned next to the bed. An elderly servant stood and gave a brief nod before skirting past them. Kenric assumed she'd been left to tend to Roland in case he needed anything.

His eyes fell to his twin. Kenric's jaw clenched as he saw the bag of bones lying there, swallowed by the bedclothes. Roland looked as if he'd aged a score in the few months since Kenric had seen him. His thinning hair was streaked with gray and plastered to his scalp. No color rested in his sunken cheeks. His cracked lips were split and bloodied. The rest of him looked as if a skeleton had bits of flesh wrapped about it. Always thin to the point of frailty, Roland had wasted away, a victim of this latest illness.

Doria went to stand on the opposite side of the bed from the priest. Kenric remained at the foot as Father John opened the vial of consecrated oil. Though Roland's eyes burned brightly with fever, he said nothing.

"I have come to give you extreme unction, my lord. Through this holy sacrament, the gift of the Holy Spirit is given to you in grace. 'Twill renew your faith in God and give you the strength, peace, and courage to endure these last minutes as death approaches."

Roland merely glared at the man of God—and then turned his angry gaze upon Kenric.

In that moment, as their eyes met, Kenric absorbed all of the hate his brother hurled at him. Kenric realized that Roland, knowing he was the second born son, had never believed himself worthy or adequate of the role Gussalen thrust him into on the night of the brothers' birth. Roland had tried to play a part for which he wasn't destined and still clung to it now, even as he stood at Death's door.

A peace descended upon Kenric. Roland had merely been a child when Gussalen divulged her dirty secret to him. His twin was a pawn in the game perpetuated by that evil woman. Kenric knew that, despite being denied his birthright, he'd already lived a full, interesting life, one of no regrets and great adventure.

And soon to be one filled with love—with Avelyn.

Father John continued now in Latin. Kenric translated the words in his head as the priest anointed the seven parts of Roland's body as he spoke.

"Through this holy unction and His own most tender mercy, may the Lord pardon thee whatever sins or faults thou hast committed by sight, by hearing, by smell, by taste, by touch, by walking, by carnal delectation."

The priest resealed the vial of consecrated oil and set it aside. He placed a hand over Roland's and said in English, "As a Christian, you must die confessed so that you are absolved of your sins. Ease your burden, my lord, and speak of your sins."

His twin ignored the priest and focused on Kenric. "You know," he croaked, his voice sounding rusty with disuse.

"Aye," Kenric replied.

Roland glanced to Doria, a sneer on his face. "So much for trusting you, my lady."

"Your sins, my lord," Father John prompted again. "You go soon to Paradise. Shrug off the mantle of sin and arrive at the gates of Heaven—"

"I'll never enter those gates, Father," Roland wheezed. "I've lived a life of sin and taken pride in it."

"But your Heavenly Father forgives all of that, my lord. You have only to admit to wrongdoing and He will welcome you into His loving arms."

Roland coughed violently. Blood dribbled down his chin, mixed with a black mucus.

Kenric knew that Roland would never admit to the truth. And if he didn't, Wymund—his son by law—would become the next Earl of Shadowfaire.

He saw the crooked smile cross his brother's face and knew his guess proved correct. Even as he hovered between life and death, Roland would best him.

The trio hovered over the bed as Roland's labored breathing finally ceased minutes later. Kenric turned away in disgust and disappointment. He left the bedchamber, frustrated and angry that his brother had the last word.

Doria and Father John joined him. She took Wymund and sat, silently weeping. Avelyn came and wrapped her arms about Kenric.

The priest looked at Doria, shaking his head sadly. "I only worry about my lady and her reputation, not to mention the cloud young Wymund will grow up under, being called a bastard—or worse."

"If I may speak, Father?" Lord Geoffrey said, turning to Doria. "My lady, I know you don't wish to stay at Shadowfaire."

"Nay, my lord. I would be most uncomfortable living here."

"Then may I offer a suggestion? I'm always in need of good men. I would offer you and Sir Heymon a home at Kinwick. It's a wonderful place to raise a child. Unless you prefer—"

"Thank you most kindly, Lord Geoffrey. I would speak to Heymon of it, but he will do whatever it takes to make me happy." She paused. "But how am I to leave Shadowfaire when my son is now its heir and the new earl? I fear I'm forever trapped."

Geoffrey raised a hand. "I'm sorry to inform you that your infant son caught the same fever your husband had and that neither of them survived. Being heartbroken at these deaths, you have decided to enter a convent. Immediately."

Kenric understood what Geoffrey de Montfort suggested. He watched understanding dawn on Doria's face.

"So I would leave Shadowfaire and let its people think I go to a convent—when, instead, I would come to live at Kinwick with my new husband and son?" Her smile lit up the room.

Geoffrey glanced to Kenric. "Is that a suitable plan, my lord?" he asked.

Kenric turned to the priest. "Only if Father John agrees."

The priest nodded. "I see no harm in this. Lord Kenric is the true Earl of Shadowfaire. This will allow Lady Doria to marry her child's father and escape to a new life."

"Then we have much planning to do," Kenric said, taking charge. He glanced down at Avelyn, his arms still about her. "And my bride-to-be will be my first and best adviser."

CHAPTER 27

They arrived in London a day behind schedule due to their sojourn at Shadowfaire. Avelyn tried to calm her nerves, knowing that, in a short while, they would be before the queen. The first person they saw inside the palace was Lord Sewell Talbot, who greeted them with a surprised glance as he gazed at Kenric.

"I didn't expect to see you here, Sir Kenric. How did my son fare on the road?"

Kenric said, "Drew made the trip an interesting one, my lord. He's quite a talkative lad. Before I departed Sandbourne, he'd already made a few friends."

Geoffrey added, "We called at Shadowfaire on our way to London. The earl passed away from a fever and Sir Kenric is now Lord Kenric—the new earl."

Lord Sewell offered Kenric his hand. "My congratulations." He glanced over at Avelyn. "Something tells me you will soon have a new countess by your side."

Avelyn's cheeks grew warm at his gaze. "If the queen releases me from her service and allows the betrothal, you will be correct, my lord. We have an appointment with her this afternoon."

"She and the king came back in the best of moods. All went well on their summer progress, especially at the last estate they called upon." Sewell looked to Geoffrey. "In fact, it was your cousin they visited at Ashcroft, Lord Raynor and his lovely wife, Lady Beatrice."

Geoffrey laughed. "I knew they planned to stop there. Raynor rode to Kinwick a month before the royal visit and pumped Merryn for information. What their favorite dishes were. The way the king liked his mattress stuffed. I'm glad that Raynor absorbed the cost of a royal stay. I've done so multiple times."

"I wish you good luck in your conversation with the queen," Sewell told them. "And do not worry. I took care of the other matter."

Avelyn and Alys returned to the chamber they'd shared during her time at court. Alys called for hot water and helped Avelyn lay out the kirtle and *cotehardie* she wanted to wear for her audience with the queen. Both were of a dark blue with slashes of lighter blue that brought out the color in Avelyn's eyes.

She glanced at her bed. Despite Lord Sewell's assurances, she decided to check for herself. Avelyn ran a hand under the mattress and then lifted it to assure herself the queen's stolen necklace was no longer in her possession. She also checked her drawers, looking for anything that Sela might have placed in them. Thankfully, she found only her own belongings.

Avelyn washed away the stains of the travel and then Alys helped her to dress. She allowed the girl to brush her hair till it shone and then let her plait it, weaving blue ribbons through it before tying one at the end of the long braid.

"I'm happy you finally found out Lady Sela was up to no good," her cousin said as she embraced her. "I wouldn't worry about the queen. She adores Mother and Father."

Avelyn nodded and ventured to the queen's rooms. During her long walk, she thought how well everything had turned out. They'd stayed for Lord Roland's funeral mass. The people of Shadowfaire believed his young son buried in his father's arms, but the healer who had aided Lady Doria had been privy to their plans. She awaited them, along with Sir Heymon, a half-hour from Shadowfaire, tiny Wymund in a basket. The healer returned to the estate, while Heymon and Doria took their young son to Kinwick.

They'd all met with Merryn, sharing the complicated tale with her. She was delighted to take the new family under her wing and sent immediately for Father Dannet. The priest married the couple that very day. Avelyn remembered the love reflected on Heymon's and Doria's faces as they waved goodbye to the escort party bound for London. It brought Avelyn a sense of peace.

She arrived and found her uncle and Kenric in conversation with Lady Agnes, the queen's head lady-in-waiting. Both men had changed clothes, Geoffrey to hunter green and Kenric to dark brown. His hazel eyes appeared greener as he gazed at her in admiration.

"Greetings, Lady Avelyn," Agnes said. "I was telling your uncle that the queen has decided to take a turn in her gardens. She missed them, as usual, and asked for you to meet her there."

"I can show you the way," she told Kenric and Geoffrey, leading them through the Palace of Westminster until they reached the outside.

They continued on to the gardens. Avelyn's heart began pounding when she spied Queen Philippa seated on a bench, basking in the warm sun.

Geoffrey said to Kenric, "Stay here, my lord. We will call you over if it's necessary."

Kenric looked at her and Avelyn's confidence soared. He winked at her, causing her heart to skip a beat.

"Are you ready?" Geoffrey offered her his arm and they went to meet the queen.

It surprised Avelyn that she sat alone. Usually, many ladies-in-waiting hovered nearby. They approached her and Geoffrey discreetly cleared his throat.

The queen opened her eyes and awarded them with a gracious smile. Geoffrey bowed to her while Avelyn made her curtsey.

"Rise. Take a seat. Lady Avelyn, sit next to me. Lord Geoffrey, you may sit there." She indicated another bench to her right.

They did as she requested.

"I must say you look younger than when I last saw you, your highness. The country air has done you good this summer."

Philippa bit back a smile. "You've never been a flatterer, Geoffrey de Montfort. It's one of the reasons I actually like you."

Geoffrey smiled. "I only tell the truth, your grace."

"And I shall do the same." She turned to Avelyn. "Did your sister have her child?"

"Aye, a fine boy named David, your grace. Everyone at Sandbourne has fallen madly in love with him."

The queen smiled. "Children have a way of doing so. Did you enjoy your visit? You seem older to me. More confident."

Avelyn swallowed. "While I enjoyed being in your service, I've realized how much I love the country."

"You've fallen in love, I'd daresay." The queen studied her. "I know that glow." She looked around. "I suppose that handsome young nobleman standing over there is the reason for it?"

"Aye, your grace," Avelyn admitted. "He is Lord Kenric Fairfax, Earl of Shadowfaire."

"Hmm." Philippa eyed Kenric carefully and then motioned him over.

Avelyn watched Kenric come toward them and her heart almost burst with love.

He bowed low to the queen.

"Have a seat, young man," she ordered brusquely.

Kenric sat next to Geoffrey.

"So, Lord Geoffrey, I believe you're here to tell me I no longer have to hunt for the perfect match for your niece."

"That's correct, your majesty."

"Even though I thought I'd found the ideal man for Lady Avelyn."

Panic swelled through her. Her nails dug into her palms.

The queen laid a hand atop Avelyn's. "Never fear, my dear. No contract has been drawn up. I haven't even spoken to this man. If you remember, I told you we'd speak again when you returned to court." She looked from Avelyn to Kenric and back again.

"Lord Geoffrey, as head of the de Montfort family, you have the final decision in the suitability of this match. I yield to any decision you make."

Her uncle smiled. "I believe that Lord Kenric and Lady Avelyn are meant to wed," he explained. "They are a love match."

The queen's eyebrows rose. She looked at Avelyn. "You told me this was the practice in your family. I've seen it with your uncle and Lady Merryn. And I visited with Lord Geoffrey's cousin, Raynor, and his wife, Beatrice, recently."

"And my sister Elysande and Lord Michael are also a love match, your grace," Avelyn added. She shrugged sheepishly. "I suppose it runs in our family."

The queen looked to Geoffrey. "Lady Merryn also approves of this coupling?"

"Wholeheartedly, your grace."

"Then I suppose we cannot stand in the way of true love." She rose and the three of them followed suit. "I offer my congratulations to this happiest of couples, for I see in your eyes a love that shines. May you enjoy as many years together as the king and I have, and may your union be blessed with many, many children."

They thanked the queen, who then said, "Lord Geoffrey, the king asked that I bring you to his chambers when we finished our conversation."

"That would be most agreeable, your grace," Geoffrey said.

"And you two—you may remain in my gardens till Lord Geoffrey returns for you."

Philippa stepped away, keeping a fast pace for a woman of her age, allowing Geoffrey to guide her from the gardens. They watched until the pair turned and were gone from sight.

Avelyn found herself enveloped in Kenric's arms.

"She quite frightened me," he admitted to her.

"She has that effect on most people, but the queen has the kindest of hearts."

He gazed down at her in love. "So where shall we marry, now that the queen has granted us permission? At Sandbourne, where your mother married? Or Shadowfaire, your new home?"

Avelyn thought a moment. "I believe we should wed at Kinwick. 'Tis where Elysande and Michael made their vows. And without

Uncle Geoffrey's quick thinking, Lady Doria would have been stuck at Shadowfaire, raising Wymund as the earl when you were the rightful owner."

Kenric cupped her face tenderly. "I look at Lord Geoffrey and Lady Merryn and see their lives are full of love. I would have us be as they are—deeper in love with each passing day. Here's to a lifetime of happiness, my love."

His mouth captured hers in a kiss that signaled a new beginning. They had started their journey to love here in London and now they'd come full circle. As Avelyn returned Kenric's kiss, she looked forward to all of their tomorrows.

EPILOGUE

Kenric rushed Avelyn into the de Montfort's solar and closed the door. A fire burned in the hearth, bringing warmth to the room. He took her in his arms for a lingering kiss. As he pulled away, he stared at her, drinking in her beauty.

"I cannot quite believe you are mine."

She teased, "You are stuck with me, my lord. For now—and till the end of time."

He cupped her face in his hands. "'Twill never be enough for me. I could love you from now through eternity and 'twould never be long enough for me."

Kenric bent and kissed her then, a gentle, reverent kiss that spoke of his great love for her. He would never be able to get enough of the woman before him. His wife. His life.

Avelyn broke the kiss. "I have something for you. A wedding present of sorts."

"You do?" Curiosity caused him to scan the room. He spied a small bundle on the table, something wrapped in a linen handkerchief that stood next to a carafe of wine and two goblets.

"I hope it will please you." She moved toward the table and poured both of them some wine. She handed him his goblet and took her own before tapping it gently against his. "To our life together."

"Together. Forever." He downed the wine and placed the goblet back on the table.

She sipped at hers before setting it down and picking up the wrapped cloth in both her hands.

"I had this made for you. Ancel helped with it. He is quite talented with engraving. I hope you will wear them with pride."

Avelyn handed it to him. It was heavy, which only raised his interest. He placed the cloth in his left hand and unwrapped it with his right.

Lying in his hand, he discovered a pair of silver spurs, finely etched. Tears stung his eyes as he stared at them.

She wrapped her arms about him. "I know you kept the spurs that you hacked off, but they could never be attached to your boots again. I thought, since we were starting a new life together, you could begin again with a different pair of spurs."

His throat grew thick. "Thank you, sweetheart."

Avelyn squeezed him affectionately. "You are the most honorable man I know, Kenric Fairfax. I thought it only fitting that your long journey to honor should be recognized. And rewarded. I give you these silver spurs as a sign of my love and to confirm my belief in you as a man, a knight, and loving husband."

Kenric's arms encircled her. "I will wear these every day of my life, my love, and think of you each time I see them. You helped me find things in myself that I had forgotten. I know you will help me discover things I have never known."

He kissed her long and hard and then swept her up into his arms and carried her to the bed. They would discover even more of themselves in the coming hours, days, and years.

And always be united. As one. In love.

The End

About the Author

As a child, Alexa Aston gathered her neighborhood friends together and made up stories for them to act out, her first venture into creating memorable characters. Following her passion for history and love of learning, she became a teacher who began writing on the side to maintain her sanity in a sea of teenage hormones.

Alexa's historical romances use history as a backdrop to place her characters in extraordinary circumstances, where their intense desire for one another grows into the treasured gift of love.

She is the author of *The Knights of Honor*, a medieval romance series that takes place in 14th century England during the reign of Edward III and centers on the de Montfort family. Each romance focuses on the code of chivalry that bound knights of this era.

A native Texan, Alexa lives with her husband in a Dallas suburb, where she eats her fair share of dark chocolate and plots out stories while she walks every morning. She enjoys reading, watching movies and sports, and can't get enough of *Fixer Upper* or *Game of Thrones*. Alexa also writes romantic suspense, western historicals, and standalone medieval novels as Lauren Linwood.

Alexa loves to hear from her readers. You can connect with her through FB, Twitter, and her website: alexaaston.wordpress.com.

Facebook:

facebook.com/authoralexaaston

Twitter:

twitter.com/AlexaAston

Newsletter sign-up:

madmimi.com/signups/422152/join

Amazon Page:

amazon.com/author/alexaaston

Made in the USA
Middletown, DE
02 August 2017